NORSEMAN'S DECEPTION

THE NORSEMEN SAGAS: BOOK 2

GIANNA SIMONE

Gianna Simone

Rosavin Publishing
Contact: rosavinpub@optonline.net

Norseman's Deception

ISBN: 978-0692674604
ASIN: B019NK6GXW

Cover Design: Gianna Simone

Gianna Simone

DEDICATION

To Kat Attalla – I miss you, my friend, but I am holding tight to all you taught me, and it was a hell of a lot over the years – I have the notes and papers from critique to prove it!!! And thanks to you, I made the leap we spoke about many times. You inspired me in more ways than I could ever count. There will always be a piece of you in my writing.

To my wonderful mentor and editor, Janet Lane Walters. I don't think I can every truly express what your support and encouragement has meant to me over the years, but I'll keep trying. And you know, someday, I am going to re-write that Western! ;)

Gianna Simone

Also by Gianna Simone

The Norsemen Sagas
Norseman's Revenge – Book 1

Medieval Warrior's Series
Warrior's Possession – Book 1
Warrior's Vengeance – Book 2
Warrior's Possession – Book 3

The Bayou Magiste Chronicles
Claimed by the Devil – Book 1
Claimed by the Mage – Book 2
Claimed by the Enchanter – Book 3
Claimed by the Zyndevine – Book 4

Praise for Gianna Simone:

Warrior's Possession

BDSM Book Reviews: Gillian is keeping secrets and Royce will use everything in his sexual arsenal to make her tell him all of them. A BDSM bodice ripper… if you enjoy spanking, bondage, subduing and sexual interrogation you'll have plenty to enjoy.

The Romance Reviews: As a period piece, I was impressed with the author's research into all aspects of the story (language, clothing, food, activities, etc.). And in typical period fashion, Lady Gillian is treated more as an object to be controlled than a partner. Something she wants nothing to do with. Well, mostly. For the Panther has a knack for turning his lady inside out. The sex scenes and the BDSM scenes are scintillating as it's easy to imagine your own skin warming under the Earl's capable hand.

Warrior's Vengeance

The Romance Reviews: The plot is so captivating that the reader feels compelled to know more. The story, the development and the end are, to put it mildly, peculiar and original. This is my first Gianna Simone novel and I must say, she did a great job.

Goodreads: Impressive and totally hot bodice ripper!

Warrior's Wrath

BDSM Book Reviews: This story combines the richness of the 14th century history, meshed along with the stories of betrayal and the stories of love. There is a sweetness of Aeron as she is immersed in a sexual education she never knew existed.

Goodreads: The menage scenes were H.O.T.! Ms. Simone really does well with the heat and creativity of the triangle in action.

Claimed by the Devil

BDSM Book Reviews: The story leads you on an emotional rollercoaster, but it is well worth the ride. As Helene and Devlin get older their past is ever present, but Devlin works at gaining what he desires. Devlin fed into Helene's needs giving her what she wanted. Sex is here, often and hot, well written and intense.

You Gotta Read Reviews: This is one intense and hot story that grabbed my attention from the start and would not let go. While we are treated to the romance between Helene and Devlin we also get to find out about their lives outside of the bedroom, which include both friends and enemies. I loved watching the attraction between the two become so much more. Helen blooms with the help of Devlin and his love.

Claimed by the Mage

The Romance Reviews: Gianna Simone does an excellent job with Aiden's seduction of Lily. He reads her well and understands, most of the time, when to push and when to give. He takes care not to overpower or frighten away his healer as he carefully reveals her submissive side to her. My favorite parts of the book are those moments when he uses everything at his disposal to make love to her, and magic can allow for some sinfully erotic maneuverings.

Claimed by the Enchanter

BDSM Book Reviews: The author did a wonderful job of contrasting Regine's need to control and be dominated. She also showed how much trust plays into a relationship. Once Cameron and Regine get together, the sparks fly. The chemistry between the two is intense and the scenes between the two, and later with David, are very hot.

Coffee Time Romance: Claimed by the Enchanter is published by a suitably named publisher, because it is a sizzler of a story. The struggle between self-perception and self-awareness is strong and the emotions it invokes mirrors the struggle between who a person thinks they are, and who they are afraid to be. The internal struggle was as strong as the struggle to solve the mystery. I fell right into the story and lived as the characters lived with every emotion magnified. I'm happy to say I'm a new fan of Ms. Simone and look forward to reading more from this talented artist.

Claimed by the Zyndevine

BDSM Book Reviews: This is a fast moving magical story with many twists and turns. I enjoyed this book with its feisty characters, spells and hexes, evil forces and new lands. The romance was inevitable and the sex was hot. Even though BDSM was the main element to all romantic encounters, the prominent feel for me was one of true love conquers all. If you like magic, fantasy and happy endings this is the story for you.

He saved her Life – Can The Gods save her Heart and Soul from the mysterious loner's Dark Desires?

Fearing an arranged marriage, Thora Korisdotter flees her village, vowing never to return. With her two pet wolves beside her, she is confident in her safety, protected by the loyal animals. But outlaws attack, wounding one of her beloved pets. Only a mysterious stranger saves her from certain death. Now in his debt, she must repay him as he asks – with her body.

After being cast out of his clan as an outlaw, Ari Hugisson has wandered for years. The time of his banishment is nearing its end, and Ari has the proof he needs to clear his name and unmask the real murderer – his brother. His journey is delayed when he comes across a beautiful woman under attack. Compelled to save her, he also knows exactly how to claim the debt she owes, using the passion lurking under the surface of her fiery nature.

Betrayal cuts deep with the revelation Ari has lied and knows well the man Thora was to wed. But the passion he stirs is unlike anything she has ever known, even if he insists on treating her as little more than a slave.

When Ari confronts those who would see him killed, will Thora stand beside him, even at the risk of losing her family – and her heart?

** Contains explicit love scenes featuring A Kinky Twist on History! bondage, spanking and more!

CHAPTER ONE

Thora crouched in the small enclosure she'd created between the boulders and trees on the side of the mountain. Beside her, Kata and Kati pressed close, their warm furry bodies assurance of her safety. She held her breath. The sounds of the men faded as they moved further away from her hiding place.

How had she failed to notice them before they were nearly upon her? The location of her shelter was far from the main road, tucked away and out of sight. Only Kati's growl alerted her to the intruders' presence. She'd tried to escape into the thick grove of trees, but their shouts revealed they'd seen her. But she was fast, always had been, and luckily eluded them, finding this crevice in the mountainside.

She let out a deep sigh. She'd had no choice but to take a path far from the regular roads. With so many traveling to Tingwalla for The Thing, the dangers were more than she'd first anticipated. At the time of her flight, her only concern had been to avoid her father and those who might search for her. For the first three days of her journey, she'd encountered no one. In the last three days, however, she'd heard travelers nearly every day. Today was the first time she'd been seen.

After waiting until silence reigned in the area around her, she crawled from the rocky enclosure and dared a look around. No one appeared in the surrounding forest. Taking a few moments to ensure she was alone, she stood, dusting off her *smokkr*. Time to move on. She returned to her camp to gather her meager belongings.

In the interest of traveling light, she'd packed only two extra dresses, a couple of blankets, and an assortment of tools, such as a short spear for fishing. Her axe she kept tucked in her belt. The large sack also had room for the smoked lamb and dried fish she'd hidden away before her flight, as well as personal items to maintain her appearance, like her favorite combs. She'd dared a bath last night in the nearby river and the dress she'd washed at the same time was now dry enough to pack.

Tying the sack closed, she lifted it over her shoulder and turned to the wolves. Panic stiffened her spine to see them standing on alert, teeth bared and growling. She spun about, eyes widening to see the two who had pursued her earlier standing not ten feet away.

Both men, tall and dark, grinned maliciously at her. The one on the left dared a step, halting at the warning bark from Kati.

"Call off the wolves," the man said.

Thora shook her head. "Stay where you are and you won't be harmed."

Both man laughed and moved closer. Kati and Kata both barked now, more like menacing howls that sent shivers along Thora's spine. She'd never heard them sound that way. The wolves had always protected her, but then, she'd never been in any real danger at home. This situation was very different.

Her hand dropped to her axe, pulling it free from the pocket in her *smokkr*. She was no shield maiden, but her father had taught her well how to protect herself and how to dispatch any opponents she might face. Despite the way her legs grew suddenly weak, alarm also bolstered her strength.

When the same man took two more steps, Kati lunged. Though he lifted his axe in an attempt to fend off the animal, Kati was much faster and with a terrifying growl, clamped his powerful jaws around the attacker's arm. He screamed and punched at Kati, but the wolf maintained his grip, easily driving the man to the ground.

The other took the moment to run toward Thora and she raised her axe, at the same moment Kata leaped toward him. This time, the wolf wasn't as lucky and the aggressor struck the animal, opening a gash on her side. Thora screamed her outrage as Kata fell to the ground with a pained whine. She had no time to determine how badly the she-wolf was wounded when she found herself raising her own weapon against the man rushing toward her. Behind him, she barely registered the agonized screams of his companion as Kati continued to maul him, snarling and snapping all the while.

She blocked another of her foe's strikes and swung her axe toward his belly. He leaped back, narrowly avoiding the blow. She darted away, lifting her weapon once more and wishing she had thought to bring a shield. The last step found her foot caught in a root. Her already precarious balance crumbled. She waved her arm in an attempt to remain upright, heart racing with panic. Her attacker realized the vulnerability and surged forward.

A moment before he reached her, Thora gave in to the momentum of her fall and he stumbled, his rush sending him tumbling over her. She quickly untangled her foot and jumped up, her crouching stance defensive, axe raised. He sneered and stalked toward her. She turned, knowing she could outrun him. Again, her speed gave her an advantage, but when she looked over her shoulder, he no longer pursued. In fact, he seemed to have vanished. She slowed a half-pace, her gaze darting through the clearing.

A strange silence hung in the air, not even Kati's victim whimpering, though the wolf continued to growl at the bloodied and motionless man beneath him. Her breath rasped out of her and she turned slowly, seeking every dark corner and crevice in the forest. A rustle to her left and she spun about, only to find Kati trotting toward her. Still, she knew her attacker hunted her. If only she could see him.

A rumble from the wolf drew her focus, again behind her. Rustling in the trees sent her spinning. Too late, the shadow in the corner of her eye lunged. A sharp blow to her lower arm drew a cry of pained anger, her fingers suddenly numb and useless, dropping the axe to the forest floor. When Kati moved to attack, the man swung at him. The wolf's instincts kicked in and he twisted out of the enemy's range.

Thora made a move toward her axe, but the man's fingers caught in her hair, halting her. He yanked her toward him, laughing at her shriek of pain. Holding her beside him, his tight grip wrenching her head back, he ran the blade of his axe along her neck. She stilled, the cold of the metal biting already, threatening to slice her skin.

"Call off the wolf." His low voice held menace and a sick lust. Thora looked at the wolf circling them. Did Kati have enough time to take down her captor before he cut her throat open? At the moment, she had no leverage. She held her hand out to the wolf.

"Kati. *Létta*!"

For a few frantic moments, Kati remained in an aggressive stance, teeth bared, hair along his spine standing straight up. But the animal made no attempt to attack. He pawed at the earth, prancing, clearly agitated.

Her captor yanked her head back. Breathing came easier when the axe slipped away from her throat. She recognized the lust in his face, knew what he intended. So predictable. He'd leave himself vulnerable enough in a moment, so she let him press his lips against hers, fighting the urge to retch.

A moment later, he jerked back, fingers tightening still more against her scalp. She bit her lip against the cry, grabbing the hand caught in her hair. She froze. An axe protruded from his chest. He gave an odd wheeze at the moment his grip released, falling away to land with a thud on the forest floor.

Thora spun about, only able to gape at the man who stood framed in the arch of trees. The warrior stood tall, sword raised. His gaze caught hers, holding her motionless and breathless.

With a shake of her head and a flick of her fingers, she summoned Kati to her side. Sparing only a glance for the man who attacked her, she turned toward Kata's still form. Thora desperately needed to see to her pet, determine the extent of the female wolf's wounds.

At the same time, taking her attention from the man standing mere feet away might prove dangerous. Yes, he'd saved her. Somehow the knowledge he posed a greater danger, one she didn't completely understand, pounded in her thoughts, in time with the rapid staccato of her heartbeat.

A whine from Kati reminded her of Kata's situation. She knelt beside the animal, placing a hand on the bloodied fur. Kata's eyes opened, meeting Thora's, revealing the pain of her wound. Thora glanced toward the man again, a moment of relief he hadn't moved any closer quickly chased by the need to tend to her pet. Still, she reached around the ground, another wave of relief when her fingers closed around the handle of her axe. She placed it close beside her, reachable in an instant, with little chance to get caught in her dress.

She searched through the fur to find the injury, tears burning her eyes at every whimper Kata issued. At least the animal wasn't dead. She gave a start of pain when Thora's fingers brushed the edge of the wound. Thora paused, taking a deep breath to steady herself and peered closely at the torn flesh.

While serious, the wound didn't appear terribly deep. All hope was not lost. Kata's injury would heal, with proper treatment. She looked over at the man again. This time he had moved nearer, but held his weapon lowered at his side. Did he mean to fool her into trusting him? Was his rescue only a means to inflict his own dark intentions?

"Don't come any closer while I tend her."

A brief moment of pride at the strength of her command flared hotter when he gave a brief nod, giving import to her order. She took a moment to study him, surprised to find herself pleased he wore a fine fur-trimmed cloak, the leather boots also indicating wealth of some sort. Had he stolen them, or did he come from a prosperous family? The latter idea briefly blunted her fear and a new plan slowly formed. Perhaps she could use his timely intervention to her own advantage, in many ways.

He walked around her, still maintaining his distance. When he pointed at the body of the outlaw, she nodded in understanding. She kept her gaze upon him as he moved the dead man further away.

With another whine, Kati nudged her face, drawing her attention back to his wounded companion. She ruffled the fur on his head then reached for the sack that had fallen away during her struggle with the outlaw. She rummaged through it, her gaze darting time and time again to the warrior, hoping he would continue to keep away once he'd finished burying the outlaw under some brush.

Finding the bone needle, her fingers also curled around the thin ball of thread to accompany it. She thanked the gods for advising her when she packed her belongings. A hand covered hers. She bit her lip to stifle her gasp and jerked away.

"What are you doing?" She grabbed the axe, raising it, ready to defend herself. Immediately, the man straightened and took a few steps back.

"I only meant to help. If you can clean the blood away, then lay heat to it, she will heal faster."

Thora considered his words, knowing well how often the warriors in her father's village sealed wounds with a searing blade, speeding recovery of the injured. Yet, there were also times where the wound festered, making the injured person more ill. She'd seen limbs and lives lost in such a manner. Icy fingers tightened around her heart at the idea of Kata suffering that way. Still, she might do better than if Thora simply stitched the wound closed. Instinct to accept the warrior's help warred with mistrust and fear of the danger he presented.

She gave a nod. "I've seen it done, but do not know how…" Letting her words trail, she returned her concentration to the wounded animal. Despite the continued bleeding, the cut was mostly clean and straight, making the stranger's suggestion more plausible.

"I've only ever done it to a man. Never an animal." He remained two steps away, his sword still sheathed. He withdrew a dagger from his belt and turned it, handing it to her hilt first.

What did he intend? She sensed sincerity, or was she just fooled by his handsome face, the concern in his odd-colored eyes? Not green, not blue, but something in between, a startling contrast to his dark hair that she found intriguing. She shook her head. Why did she think on such foolishness now? She ran a gentle hand along Kata's head, the injured animal barely moving under her touch. In order to save her companion, she had to act now. She reached a trembling hand to accept the blade.

"What should we do?" she asked.

"We need a fire."

"No. It will draw attention."

He took a small step closer and crouched on the other side of Kata. "A small one. Just enough to heat the dagger."

She looked from the blade, to Kata and back to the man. "I don't know if I can…"

"I can do it."

Did she dare trust him? "I don't even know your name!" The words burst free before she'd even considered them.

The corner of his mouth tilted, softening his fierce

demeanor. "I am Ari. I am traveling to Tingwalla."

So many questions raced in her thoughts, but she couldn't decipher a single one. "I am Thora."

"Are you going to The Thing?"

She shook her head. "My journey is none of your concern."

He gave a sharp nod. "Shall we tend your wolf?"

Thora realized Kati sat quietly near Kata's head. The male wolf never once warned Ari off with a growl or baring of his teeth. Clearly the animal didn't consider him a threat. Why? Because he had slain the attacker threatening Thora? Still, many warnings lingered in her thoughts.

"What shall I do?"

Ari looked at the wolf lying motionless on the ground. "Gather kindling for a fire. I will determine a way to keep the animal still."

Thora tilted her head. "How can you do that?"

"She'll need to be bound. And her jaw tied shut."

"No!" Thora stood, fists clenched. "How can you harm her that way?"

"It won't harm her and it is much safer for all of us that way." Ari's voice held a calming tone.

Thora once more knelt beside Kata. She couldn't let her companion die, yet the only way to save her seemed so cruel. The blood staining the wolf's gray fur knotted her gut.

"Are you sure?"

"She will bite if I don't."

Thora nodded, recognizing the truth in Ari's words. "Very well." She leaned in close to Kata's snout. Kati did the same. Tears burned Thora's eyes. "I am sorry. I must hurt you. But you will recover sooner."

She stroked Kata's head then ran her hand along Kati's back. She leaned close to the male wolf's ear. "Tell her I hate what we must do."

Kati rubbed his head against Thora's cheek. She

knew he understood her message, if not her exact words, and shared her sentiment. For a few extra moments, she held him near with an arm over his neck, until he pulled free and moved to sit beside Kata's head, his snout lightly touching the she-wolf's. The wounded animal gave a weak whimper, Kati responding with a whine and a lick of his sister's face.

Turning away, Thora wiped at the tears now rolling down her cheeks. Forcing herself to focus on her task, she surveyed the forest floor, gathering small dry sticks to start a fire. She worried still about drawing attention, but that concern seemed almost laughable when she considered what lay ahead in the next few minutes.

The sound of tearing drew her attention back to Ari. He held a tunic and methodically tore strips from the garment. He seemed unaware she watched him. Despite the serious situation, she found herself admiring his strong jaw, covered with a scruff of beard. His long dark hair hung loosely past his shoulders, instead of being braided or tied back. It gave him an untamed yet somehow regal appearance.

He looked up, catching her stare. Heat ran up her cheeks when he gave her a knowing smile. Something in his unusual eyes, now the dark slate color of a stormy sky, stirred an unfamiliar tingle deep within her. She turned back to her task, even more questions rising about her savior.

Part of her trusted him, well, the part that had no choice, truth be told. Her only chance of saving her wolf lay with the man who had saved *her* from certain rape and likely death. The worry he possessed similar intentions afterward remained, taunting her. She bent to pick up a stick, remembering the brief idea she'd had earlier. If he truly possessed the wealth he appeared to, he might be able to assist her in finding a new village far from here in which to settle. It was a large favor to ask, especially as a debt as big as she owed already hung over her. She had no means to pay him, and wondered what he might demand in recompense. The various ideas that sprang up in her thoughts didn't seem as disturbing as they should.

She forced the troubling thoughts aside, to focus upon later, after Kata's wound had been tended. Seeing to the animal was her priority. Worry for herself had no place in the next hours.

CHAPTER TWO

Ari continued to tear strips from the tunic. The wolf, while weak at the moment, would likely attack the moment the hot blade was applied to her wound. As he prepared for the upcoming treatment, he continued to watch Thora. Every now and then, she glanced his way. Even from this distance, the blush staining her cheeks was clear. He found the sight intriguing.

Why did she travel alone? Well, not completely alone, she had the wolves for protection. The animals were clearly fiercely loyal to her, so he surmised she must have raised them from pups. The male had easily dispatched the one outlaw, warning Ari to use caution around the beasts. Though, so far, the male seemed more inclined to protect his mate rather than attack him, an observation that greatly eased Ari's concerns.

Thora approached, a bundle of twigs and sticks in her arms. The distress in her dark eyes roused a need to banish her worries. He shook his head. He'd been traveling alone too long, to so quickly find himself distracted and entranced. How long had it been since he'd enjoyed a woman's warm body? Months, at least. So long ago, he could barely recall the last time.

Thoughts of ways to secure her to him answered the many dilemmas facing them both. Clearly, despite her lupine companions, she faced a dangerous journey, whatever her ultimate destination. He glanced again at the animals a few feet away. Not dark and vicious, like the legendary Fenrir, they possessed silvery gray coats and at the moment, appeared quite tame.

He stood and accepted the kindling. He nodded toward the wolves. "Go, keep them calm. I will start the fire and then we must begin."

She gave a nod, remaining silent, but tears

shimmered in her dark eyes and he again fought the urge to pull her close and offer comfort. Somehow, he sensed she wouldn't appreciate the gesture, for despite her sadness, she possessed strength. He withdrew a flint from the pouch on his belt, along with a few pieces of touchwood and quickly lit the kindling. Fanning the small flames until they grew, he gathered the strips of cloth and turned to Thora and her wolves.

She watched him warily, even while she spoke softly to the animals. Ari couldn't quite make out her words, but after a moment, the male lay beside her. Ari moved slowly, so as not to frighten the wolves, especially the wounded one, and gently drew the beast's hind legs together. He watched Thora carefully, but she didn't notice, too absorbed in watching how he tended her pet. He repeated his motions with the wolf's front legs. He leaned back and met Thora's stare.

"Hold her head in your lap while I..."

She nodded and gingerly lifted the wolf's head. Ari leaned forward and before the animal had a chance to react, wrapped a cloth strip around her snout, securing her jaws. The beast gave a few attempts to break free, but weakened as she was, quickly stilled again.

He took another strip and poured water from a skin over it. He handed it to Thora.

"Wash away as much of the blood as you can. Do you have the dagger I gave you?"

Thora nodded and pulled the knife from the pocket in her cloak. She handed it to him and he placed it into the fire. Thora gently cleaned the animal's fur. Ari peered closer at the wound. The edges were fairly even, not jagged and irregular, which would make the process easier. He eyed the blade, judging it needed a minute or two more to be hot enough to seal the wound. His skills as a smith served him well. He took the bloodied cloth from Thora and tossed it aside.

"Hold her still."

She nodded, her arms engulfing the wolf's head. Ari lifted the dagger and neared the animal. He hesitated but a moment before using one hand to hold the wound together and pressed the heated blade against the injury.

The animal lurched, her bound legs flailing, a muffled shriek escaping the cloth-wrapped snout. Ari didn't dare look at Thora as he worked, pressing his other hand harder against the writhing body in an attempt to hold the wolf still. The male jumped up, barking and howling but made no attempt to hinder his efforts. Ari heaved a deep breath, one less worry fighting to be heard. After a moment, the wounded beast went still, though the other continued to paw at the ground, whining and barking in empathy for his companion's pain. Ari worked quickly, laying the flat edge of the knife against the laceration for a few seconds before moving along the length of the gash, finally searing the last of the injury closed.

He drew away and let out his breath in a heavy exhale. Wiping the blade clean, he placed it on the ground to let it finish cooling. He looked at Thora. Tears spilled from her eyes and she still held the wolf's head in a tight protective embrace.

He rummaged in his pack, withdrawing a small jar. "Put this on it and bandage her."

He noted the way her hands shook as she accepted the salve. Her stare held his, gratitude shining clear.

"Thank you. For saving me. And for saving Kata."

He gave a nod before turning back to the fire. The afternoon sun had faded, signaling Sol had neared the end of her daily journey. He'd hoped to be several miles closer to Tingwalla by nightfall, as weeks of his journey still stretched before him. Another glance at the woman tending the injured animal roused a riot of conflicting thoughts.

Leaving her alone was not a consideration and the interruption to his plans roused a hint of annoyance. Still, he couldn't deny the fact Thora was one of the comeliest women he'd ever encountered. The thought of ending weeks of celibacy with her had his cock already half-hard. Caution must remain his ally. He eyed the healthy wolf seated beside her. No doubt the beast would attack if he thought Ari threatened his mistress.

If he was truthful with himself, he might admit he rather liked the idea of company for the rest of his journey, but suspected she might not want to accompany him. She'd indicated she had no plans to attend The Thing. He must make her think she no longer had any choice in that matter.

His stomach gave a low grumble, reminding him he'd eaten nothing since waking this morn. He rose, drawing Thora's attention. Beside her the male wolf stood. Ready to defend her, or attack Ari? The beast made no move other than to watch him as intently as his mistress did.

"Are you hungry?" he asked.

Thora blinked, clarity sharpening her gaze. "Actually, I am. I'd not given it much thought."

He nodded. "I must fetch my horse, then I will find something for us to eat. What about them?" He nodded toward the animals.

Thora ran her hand along Kati's head and Ari found himself wishing her hands were on him instead. His cock tightened further.

"Kati will hunt for them. Kata still sleeps."

He turned and strode deeper into the forest, where he'd tied his steed. The animal pranced in apparent excitement upon seeing him. Ari grinned and gave the black a hearty pat.

"Good boy, Gyllir. Come, we are making camp over here." He led the horse back to where Thora remained. At the sight of the wolves, Gyllir rebelled, his movements now jerky and filled with agitation. He dug his front hooves into the dirt and refused another step.

Ari patted the steed's neck.

"It's fine, boy. They'll not harm you." Still, he couldn't coax the animal to come closer to the clearing. With a heavy sigh, he tied the reins to a tree. He turned to Thora. "He fears your wolves. Can you keep watch over him while I hunt our dinner?"

"Yes." She turned to the male wolf and spoke to him. The animal sat, obeying what must have been an order. "Kati will not harm your steed."

"Thank you." With a brief wonderment at the way she communicated with the animals, Ari once again trekked into the forest, moving carefully as he listened for sounds of any small game. Pulling his sling from his belt, he bent and picked up a couple of small rocks. A few steps later, a hare darted out from the underbrush. It hopped away, then paused for several moments, giving Ari just enough time to load and fire the sling. The rock landed squarely on the animal's head. It toppled over and Ari hurriedly picked it up. At that moment, another hare emerged, this one running in the opposite direction. Ari quickened his pace and followed, tying the slain hare to his belt. Once more loading the sling, he kept his gaze on the animal when it slowed. A few minutes later, several more stones used this time, the second hare hung beside the first.

He made his way back to where Thora waited. She had eased the injured wolf from her lap and now tended the fire. She turned when he neared.

"How is your animal?"

"She still sleeps."

"I've found our *náttmál*" He patted the hares on his belt.

She nodded then looked over her shoulder, in the direction he'd laid the outlaw's body. When her gaze swung back to his, it held a note of revulsion.

"Is there any way you can carry Kata back to the grove where I sheltered the last two days?"

He looked over at the still form of the wounded animal. Truthfully, he could easily carry the wolf, but how far away was this grove? He posed the question to her.

She pointed behind him. "That way."

Ari turned in the direction she indicated. A thick cluster of trees lay several long paces away, snug against the foot of a rocky hill. Similar to many places he had slept during his years away from home. He found himself admiring her instincts at finding a fairly safe place for a camp.

"How did they find you?"

Her shoulders heaved with a heavy breath. "When we set out this morning. That's when we encountered them. I found a place for us to hide, and it was a long time before we came out again. I thought perhaps they'd forgotten about us. I should have waited longer."

Something about the way her shoulders slumped, the waver of guilt in her tone, roused the need to assure her she'd done nothing wrong. He clenched his fingers to restrain the impulse.

Saying nothing, he strode to the wounded wolf. He knelt beside the animal.

The beast slept. Would she wake if he touched her? He reached out a hand and stroked the fur along her back. She didn't even flinch. Beside her head, the male wolf watched him with golden eyes, a sight that might normally terrify Ari. The animal made no move to prevent Ari from sliding his arms under the she-wolf.

Gently, he lifted the beast, holding it close to his chest and taking care not to touch the bandaged wound. He stood and turned, meeting Thora's dark wide stare.

"Show me."

She gave a nod, and with a lift of her dress, headed toward the grove of pines. The male fell into step beside her and Ari once more found himself impressed with the rapport between the woman and wolf.

The animal in his arms was not heavy an it
trouble keeping up with Thora's hurried stri V
they stood within the confines of the trees, the h
them added protection. Thora guided him to a pi
forest brush, where he gently laid the she-w
animal hadn't responded in any way to being
deep in the sleep of the injured. When he stepped
Thora immediately fell to her knees beside her pe
spoke softly to the still beast, her fingers stroking th
of the wolf's head. After a few minutes she turned.

Pointing toward the hares on his belt, she said, "G
me those."

Ari handed them to her.

"Fetch our belongings. I'll prepare these."

Ari chuckled at the imperious tone of her order. Did the woman not understand what she owed him? She would, soon enough. Still, she was right. Their possessions needed to be gathered. Saying nothing, he strode out of the grove toward Gyllir and his packs.

When he returned and secured the horse, he found Thora had already finished decapitating and skinning the animals. He laid her sack beside her and she immediately reached in to remove a small bowl. A few moments later, blood from each of the hares filled the bowl.

"We must thank the gods for providing our meal." Thora dipped her fingers in the blood and ran it along her forehead and cheeks, and down her nose, then turned to Ari. "You too."

He held back his smile at the command in her tone. While he didn't usually take kindly to being ordered about, he would acquiesce. This time. Later, when he discussed the debt she owed him, he would make clear that she was not the one in charge.

He was.

***

After spreading the blood along Ari's cheeks and nose, Thora set the bowl down and waved her hands over an attempt to send the value of the sacrifice toward alhalla.

"Odin, accept this meager offering as thanks for this ood. I also thank you and all of the gods for my rescue oday and pray you will see Kata healed quickly."

She glanced up at Ari. With the hare's blood smeared across his face, he looked fierce, like the warrior she sensed him to be. Turning away, she lifted the skinned rabbits and spitted them on a long stick, and turned to the small fire that still burned. Yet, the flames were not nearly strong enough to cook the animals in a timely manner. Propping the stick against a tree, she bent and picked up a rock, motioning to Ari to do the same. She paid him no mind and gathered more rocks, setting them in a large circle around the small pile of flames. Ari handed her more of the larger stones, his hand brushing hers as she took them.

The contact sparked a strange heat that spread through her. She concentrated on her task, picking up larger pieces of kindling and feeding them into the fire, until soon, hearty flames blazed within the circle. She set two large branches upright into the ground at opposite positions of the fire then placed the spitted hares across them. Soon, the smell of the roasting meat filled the air.

She pulled a small cloth from her sack and offered it to Ari to clean his face. He accepted in silence, but his intense gaze bored into her. Now his eyes appeared a dark and dusky blue, like the sky shortly after Sol had ended her race and Mani awaited to make his appearance.

"I must tend to Kata," she said, rising to sit beside her wolf. "Make sure they don't burn."

He arched an eyebrow but said nothing. Thora focused on Kata, gently petting the animal around the bandaged wound. The wolf opened her eyes and the relief that her pet still lived swept over Thora and left her thankful she already sat, for surely her weakened legs would not have held her.

"How do you feel, Kata? Kati is hunting and will bring you food."

Ferocious pain still echoed in the animal's eyes, though now it seemed a little less intense. Was it the salve Ari provided already working? She must believe Kata would soon heal and be well enough to resume their journey, possibly even in a few days. The pace would be slowed for a time, but the need to put more distance between herself and her village stirred again.

Kati returned, two hares of his own caught in his powerful jaws. He placed the dead animals on the ground before Kata and sat, a small whine escaping. Thora smiled and put her arm around him. He licked her face, making her giggle.

"She's feeling better already, Kati. You're a good boy to bring her food."

Another lick and Kati nuzzled her neck. Kata lifted her head and sniffed, the scent of the hare rousing her. The wolf slowly rose up. It took some time before she rested on her forelegs and inched closer to the food. Kati's body shook against her, his tail wagging furiously. He moved to lay snout to snout with Kata. Certain the two would be fine for the moment, Thora ran her hand on each wolf's head then turned to the fire.

Ari still watched her, his gaze heated to a bright and fiery greenish-blue, roving her face and leaving heat in its wake. Her heart raced, her earlier worries about his intentions rising once more. Yet, the concern didn't seem as frightening as it had before. Why? Perhaps it was because she had to admit, her mysterious savior intrigued her in ways she'd never been before. He'd shown several signs of compassion, especially toward Kata. Why did she fear that kindness might prove more dangerous than if he'd attempted to rape or kill her outright?

She tore her gaze away, turning to the cooking meat. The delicious aroma filled the darkening grove, reminding her again of her hunger. When she looked toward him once more, she gasped, finding he had moved silently and quickly. Now he stood before her, making her tilt her head back to meet his stare.

Something feral in his gaze drew a gush of heat to her core. She pressed her legs together, shocked at the ferocity with which her sex swelled. Ari still said nothing, but finally hunkered down in front of her, elbows on his knees.

"We must discuss your debt."

The words hung ominously between them. Thora gulped, her mouth dry as sand.

"You saved me, and Kata as well."

He nodded, but said nothing.

"I have no coin to repay you, but perhaps we can reach an agreement."

"Perhaps. What can you offer?"

"Well, I am not traveling to The Thing, as you are, but I can give you some of my provisions. Do you have any clothing that needs repair?" She nodded to his horse. "I am also quite skilled at –"

"I was thinking of a different kind of service you can provide."

Thora bit her lip, refusing to voice the question to which she already had the answer. His rescue would cost her dearly, it would seem.

"Do you know what I am asking, Thora?"

His gaze continued to bore into her, and her heart thudded against her ribs. She knew, she was no fool, but wasn't sure she wanted to admit it. She'd not given much thought to laying with a man before, had never been drawn to any man enough to want to. But she *was* drawn to this one and the realization she half-wanted to agree to his demand frightened her.

"I do."

"And?"

She hesitated. "Surely there is something else you

will take in payment."

He shook his head. "I don't want anything else."

His words sucked the air from her lungs. "And if I refuse?"

He shrugged. "I can take what I want."

"You would rape me? Then why did you waste your time saving me?"

Again, he shook his head. "It won't be rape. You'll want it."

She forced a brittle laugh. "You are very sure of yourself."

He grinned. "I am."

"I will sic Kati on you."

He threw his head back, his laughter echoing around them. "He is more concerned with his mate."

Ari nodded toward the wolves. Thora turned, dismayed that Kati did indeed appear to be ignoring them. As if sensing her gaze upon him, the wolf looked at her, then at Ari, before resuming his protective position beside Kata. Thora frowned. Still, she had no doubt that if Ari laid a hand on her and she screamed, Kati would come to her defense.

She faced Ari once more. Again, the force of his desire, for there was no longer any doubt that's what she read in his stare now, started that fluttery feeling in her belly. His gaze roamed lower, lingering on her breasts, sparking a tingling sensation that tightened her nipples. She inhaled sharply, fingers clenching at her sides. A strange weakness swept over her.

"You want it, too."

The husky timbre of his voice spurred another flash of heat between her legs. The unfamiliar sensation wreaked havoc in the jumble of her thoughts, and she found herself staring hard at his lips. A half-smile curved his mouth and he inched closer. Barely aware of his hand moving toward her, she remained motionless, still captivated by his mouth. He drew her close, taking her lips with near-bruising force, and the little moan hovering near the top of her throat escaped.

Fire washed over her, the blood scorching in her veins. His mouth moved slowly, deepening the kiss further, his tongue brushing against her lips. Startled, she gasped. He took that moment to sweep deep inside, leaving her head spinning. Her hands moved of their own accord, sliding to his shoulders, tightening against the muscle there, as if she could steady herself against the turbulent tide of yearning that left her bewildered and breathless.

The rumble of his muted laugh vibrated through her and she found herself hauled against him, her body pressed tightly to his. Her fingers slid into his hair, the velvet of the strands rousing more of the wicked sensations assailing her. And still his mouth devoured hers. Her response strengthened and she dueled his tongue, forgetting where they were. Nothing mattered anymore, nothing but this passion he'd sparked. She wanted more.

He drew away, leaving her bereft, and breathing as heavily as he. Long fingers slid along her cheek to her throat and she arched her head back, silently urging him to continue. He chuckled, the sound jolting her from her reverie.

"You see? You want it as much as I."

She said nothing, couldn't deny the truth, even as she wanted to slap the smug smile from his face.

"Give yourself to me. Come with me to The Thing."

As if he had splashed cold water on her, her wits snapped back into place. Shaking her head, she tried to pull free of his embrace. He didn't release her.

"No, I cannot go to Tingwalla."

His eyes narrowed. "Why? What are you afraid of, Thora?"

Her reason for refusal was none of his business. She simply could not go to Tingwalla, and risk her father finding her. She would not be sacrificed for an alliance. She'd choose her own husband and only then would she return.

"It doesn't concern you."

"As you are under my protection, it does."

She gave another tug against his hold, but he held firm. "I don't need your protection!"

"If I hadn't come along when I did, you would be at the mercy of the outlaws."

"I would have disarmed him soon enough. Like every other man, his lust dulled his senses. I was waiting for the right moment, and I would have dispatched him myself."

He laughed again, sparking her anger. She shoved hard at him, relieved when he finally released her. Shaky legs carried her a few steps away and she willed the strength back into them. When she turned to face him once more, his stare, amusement mingled with desire, left her annoyed.

"And when you failed? You could be dead right now."

He leaned in close, towering over her. She refused to give in to the urge to retreat. He would not intimidate her.

"You have no idea what I'm capable of."

"Perhaps I should bind your hands then."

Her eyes widened. "You would not dare!"

"I would. And I will. But for now, I believe our meal is ready."

With that he turned away. She blinked, surprised by the suddenness of his change of mood. For several moments, she remained where she was, gawking at him in astonishment, until the aroma of the cooked meat teased her nose, making her stomach rumble. Assailed by two very different hungers, she forced her unsteady legs to obey, finally taking up a seat across the fire. He had already removed the hares from the spit and used his dagger to cut the food into portions, handing her one.

She hoped he didn't notice the way her hand shook as she accepted the food. Avoiding his gaze, she bit into the meat, the gamy juices flooding her tongue. At the first taste, her hunger escalated and she ate heartily, ignoring the urge to meet the stare she knew focused intently on her.

"Here."

She looked up to see him once again beside her, offering a drinking skin. With still trembling hands, she accepted it.

"Thank you."

She lifted the skin, taking a long swallow of ale, warm and musty from the skin but still refreshing. Thirst quenched, she returned the skin to him, dismayed when he sat beside her. When he was so close, her thoughts refused to be reined in and she needed her wits sharp.

"So, Thora, do you agree to my demand, or do I take what I want from you.?"

"I'll not lie with you willingly."

"So be it." He picked up another hunk of meat and bit into it, giving her a wink and a knowing smirk.

Damn him! He knew she would respond to him, even if she initially attempted to fight him. Heart racing once more, she found any remaining appetite had fled. She stood, determined to get away from him. Her wolves needed tending and maybe she might find a way to convince him not to take her innocence. That thought roused another burst of heat within and she knew damn well that with a few more kisses, she'd not deny him anything.

She raised her eyes heavenward, praying to Odin for the strength to resist. But even as the request solidified, another idea, one that had sprouted earlier and been dismissed, rose anew.

CHAPTER THREE

Ari watched Thora walk away, well aware of the conflict brewing within her. Rising, he turned to tend Gyllir, his thoughts filled with the intriguing woman he'd found himself with. Her passionate response to his kiss told him he would have little trouble seducing her, though the idea of binding her, rendering her helpless to his whims, remained strong. He'd indulged in such dark sexual games many times, relished the thrill of dominating his lovers, bending them to his will while also giving exquisite delight, mixed with varying amounts of pain. He wanted to torment Thora that way, watch her eyes cloud with desire, make her body writhe with pleasure. He would, he vowed silently. And she would learn to crave his touch.

Once assured Gyllir had what he needed for the night, Ari dragged his saddle and remaining packs back toward the fire. He resumed his former position against the log and studied Thora.

She knelt beside her pets, her long chestnut hair obscuring her face. He found himself jealous of the wolves, wanted her to touch him with such tenderness. The notion of her hands on him set his cock to full hardness. He would have her tonight. He would have her begging for his touch, pleading with him to take her.

His growing desire to indulge and delight in her body barely surpassed his need to know why she ran. No doubt remained that her journey was a flight. From what, or whom, did she flee? The fear in her eyes accompanying her refusal to travel to The Thing troubled him. He needed to know what threatened her, so he could protect her. *Wait. What?* Where had that startling notion come from?

He sighed, staring into the flames. Since he'd first seen her struggling with the ruffian, the need to defend and safeguard her had taken over, growing stronger with each passing moment. Bah! He'd been too long alone. Surely the gods only toyed with him, by placing such an intriguing and beautiful woman in his path.

Or maybe she was Freyja herself, come to torment him, transforming her two felines into wolves who walked beside her. He shook his head, smiling at the fanciful thought. Freyja would never let a mere mortal man survive the initial attack made on Thora. Ari was merely lonely and filled with lust. That explained the silliness making him forget the purpose of his journey these last three years.

What would Thora think if she knew he was an outlaw himself, no longer a feared yet respected and valued warrior? Granted, the crimes he'd been accused of were false, and he had proof now to clear his reputation. Others would speak for him; to protect those until the time came to face the council at The Thing and absolve him of the accusations leveled against him, those others traveled separately. For now, in the eyes of society, he remained an outlaw. True, he could wait the additional months for his sentence to end, but if he didn't remove the stain on his reputation, he would forever be looked upon with suspicion. Soon, he would be a free and honorable man once again. And those who'd tried to destroy him would see justice.

Thora neared, drawing him from his thoughts. Her lower lip, caught between her teeth, sent his lust surging once more. Something in her eyes warned him to be wary, as if she planned some nefarious act. Maybe she did. The earlier thought of binding her rose again, the idea meriting further consideration.

"May we discuss my debt?" she asked, so quietly, he almost didn't hear.

"Yes." He motioned to the ground beside him, against a log that offered a meager comfort. She knelt, a few feet away, facing him.

"If I… agree to your requirement, will you force me to go to The Thing?"

"It is where I am going. I am determined you will accompany me."

She nodded, lowering her head. "I know. But…"

He waited for her to say more, but she remained silent.

"Thora, who do you run from?"

Her head snapped up, her dark eyes blazing with anger.

"Why do you think I am running?"

He shrugged, studying the flush taking over her face. "You are alone, no family or other traveling party. You are traveling away from Tingwalla, and carry little with you, as if your flight happened quickly."

She blinked and stared at him, her face ashen, even in the glow of firelight.

"I…" She lowered her head once more, and he almost didn't hear her next hoarsely whispered words. "I am fleeing my family. My father plans to wed me to an jarl's heir. I don't want to marry any man not of my choosing."

"Surely you can refuse the match?"

Daughters doing so was not uncommon, Ari had known several who had done exactly that, though he'd often wondered whether the women who gave their consent to a marriage felt they had no choice. He'd seen fear on too many of their faces when they were presented to their husbands on their wedding day to believe most agreed with their families' choice.

She shook her head. "My father insists. He travels to Tingwalla with my family and his men. The only way to prevent my marriage is to stay away from The Thing."

"Thora, do you not worry the failure of the alliance could be a problem for your clan?"

She gave a heavy sigh, her eyes closing. Regret lined her brow. "I do worry. But I cannot wed this Hersir. He is cruel and heartless."

Ari sat up straight. Had he heard correctly? Hersir? Could it possibly be? He managed to maintain an aloof expression, though he itched to learn more of the man Thora had been promised to. Maybe her appearance on his journey had been to make his vengeance so much sweeter. Surely the gods had intervened, bestowing their blessings on his quest.

"If you've never met him, how would you know?"

She gave another sigh, opening her eyes to gaze steadily at him. "I walk with my wolves a lot." She paused and turned to look over at the sleeping animals. When she faced Ari again, she drew her knees up, wrapping her arms around them.

"Something tells me you are quite the eavesdropper."

The glow of the fire now revealed the flush in her cheeks. He chuckled. This woman was enjoyable to be near, unlike many he'd known over the years. She piqued his interest in so many ways. Most likely, she was quite the troublemaker. He found he rather liked it, and wished to see her antics for himself.

"I do hear things. And what I've heard mentioned of this man is bothersome."

Ari somehow managed to maintain an air of casual interest, but his excitement built at the thought of snatching away his brother's bride grew near as strong as his need to clear his name.

"What have you heard?"

She hesitated, her hands once again twisting in her lap. "That he once killed a boy who stumbled in front of him. And that he uses his power to take whatever he chooses from those not as strong as he."

That sounded like his brother. Hersir always took what he felt should be his, whether it was right or not. Having the ear of the jarl made it unlikely most would protest. Ari remembered one time when Hersir had helped himself to a family's harvest, claiming it for the jarl. The man had dared to refuse and ended up dead, leaving a widow and four orphaned children, without their crops to feed themselves. Hersir then availed himself of the widow's body for months afterward, until she finally gathered her children and fled the village, seeking refuge with family from another town.

"So you are to wed him, then?"

She nodded. "My father has made the agreement. After The Thing, he was to bring Hersir back to Grindafell for the wedding."

"You fled before they could return."

She nodded. "I won't go back. And I can't go to Tingwalla."

"An impossible dilemma." Ari leaned back against the log once more, his thoughts racing with ideas. "But I must be compensated. Don't you agree?"

Again, she nodded. "I've given your demand some thought. If I were to… offer myself to you, then afterward you can continue to Tingwalla, and I will go my way. But I will no longer be valuable as a bride. I would ask that you take a message to my father and perhaps he will stop searching for me."

Ari sucked in a breath. The wench was cunning and his admiration for her grew even more, as did his yearning. He shifted, his cock now hard and uncomfortable. He cleared his throat.

"Aren't you worried your father's honor will be ruined? You place him in a difficult position by refusing a marriage he's agreed to."

Thora shrugged. "I know. But I have no choice. My father married my mother for love, and when she died, he found another, and their love is strong. I only want the same for myself."

Ari nodded in understanding. Thora was like most other women, wanting a love match, rather than an alliance to ensure the strengthening of both families and clans. He also knew full well that she would never have that while wed to Hersir. But Ari had no intention of letting Thora leave his side. She'd likely be furious when she realized his lies, and again the idea of binding her so she couldn't flee poked at him. Hel, once she learned the truth, he'd have no choice. He held back the eager grin and thought carefully on his next words.

"Very well, Thora. I will accept your offer of payment, however, there are conditions on this agreement."

Her lips pressed together, her eyes flashing with suspicion. "What are your conditions?"

"I decide when it is time for us to part ways."

She nodded. "What else?"

"You will obey my every order. Please me and you shall be rewarded."

"And if I don't?"

He shrugged. "You'll be punished."

Only the crackling of the flames broke the abrupt silence. Even the creatures of the forest had quieted, as if all waited to hear her reply. He held her stare, daring her to refuse.

She didn't. In fact, he wasn't sure he managed to completely contain his surprise when she nodded again.

"Very well. I accept your terms." She looked away for a moment, then leveled her dark stare on him once more. "When… I assume you want…"

He chuckled. "Yes, Thora, I want you. And I will have you. Tonight."

***

Thora sucked in a breath. The husk in his voice sent heat pulsing through her veins. Her sex throbbed, growing hot and damp, her breasts swelling and tingling in anticipation. While she'd not wanted to give herself to a man she didn't love, Ari did stir a fierce yearning, one she found herself curious to explore further. She would get much out of this, even if she did it only to repay her debt.

Strangely, the biggest relief came at the idea of her ruination, making her unwanted as a bride for a jarl's heir. Ari's point about dishonoring her father had stung, but little choice was left to her. Her father was prepared to barter her away as if she were no more than livestock, and that knowledge still cut deep.

All thoughts of her father vanished when Ari stood and walked over to her. He held out his hand and she hesitantly placed her trembling fingers in it. He pulled her up and close, his mouth coming down hard on hers, muffling her surprised squeak. Already, the fever he'd sparked earlier roared back to life, rushing through her with such force, she would have fallen had he not been holding her. His tongue swept between her lips and she responded eagerly to the velvety caress.

His hands slid down her back to her ass, cupping her and pressing her even tighter against him. Even through their clothes, his hard shaft pressed against her core. Need rose, a hunger she'd never known taking over her senses. She held tight to him, her tongue dueling with his and not caring when he reached for the laces at the back of her neck. The brush of his fingers as he untied them was a teasing torment, one that left her breathless, her head spinning.

Finally he drew away and she opened her eyes to find him studying her with a gaze that near scorched her on its own. A ragged breath shuddered through her. He trailed a finger along her cheek before moving to open her brooches and beads, allowing him to slide the *smokkr* from her shoulders.

A moment of alarm rose, for an instant cooling her passion. But when he continued to hold her gaze, in another second the panic faded, replaced with a surge of longing when he slid the dress down her arms, followed immediately by her undershift. The chill of the evening air raised gooseflesh on her skin and finally, the dress slid still further, now baring her breasts. Her nipples hardened almost painfully, yet she relished the tingling in her flesh.

Ari's stare drifted to gaze on her breasts. Her hands tightened on his shoulders at his low groan. Was he pleased? Why should it matter?

"Beautiful," he murmured, right before cupping her breasts in his hands. Another trembling breath rasped through her at the touch. She half-expected to see sparks along her skin as he explored her, his fingers like a hot blade leaving fire in their wake. He caressed and squeezed, and Thora's fingers tightened on his arms. Her legs wobbled ominously, the intense delight overtaking all her senses. The taste of his lips still lingered on hers and with each breath, she inhaled his rich musky scent. She only wished he would look at her, so she could get some sense of what he felt. Was it only she who thought the world spun madly about them?

Her thoughts grew into a muddled mess, fading under the ever-growing lust Ari's caresses caused. Passion had hold of her now and it rocked her very soul, leaving her whirling in the maelstrom.

When his fingers tightened around her nipples, a low moan finally escaped, her entire body quivering under the intensity of the sensations robbing her of her wits. Flashes of bliss pulsated through her, her only awareness of the delight consuming her body. Her sex throbbed, hot and wet, the tumultuous pleasure sucking the breath from her lungs. Finally, knees no longer able to support her, her legs buckled and she leaned heavily into him.

He wrapped his arms around her, a soft chuckle escaping. The feel of his kisses pressing against her forehead drew her from her stupor. She sucked in a deep breath, echoes of the pleasure he spurred quivering through her.

"You are quite passionate, Thora."

His low voice, heavy with desire, seemed a heated

caress against her ear. Another tremor jolted through her. She gulped deep breaths of air, but it did nothing to cool the ferocity of the desire still holding her in its tempting grip.

Awareness returned when Ari guided her back to sit beside the fire. He tilted her head back and placed a tender kiss on her lips.

"Wait here."

She blinked several times, the loss of his nearness drawing a different kind of shiver in the cool evening air, yet she made no move to cover herself. Her gaze never left him as he moved to his pack and removed several items, though since he kept his back to her, she had no clear view of what he did. Each breath came heavily while she waited for him to return to her side.

After what seemed an eternity, he finally turned. The heat in his eyes warmed her anew. Anticipation for what else he planned set her heart to racing again. The sliver of alarm that remained added to the tumult, another layer of delight tinged with dark promise. His earlier words about obeying him whispered through her thoughts, spurring tremors of eagerness. What did he mean by punishing her if she disobeyed? And why did she so badly want to discover his intentions?

He lifted his arms holding up several fur blankets. He gave her a smile before carefully laying the skins on the other side of the fire, creating an enticing bed. Her gaze held his when he approached, his pace quick and purposeful until he stood before, taking her hand and pulling her to her feet. His mouth crashed onto hers and she wrapped her arms around his shoulders, needing to ground herself against his passionate onslaught.

The fierce sensations assaulted her wits, as if the heat from Sol's summer chariot shone within her, making everything inside squirm with delight. When he set her away, their harsh breathing mingled like erotic off-key music in the quiet of the secluded glen. Desire glazed his eyes with a deeper green. Desire for her. The realization set off a giddy whirl of excitement and eagerness. All the reasons she shouldn't give herself to him briefly poked through her haze of passion. The reasons for doing so overwhelmed the doubts, her own yearning taking over most of her awareness. She wanted this. Wanted him. And he knew it, too.

Thora didn't care. She longed for more of his kisses, his caresses. As of he read her thoughts, he gently cupped her bared breasts once more. She arched toward him, a groan of pleasure escaping. The groan quickly turned a soft whine when he withdrew.

"We have all night."

His whisper contained a dark promise she had no strength to resist. How could it be that mere hours ago, she'd not even known this man existed and now she craved his touch as if it were the air she breathed? Still, she remained motionless, waiting for him to guide her. She needed to maintain some of her dignity, not fall upon him as though she was Kata in heat.

He reached for her again, but only to slide her kirtle further down, past her hips, until it drifted to the ground around her ankles, leaving her bared before him. A wave of heat suffused her at the force of the fire blazing in his eyes.

For several moments, which to Thora seemed an eternity, he simply stood before her, his gaze moving over her. She fought the urge to cover herself, instead lifting her chin and straightening her spine. Her reward was a pleased smile that left her breathless.

"You tempt me beyond my endurance."

His words came out on a growl and she barely had time to savor the delight before he once again pulled her close, devouring her mouth with a kiss that left her head spinning. Her breasts mashed against his tunic, the fabric another tantalizing sensation added to the riot in her body. Her hands moved to his shoulders and she pushed him away. The confusion in his eyes almost drew a laugh.

"What's wrong?"

"I'm naked. You're not."

A grin brightened his face and near stole her breath. He truly was one of the most fetching men she'd ever known.

"Very well," he said, his voice still heavy and deep with desire. When he moved to undo his belt, she reached for his hands, stilling his motions.

"What now?" he asked.

With a sly smile she said, "I wish to do it."

Another grin, and a nod, and Ari dropped his hands to his sides. Before her boldness faded, she reached for his belt with trembling fingers. The buckle and tail of the belt were made of what appeared to be gold, but she had no time or inclination to study it now. She quickly opened the belt and pulled it free of his pants, pushing them down as he had done to her dress. Aware he watched her, she forced her focus to remain on his clothing. With a deep breath to steady her trembling fingers, she stood, reaching for the laces at his neck. They opened easily enough, but Ari remained motionless, hindering her progress. She paused, meeting his stare. The hunger there almost undid her determination to keep some semblance of control. Somehow, she managed, composing the errant need to offer herself without protest. Instead, she lifted her chin, arching an eyebrow.

"Raise your arms."

"Are you giving me an order?" He arched an eyebrow, his mouth set in a grim line.

A momentary recollection of his earlier words poked through her concentration. She forced them aside. If he meant to intimidate her, she'd not allow it. Meeting his gaze steadily, she nodded.

"I am. I cannot remove the tunic if you don't. Unless

you'd prefer to end this now."

Another hearty laugh echoed around her. Several moments passed in which he kept his stormy gaze upon her, but finally, he did as she asked and raised his arms.

When she bent to grab the hem of his tunic he thrust his hips toward her. A hint of the solid bulge against her core startled her, forcing her back, the tunic gripped in her fingers. The movement pulled the garment up and over his head and upraised arms, leaving him nearly nude before her. She tossed aside the tunic, her gaze hungrily absorbing the sight of his firm muscled shoulders and chest glistening in the firelight. For several moments, she kept her focus above his waist, but curiosity soon took over. Daring a glance into his smug expression, she ignored the twinge of annoyance and let her eyes drift lower. She gulped, hoping her expression didn't reveal her sudden wariness.

His shaft rose long and thick from a bed of dark curls. While she found the sight impressive and intriguing, she feared he would split her in two. Surely, he didn't intend to… her eyes snapped back to his face.

"Don't worry, Thora. It will fit."

Heat scorched her cheeks. Had he read her thoughts? "I… maybe this wasn't the best –"

He pulled her close, knocking the breath from her lungs. His hard cock lined up perfectly with her damp sex, her core clenching with spasms of desire.

"I assure you, you will enjoy all of it. Well, there may be a moment or two of pain, at first. But it will soon pass."

"How would you know?"

"I've bedded my share of virgins."

Thora had nothing to say in response. He pressed another bruising kiss against her lips and soon she forgot her worries. He drew away, cupping her face in his hands, his fingers moving gently over her skin and sparking all the banked fires back to life.

"Come, I will show you."

He took her hand and led her to where he'd arranged the furs. She took a moment to look over at her pets, relieved to see that both appeared to sleep. A twinge of guilt for not being at their side now, when Kata needed her most, made her tug on Ari's hand. He turned to face her.

"I should check on them. One more time."

His lips twisted in a half-scowl, but he gave a slight incline of his head and released her hand. "Go. Return to me quickly."

She turned, feeling oddly exposed. Walking naked in the forest was not something she had done before, especially not with a fierce warrior watching her every move. She tip-toed to the wolves, pleased when both lifted their heads. She knelt beside them, gently stroking their fur. That Kata seemed comfortable soothed her worries.

"I will be with Ari if you need me. Kati will come, right boy?"

The male pressed his nose into her hand and gave her an acknowledging lick. She smiled and leaned close.

"I will call if I need you."

Kati's eyes possessed a message, telling her he understood. Stroking Kata once more, she rose and turned to face the man waiting for her. Her agitated worry returned and she gingerly made her way back to him, ignoring the bite of twigs and pebbles under her feet.

When she was a few steps away, she paused. After tonight, everything would change. She took a deep breath. And the next step.

CHAPTER FOUR

The sight of Thora walking toward him, head held high, set fire raging in Ari's veins. The tease over the last hours had only inflamed his senses and his lust neared its breaking point. Control lay in frayed threads around him. He needed to slow down. While he anticipated his domination of her, he didn't want her to truly fear him. Well, maybe he did, just a little. Still, ensuring her loyalty to him when the time came to reveal the truth before the council was another facet of his revenge that he must not forget.

Yet, somehow, something about this woman screamed that his life would be forever changed once he possessed her. At the moment, he didn't care. In the morning, he would ensure his control and dominance over her. But now, tonight, he wanted nothing more than to sate himself with her body.

She paused a few steps away and her shoulders lifted with a sharp breath. His gaze was immediately drawn to her full high breasts, the pink tips hard. His fingers itched with the need to touch her. He moved toward her at the same moment she took another step closer, bringing them mere inches apart.

He placed his hand on her shoulder, savoring the way she quivered beneath his touch. She possessed a deep passion, one which had likely never been tapped, judging from her reactions. His hands on her breasts alone had brought a fiery climax he'd not expected, and clearly, neither had she. What would happen when he finally explored the depths of her body? Anticipation of the eruption of Thora's deepest passion also held a warning, one he heeded by composing his thoughts. For the coming hours, nothing mattered but the physical connection. The rest would follow.

He drew her near, pressing a kiss against her full lips, his cock hard and seeking her damp heat. Her eager response spurred him to slide his hands along her hips, fingers drifting lower to find the soft tangle of curls hiding her secrets. Secrets he meant to uncover, and claim for his own.

Beneath his touch, her body tightened. In pleasure or fear? He paused in his exploration, using his tongue and his lips along hers to once more soften the muscles in her shoulders and arms. When he slid his fingers along her pussy, she gave a little moan and leaned heavily into him. Her slick flesh near scorched his hand and the heavy sweet scent of her arousal surrounded him, overtaking his senses.

Each tremble of her body echoed within him and the need to possess her, now, took over his thoughts. He drew away, sucking in his breath at the way her heavy-lidded eyes fluttered open, revealing her need. Pride that he'd been the one to cause such passion gave him the strength to hold back. He wanted to hear her beg, plead for her release. He wouldn't oblige her, not until he was deep within the warm depths of her body and he could watch and feel her come undone when he drove her over the edge.

Stepping away, he took her hand. "Come."

She followed quietly when he drew her down to the furs. Easing her to her back, he stretched out beside her, propping his head up on one arm. Her dark eyes remained fixed on him and he had the errant thought he could drown in their depths. Leaning over, he pressed a soft kiss to her lips, then trailed his mouth along her cheek down to her neck.

A soft sigh escaped her, but to Ari's ears, it sounded like a roar. He slid his hand across her breast, relishing the way she arched against him, as if seeking greater contact. He held back a grin and continued the teasing caresses, finally catching her nipple in his fingers. She moaned, reaching for him. He grabbed her wrist, halting her, enchanted by her confused gaze.

"I want to touch you."

Her husky words shivered through him. If he allowed that, he feared he might not last long enough to be inside her when he came. He shook his head.

"No."

"Why?"

Some of her bewilderment faded, replaced with a hint of hurt. The need to assuage it rose up swift and sharp.

"If you do…" Telling her he feared losing control and acting like an untrained lad seemed somehow a weakness. "I want no distractions while I take my pleasure."

A sharp intake of breath accompanied the tensing of her body. "And what of my pleasure?" Anger sharpened her tone and she tugged against his restraining hand.

"You'll receive plenty of pleasure, *ástin minn*, I promise. But my pleasure comes before yours."

Sparks of annoyance flared in her eyes and she pulled her wrist free, sitting up. Ari placed his hand on her chest and pushed her back down, straddling her. He barely had time to duck the hand flying toward his face before again catching her arm. Her cry of frustration accompanied another attempt to hit him, but once more, he stopped her, pinning her arms above her head with one hand. She bucked against him in an attempt to dislodge him, but he leaned heavily atop her, holding back his groan when his cock came up against her damp sex. Her eyes widened as she also realized the position they now held and she stilled beneath him.

"Release me," she demanded.

Heart racing with excitement, Ari shook his head, grinning at her cry of outrage.

"I agreed to repay the debt as you wanted, but I'll not be treated like a lowly thrall!"

Her full lips, still swollen from his kisses, drew his focus and he lowered his mouth to hers. When he slid his tongue along her lips, a sharp nip sent him reeling back. She'd bitten him! He held back a laugh. This feisty hellion promised him great satisfaction.

"I like your fire. Taming you will be a delight." He spoke slowly, watching her eyes closely for her reaction. She didn't disappoint.

Fury flashed in her dark gaze and she again tried to buck him off. He held firm.

"I am not an animal to be broken! Let me go!"

Again he shook his head. "You owe me, remember? And I set the terms."

She looked past him. Toward the wolves. Would they attack if she called them? He dared a glance over his shoulder.

Both animals remained where they were, the female still weak from her wounds, the male hovering protectively over her. But Ari knew Kati watched them. He turned back to Thora.

"Don't. You will regret it."

"I already regret agreeing to this madness. Let me go!"

He shifted his hips, his cock achingly hard against her wet pussy. The movement drew a sharp gasp.

"You don't want me to let you go."

She closed her eyes and looked away, a clear refusal to admit what he already knew. With his free hand, he reached for his discarded belt and wrapped it around one of her wrists. The moment she realized his intention, her eyes snapped open, her shout echoing in the clearing. Before she had a chance to break free, he secured the belt firm around both her wrists. He leaned back, his cock still hard against her damp heat. He pulled on the trailing end of the belt. She swung her bound hands toward him but he tugged, halting her movement and drawing her flush against him.

"Until your debt is fully paid, you belong to me, and I will make the decisions. You agreed, but insist on fighting me. So be it."

"I should have known you are no better than those foul outlaws you "saved" me from."

He ran a hand over her hair, not surprised when she jerked away. His cock grew harder than ever and he knew he had to be inside her soon. But first he wanted to remind her of the passion that existed between them.

He reached for her breast, cupping it, his finger rolling lightly over her nipple. A shudder rippled through her, but she clenched her jaw. He smiled. Her resistance would soon crumble. He pinched the hardened tip and smiled at her sharp intake of breath. When he repeated the motion, a low moan escaped.

"You see, Thora, what I can do to you?"

The husk in his voice betrayed his own lust, and he noted the awareness glowing in her gaze. A hint of a smug smile hovered on her lips. He longed to kiss her again, but decided against it for now. As it was, she'd earned a punishment for her earlier bite, but he wouldn't bring that to her attention just yet. He gave her breast another squeeze, delighted at how her mouth opened to suck in a ragged breath. With a quick movement, he shifted away from her. She stared defiantly at him, once more tugging against the belt binding her wrists. He wrapped the end tighter around his hand. Without giving her any warning, he yanked her forward and across his lap, face down. For a moment, she remained motionless and silent before erupting in fury.

"You vile bastard! What in Hel's name are you doing?"

She bucked and writhed, trying to escape his hold, but he caught her flailing legs between his. She gave another shriek when he pinned her bound wrists to the ground. With his other hand, he stroked the sensuous curves of her ass, drawing another outraged yell.

"You bit me," he reminded her in a casual tone. "I warned you what would happen if you didn't obey."

"How dare you!" She heaved against his hold once more, her movement further tormenting his aching cock. He pinched her trembling flesh, holding back a chuckle at the strangled cry that escaped her.

With no warning, he raised his hand and brought it down harshly against her ass. For a moment, she stiffened, then her writhing attempts to free herself began anew. No sounds escaped and he found himself disappointed and a little annoyed. He wanted to hear her cries. He merely tightened his hold and landed another blow. The blood roared in his ears, the feel of the warm skin of her belly rubbing against his cock driving him to strike again and again.

Finally, a whimpering sob broke through the haze engulfing him. He paused, resting his hand lightly against her reddened flesh. She still squirmed, but her movements had taken on a sensual rhythm. He noted the way her shoulders shook with each shuddering breath and the sounds of her little moans. With a knowing smile, he reached between her legs, sliding his fingers slowly through the curls covering her charms. Her body tightened, but she didn't resist as he found her pussy and stroked lightly against her swollen and soaked flesh.

"You little minx! You like this!" He'd never imagined it possible, but his cock grew still harder, his balls tightening in need.

She said nothing, but a low groan escaped. He continued to caress her sex, sliding along her slick heat and finally to her clit. At the first touch, her head shot up and she wriggled wildly. He gave a tender pinch and another violent quiver swept over her. His mouth went dry as sand. He'd never known a woman to possess such lust. How many ways could he play with her? The idea took hold and he knew he had to keep her long enough to find out.

A few more strokes along her cleft and her panting hung heavily in the still of the forest. He withdrew, chuckling when she gave a disappointed moan.

"I told you, Thora. Your pleasure comes after mine. Now, I shall finish your punishment then we will proceed."

"I hate you!"

Despite the harsh words, her voice possessed a hoarseness that sounded more like passion than anger. Ari suppressed a shiver.

"I'm sure you do."

He brought his hand down hard again, noting that this time, her cries held desire, need. The knowledge he'd brought her to this state fired him to rush through the last strikes, finally stopping to caress her heated skin. He soothed her a few more moments, then softened his hold and gently eased her up, turning her to face him.

He sucked in a breath at the sight of her tear-streaked face. This woman let her emotions out to the fullest. He suddenly feared getting lost in the powerful maelstrom.

***

Thora hitched a breath, her vision blurred with tears. Despite her anger at the way Ari had spanked her, need ran through her with such force, she had little strength to resist. How could the pain of his punishment spark such hunger, make her want to once again feel the blinding delight he'd given her earlier?

The intensity of her desire frightened her. She'd never imagined such passion truly existed, despite seeing the deep love her father and stepmother shared. To experience some of it for herself left her stunned and exhilarated, excited and terrified, all at the same time.

When Ari's fingers gently wiped away her tears, she nearly threw herself on him. What was wrong with her? She should be furious with how he'd treated her, but the burning soreness in her bottom throbbed through her in an oddly pleasant manner, feeding her desire instead.

Silence hung heavily between them, only her ragged breaths breaking the quiet of the night. He pulled her near and she made no attempt to resist, seeking the heat of his lips as they neared hers.

At the first contact, he devoured her and she let him, meeting the harsh thrusting of his tongue driving deep into her mouth. A growing awareness of what she wanted, no, needed, sparked within, and the desire to resist faded further.

For what seemed hours, he did nothing more than kiss her with a hunger she feared might consume her. When he finally drew his mouth from hers, she opened her eyes to find in his a lust that surely matched her own.

Why did it seem that he roused something in her she had never even realized she had been missing? Even with her hands bound, after he'd spanked her, she wanted nothing more than to lose herself in the fire of passion. As if something had been absent within her, something Ari brought to life in a way that left her reeling.

The last of her determination to resist crumbled to dust. She wanted the fire he stoked. Having tasted the bliss his touch could bring, she found herself with a hunger for more. The last vestiges of embarrassment floated away on the evening breeze. Why shouldn't she seek her pleasure? No longer did she resent the leather binding her wrists. Despite the way his lips and tongue wreaked havoc on her senses, she had the presence of mind to realize he no longer held the trailing end of her bonds. She lifted her arms, letting her bound wrists settle against the back of his neck.

The sudden tensing of his body sent a shiver along her spine. The surprise in his stare sparked an instant of humor, one quickly chased by the untamed gleam that arose a moment later. Thora's heart tripped in its rapid rhythm.

"I think you like acting my slave."

The deep husk in his voice drew a responding heat

in her core. She pressed against him, her sex needing the contact with his own hard and hot flesh.

"No, I merely seek my own pleasure."

The grin lighting his face grew positively feral. The sight called to her in a way that left her anticipating what was to come with an eagerness she'd never known before.

"Well, then, I shall do my best to give you that. After I've reached my own."

The brief spark of annoyance flared and faded. She didn't care anymore, she only wanted what he would give her. He'd already proven his masterful touch could inspire a ferocious desire that shattered her awareness of everything but him. She found she rather liked it, though the tiny voice of reason continued to warn of the danger that lie in such feelings. At that moment, he thrust his hips toward her, the heat of his hard shaft sliding along her sex chasing any remnants of caution to the wind.

Ari continued to move slowly against her, stirring her to the fever pitch of moments before. She arched toward him, pressing her mouth against his neck and kissing and licking the salty, heated skin. A wild quivering swept over him before he stilled.

She drew away and lifted her questioning gaze to his.

"Why did you stop?"

***

Ari ground his teeth to hold the climax threatening to explode at bay. The husky question, laced with frustration, combined with the feel of her slick and hot pussy, threatened to sever the already tenuous hold on the reins of his control and he wasn't even inside her yet. Her feisty passion combined with a healthy portion of innocence unleashed something primal within him he couldn't name.

"I am not yet ready." He forced the words through his clenched jaw, inhaling sharply when she undulated toward him, the flesh of her sex surrounding him nearly as delightful as if he were fully engulfed in her sheath.

He grabbed her hips. "Remain still."

The fire of annoyance flared in her dark gaze, but she said nothing. Was that a curt nod indicating he should continue, or merely a way to protect herself from more discomfort? Strangely, he sensed a struggle within her, one to hold back. How he understood she was as caught in the torrent as he, he'd never know for sure, but the instinct gave him the strength he needed to contain his riotous lust. A few more deep breaths and he was once more eager to continue without the threat of ending the joining too soon.

He slid one hand to her pussy, stroking the swollen flesh surrounding him. In a few moments, he would be completely inside her, her sweet sheath completely enclosing his cock. Beneath him, Thora moaned and trembled, her legs wrapped tight around his back. He barely had room to move, but somehow managed to shift enough so the tip of his cock rested at her opening.

He reached up and brushed the hair from her face. Her gaze snapped to his and in the depths of her dark eyes, he read the same passion that held him just as tenaciously.

"This will hurt."

Several moments passed before she responded.

"Do it. Now."

He wasted not a second more and thrust hard, taking her innocence in one stroke. She cried out. Now embedded within her heat, Ari forced himself to remain motionless to allow her to adjust to his invasion, though he desperately wanted to drive still more deeply into her body.

He studied her, eyes tightly shut, vestiges of pain lining her face. "Thora, look at me."

Slowly, her eyes opened and despite the pain pulling taut across her cheeks, he saw passion still flaming in her stare.

"Only pleasure now. I promise."

He didn't wait for her response, merely shifted inside her, a hint of the way he wanted to take her. Her eyes widened, a hoarse moan shaking out of her. He eased back, savoring her cry of delight, then slowly slid deeper within her.

"Oh, yes!"

Her shout surprised him, encouraged him to increase his tempo, to take them both to the pinnacle promised by the sensations already assaulting them. The feel of her fingers scratching along the back of his neck enflamed him further. He took her mouth in a bruising kiss, silencing her needy cries as he stroked within her. Her tongue thrust against his, mimicking his own actions, driving him on. Each of her muffled shouts vibrated within him, in time with the furious rhythm that tossed him in every direction, until the feel of her sex clenching hard on his cock sent him into a blinding release. He pulled away from her mouth, his exultant cry echoing with hers, the force of his climax filled with a force that made him feel as though he soared high above Midgard. Beneath him, Thora rocked and shuddered, her own cries resembling the sharp sound of the long lur horns, sending shivers along his spine and adding to the tumult overtaking him.

It seemed hours passed before Ari's breathing and heart steadied, and he resisted the urge to collapse upon her. Her lips sought and found his once more, a sweet ending to the fiery passion that had consumed them both, one that left him sated and complete. Content. Relaxed in ways he hadn't been in years. He forced his trembling arms to hold him as he shifted, not yet willing to relinquish the warmth of her body. As if attuned to his desires, she tightened herself around him. Somehow, he managed to slide to his back, his softening cock still buried within her. With a shift of his hips, Thora now rested atop him, her head nestled against his neck. He drew her bound hands from around his neck. She snuggled closer, somehow finding his fingers and twining hers with them.

Why did he find himself wishing he could savor this delight for the rest of his days?

CHAPTER FIVE

Sunlight filtered through Thora's sleep. She'd much prefer to remain in slumber, but the lick of a raspy tongue on her cheek roused her. An attempt to stretch stopped when she butted against the warmth of a solid chest. A man's chest. Ari's chest.

She forced her eyes open, squinting against the bright sun. Kati loomed over them. Thora noted the way Ari's arms held tight around her waist, pressing her close. Her hands, still bound by his belt, rested on his chest. He no longer held the tail of her bonds.

Her eyes slowly adjusted to daylight, brighter than it should be for early morning. How long had they slept? At the very moment she lifted her head from his shoulder, Ari tightened his embrace.

"Where are you going?" He didn't open his eyes and his voice was thick with sleep.

"Kata needs me."

Several moments passed before he responded, his grip on her body easing. She watched him closely, sucking in a gasp when he opened his eyes and pierced her with his lustful stare. Silence hung awkwardly between them until Kati gave a whine, momentarily drawing her gaze from Ari's.

"Please."

Several moments passed before he briefly tightened his hold, then disentangled himself. A chill swept over her, but she managed to suppress it while he gripped her bound wrists and undid the belt keeping her tied. Thora bit her lip to hold back the cry when returning feeling painfully eradicated the numbness in her fingers. Ari gently rubbed her tender wrists until the sharp discomfort faded.

Once again, she focused her attention on the sky. Sol

had already completed half her journey. Never had Thora slept so deeply and for so long into the day, unless she was ill. Ari had truly wrung all strength from her with his wicked attentions. She lifted her head to meet his gaze.

He said nothing, but she read a host of confusing emotions in his stare. Regret, hunger, apology. Her heart thudded heavily. Somehow, she managed to draw her attention away from him and to Kati who stood waiting, his golden eyes focused firmly on her face. She ruffled his furry head.

"Yes, I am coming."

Every muscle in her body ached when she stood, especially her inner thighs. Flashes of the way Ari had taken her throughout the night sent waves of heat through her veins. No wonder she'd slept so deeply and for so long. She shook her head. She had no time to dwell on that. Kata needed her.

Pulling her shift over her head, she went to the wounded wolf, kneeling beside her. A rush of relief burned her eyes when the beast lifted her head and licked Thora's hand when she reached out.

"Feeling better, girl? Good. Kati is getting you some food." She ran her hand along the wolf's back, keeping her voice soft and low. "I'm going to look at your injury."

She slowly drifted her hand toward the bandages covering the wound. Pulling the fabric away, she heaved a sigh of relief. The wound healed nicely. So far, no sign of infection. Maybe because the gash was not so deep. Kata might heal enough to travel in a couple of days.

"Here."

Ari held the small jar of salve before her. She looked up, shivering under the intensity of his stare. Knowing that he'd likely remain over the next days until Kata recovered enough to travel set her heart to racing again, as well as her thoughts, imagining what would pass between them in that time. She took the salve, suppressing a quiver when their fingers brushed.

She forced her focus on Kata, applying the paste to the wound. The wolf whined, but made no attempt to evade Thora's attentions. When she drew away, Ari handed her a fresh strip of cloth to cover the injury.

Sitting back, she spotted Kati approaching, threefat squirrels dangling from his jaws. He trotted over, laying the animals before his sister. He nuzzled Thora and sat, watching Kata as intently as she.

Kata's head rose up and she rested her forelegs before her, ears perked forward. The sight encouraged Thora's heart. Tears burned her eyes when Kata leaned toward the squirrels, taking one in her mouth and eating eagerly. Thora stroked Kati's head, thrilled the she-wolf's appetite had returned, and so quickly. Another sign her pet would recover.

"Go, find yourself a meal." She whispered the words against Kati's ear and turned to find Ari watching her. A wave of heat ran along her spine seeing the force of his stare. Flashes of the night before, of his wicked and dark games, roused a hunger that startled her with its ferocity. Ari had introduced her to delights she'd never imagined, never thought to want so deeply, even as she also resisted the urge to offer herself completely to his control.

Yet a frightening aspect cooled the heat. How had he, in less than a day, found a way to make her want to give in to every one of his debauched demands? Yes, he most definitely posed a greater danger than her attackers. She must attempt once more to free herself from his claim. She took a deep breath and stood, holding the jar out to him.

"This is very powerful salve. Where did you get it?"

He shrugged. "At market somewhere. I can't recall."

"In my village, we have a woman who creates similar healing draughts and ointments, but I don't think she's ever made this."

She twisted her hands before her. She doubted he would go along with her suggestion, but she had to try.

"Kata is healing nicely, but it will be at least another several days before she can travel again." Truthfully, she worried even that wasn't enough time, but she kept that concern to herself. Here was another chance to separate herself from him.

Ari nodded. "I understand."

"So, we shouldn't delay you anymore. In the morning, you can be on your way. Staying here with me *will* hinder your journey, perhaps ruin your chance to reach The Thing."

He chuckled, walking to stand before her. He was still naked and Thora forced herself to look only into his face.

"I'm not going anywhere, *ástin minn*."

Did he think to soften her by using wooing words and calling her his dear? "But The Thing –"

"Have you forgotten my conditions? I am to decide when you've fully repaid me."

Her eyes widened before she scowled. "Last night wasn't enough for you?"

"I fear a thousand nights may never be enough."

He spoke so quietly, she wasn't sure she'd heard him. "What?" Why did a thrill linger upon noting the unwilling sincerity in his voice?

He said nothing for several moments then smiled. "I think I've only tasted the very tip of your passion, Thora."

She sucked in a breath, fighting the urge to throw herself upon him. He cupped her cheek, threading his fingers through her hair to hold her still while he lowered his mouth to hers. He moved slowly, too slowly. Each passing second felt like an eternity until the heat of his lips finally brushed against hers. She held herself still when he moved over her, sliding his tongue along her mouth. Despite her intention to resist, she parted her lips, allowing him inside. Fingers clenched to fight the desire to wrap her arms around his neck and hold on tight.

A moment later, his arms encircled her and he hauled her roughly against him. Through the thin shift, his hard cock scorched her sex. The now-familiar rush of wet heat pulsed through her; still, she made no move to touch him.

The kiss deepened, his moan rasping through her, his hands tight on her ass, squeezing and pressing her still closer. Bliss poured through her veins, her heart slamming so hard against her chest, surely he felt it too. The last of her intent to defy him crumbled and soon she responded to the kiss, her tongue dueling with his in an erotic dance that left her breathless.

When Ari tore his mouth away, Thora sucked in gulps of air in an attempt to steady her whirling senses. But when his mouth moved along her cheek to her throat, licking and nipping at the sensitive skin, she found the slight hold she'd regained on her wits rapidly disintegrated. Knees trembling, she sagged against him, arching her head to allow him to continue. His soft chuckle vibrated against her skin, adding to the tumult in her body.

Abruptly, he let her go and stepped back, a hint of a smirk quirking his lips. Overcome by astonishment, several moments passed before the lustful fog cleared. A cool breeze wafted over her heated skin, drawing a shiver and clarifying her awareness. Once again, she scowled.

"You toy with me."

He shrugged. "Perhaps. But you like it."

Heat scorched her cheeks. Damn him to Hel, he was right. She fought the urge to stamp her foot and punch him. Remembering how he'd spanked her last night sent another wet rush of heat to her pussy. How could the recollection of his uncomfortable punishment spur still more desire? It made no sense, but he'd upended her world in so many ways in such a short time, she no longer trusted her own thoughts.

"When your wolf fully heals and is ready to travel, I

will decide then if your debt is paid."

He turned toward the furs and reached for his pants and tunic. Thora found herself drawn to the sight of his powerful shoulders, her mouth dry and her heart thumping loudly. With a shake of her head, she forced her trembling legs to the bed of furs to retrieve her own clothing. Even after donning her dress, her fingers shook and it took several attempts to clip the *smokkr* so it hung straight. Purposefully avoiding looking at Ari again, she reached for her pack and pulled out the last of her flatbread and dried lamb. There was enough for them both, but Ari would then have to hunt for more game for the rest of their meals. Sensing his gaze on her, she looked up.

"Fear not, Thora, I have food as well. And I will hunt again. Fish in the stream nearby are plentiful. We'll not starve while we're here."

The easy warmth in his voice and eyes soothed her wild trembling. Yet, her relief remained tempered by the worry her wits would always be so addled around him.

***

Ari fastened his belt, the image of the leather wrapped around Thora's wrists last night seared into his thoughts. The depth of her passion still astounded him. Anxious for more, he'd forced himself to stop before he took her again, there in the dirt. Flashes of the night before came at him with dizzying speed and he kept his back to her, worried she might recognize the hunger churning through him. He slipped his axe into his belt and reached for his sword. He would feed and water Gyllir, then ride along the stream he mentioned. Maybe by the time he returned, his head would be in more control than his cock, which ached in the confines of his trousers.

Even now, he felt her gaze on him, her eyes seeming to touch him as if they were her hands gliding along his chest and shoulders. He turned and knew immediately he shouldn't have. The combination of uncertainty and desire had his dick hard as the steel of his sword. How he resisted the urge to go to her and haul her against him, bury himself in her body every way he could, he realized he'd never know. This strength could only have come from Odin himself. Gritting his teeth, Ari gave her a nod and turned to the tree where Gyllir remained tethered.

The steed nickered in greeting, butting his head against Ari's chest when he neared. Chuckling, Ari gave the horse a hearty pat then released the ties holding him in place. He quickly saddled the animal and mounted, guiding him toward the stream.

His thoughts remained filled with the woman waiting at their small camp. For him. Bah! Who did he try to fool? No one but himself. If the wolf wasn't injured, Thora would take this opportunity to flee. He gave a silent prayer of thanks to the gods in Valhalla that the wolf needed more time to heal, thus forcing her mistress to stay. Maybe by the time her pet recovered, Thora would no longer wish to leave.

From where did such nonsense come? One night of passion and his wits had scattered. Admittedly, what had passed between them last night had been unlike anything Ari had ever known before, but still... He must remain focused on his goal. She merely played a small part in his scheme. He inhaled sharply, savoring the musky earthen scents of the forest, the crisp aroma of the pines strong enough to clear his head.

The dappled daylight's muted tone sharpened as he neared the edge of the forest. He squinted against the past-midday sun, taking a few moments to scan the area. He saw no one, though wasn't surprised. Most people had set out weeks ago, were already on the main road to Tingwalla, a few hours' ride to the north. A road he hoped to be on himself in the next couple of days. With Thora beside him.

He stifled a groan and guided Gyllir to the stream.

The horse pranced eagerly and stepped into the water the moment Ari dismounted and removed the packs and saddle. With a frown, he noted that Gyllir's splashing chased the fish that moments ago had swum in abundance. No fresh fish for *náttmál*, their night meal, tonight. Allowing Gyllir his play time, he turned to his belongings, retrieving the small bow hanging on the saddle. He'd acquired it early in his journey and it had come in handy many times over the last years. Retrieving several arrows, he hooked them into his belt. Notching one arrow, he headed toward the brush. A few stomps and shouts sent three grouse and a cluster of squirrels fleeing from under the bushes. He lifted the bow and took aim, hitting one grouse in its side. The others clucked frantically, their short legs scurrying over the forest floor in their attempts to flee. Ari loaded the bow again, his aim once more true. The remaining fowl ran, now nearly shrieking in fright. Ari gave chase, notching a third arrow and taking the bird down.

His heart raced with his success. He'd become a skilled hunter during his travels. Very few beasts survived once he'd set his sight on them. A few steps ahead, the first bird lay on the ground, still alive, screeching in pain. He picked it up and gave a quick twist to the grouse's neck. The body fell limp. Securing the remainder of his catch, he turned to Gyllir and laughed. The steed emerged from his play in the water, and while he waited patiently, he still shifted excitedly. Ari secured the birds to the saddle and mounted, his hunger growing. They'd slept nearly half the day away, no wonder his stomach ached for food. He turned Gyllir back toward the small camp, where Thora awaited him. He found himself suddenly eager to be beside her. Giving his head a shake, he forced the thoughts aside. Must be the lust speaking, for he found his hunger to be inside her warm body again just as strong as that for a meal.

Once more his thoughts turned to exactly how he

might use her against his brother and prove himself a victim, rather than the criminal. The men who would speak on his behalf had once been powerful warriors, several with fearsome reputations. Though he did still harbor some doubt that any or all of them might change their minds and refuse to speak about what they knew, his last meeting, in Myrka, solidified his confidence that he had truth and honor behind him. The fact he could now also use Thora in his plan added to his anticipation of success.

When he neared, she still sat beside her wolves. Clearly the male had hunted, for both animals ate heartily of several squirrels, though the wounded she-wolf needed some help from her partner, who nudged the catch toward her. Ari's gaze settled on Thora. Her hair fell in long waves around her face and shoulders and he found himself longing to tangle his hands into the dark locks while he pulled her mouth to his.

Gyllir pawed nervously at the ground when they neared. The wolves clearly still agitated him. He dismounted and tethered the stallion to a tree a short distance away. After tending to the steed's comfort he turned back to the still smoldering fire.

He hoisted the grouse in the air. "Gyllir chased all the fish, but we'll still eat well."

Thora stood, nodding. "I'll gather more kindling."

"I'll do it. Tend these." He handed her the birds. For a moment, he hesitated, studying her in the late afternoon light, quickly fading in the shade of the forest. The urge to kiss her again came on strong but he resisted and turned to gather the sticks. Sensing her stare on him, he paused, but didn't turn. Gazing upon her left him with addled wits and he needed to regain control of himself.

When he returned to the fire, he avoided her gaze and dropped some of the sticks and twigs into the dying embers. He added some touchwood from his pouch and flames flared at the addition of the treated fungus from tree bark. The supplies dwindled. He must use the rest wisely, for obtaining more of the fire-starting aid would have to wait until he reached The Thing.

He looked up to see that Thora had expertly plucked two of the birds and had begun on the third. He took out his axe and gathered one of the plucked birds, laying it across a stone where he chopped off the head. He gathered some of the blood in a small bowl he'd removed from his pack and offered a prayer of thanks to Odin for providing them the plentiful food. Dipping his fingers into the blood, he ran it down his nose and across his cheeks, motioning for Thora to lean over so he could do the same for her. After pouring the blood into the fire where it sizzled and popped, he set about preparing to spit the birds. He did the same with the next two birds and soon the heavy gamy aroma of cooking grouse filled the air, sending his hunger raging once more. He almost tasted the cooked meat already.

"I have some dried berries," she said, breaking the silence that hung over them.

"A fair enough *náttmál,* though perhaps this one is a bit earlier than usual."

She nodded, her gaze steady and bold, yet wary as well. He smiled. After they ate, he planned to slake his lust on her body once more, anxious to once more stoke the fire of her passion.

Would she give in easily, or attempt to resist as she had last night? He found himself looking forward to reddening her ass again, binding her wrists and spreading her out helplessly beneath him. Somehow he sensed she had enjoyed it near as much as he and wouldn't protest. Not much, anyway.

"How far is the stream?" she asked.

"Just beyond the edge of the trees." He pointed. "Why?"

She stood, pressing her hands against her dress. A slight tremor passed over her, though Ari sensed the effort she exerted in an attempt to conceal it. Her gaze darted everywhere, except toward him. He stood, taking two steps so he stood a mere breath away. She smelled of forest and flowers, the sweet scent intoxicating. His scowled when she backed away from him.

"I would like to bathe. I will take Kati with me, if you will stay with Kata." She looked over at her wounded pet. Her concern for the animal gave her a vulnerability he almost felt guilty about taking advantage of. Almost. Not enough to change his plans for tonight.

He nodded. "You may go. Don't take long. The birds will be done soon."

"I know."

He bent and picked up another waterskin, this one only half-full. "Take this with you and fill it."

She took the pouch and lifted her pack. With a snap of her fingers, Kati trotted over to stand beside her. He gave a long look at the injured she-wolf then fell into step beside Thora when she turned in the direction of the stream.

He watched until she disappeared from sight. The stream wasn't far, and he knew she wouldn't abandon her pet with him. The animal kept her tethered to Ari. He sat beside the beast and gently stroked her head. While still weak, a brightness sparked in her eyes, telling him she would eventually heal completely.

"I wish you could talk, so you could tell me about your mistress."

A little whine was Kata's response, right before she twisted her head and licked his hand. He smiled. He'd never been this close to a wolf without either of them trying to kill the other, but he found he rather enjoyed the animal's presence. Both of them. The male had not attacked or menaced once, but Ari knew winning Kati over would be more difficult than Kata.

CHAPTER SIX

Thora stepped out of the stream and after drying off with a small cloth, reached for the undershift she'd laid out from her pack. Beside her, Kati stood guard, his senses attuned to the surrounding area. She smiled.

"Good boy. Thank you for watching over me."

The animal's tail wagged and he gave a responding yip. She wrung out her wet hair, grateful for feeling clean and refreshed. She looked up at the sky. Sol's chariot had nearly disappeared into the horizon. She pulled her dress over her head and hooked the brooches into place. She slung the clothes she'd attempted to wash over her arm. The soft leather boots soon covered her feet, her belt fastened, the axe hanging within her reach. She lifted her pack and slung it over her shoulder. Ruffling Kati's head, she turned, her wolf at her side. If felt strange without Kata on her other side.

"When we return to camp, you will tend to Kata."

Another soft sound, a clear assent. She continued to stroke his fur, trying not to think about the man waiting for her back at the camp. So much about him enthralled her, denying it was foolish. But she had to remain cautious. She knew little about him. That must change.

The remnants of daylight faded completely as she walked further into the woods. The glow of the fire of their camp made it easy for her to find her way back. Soon, she laid her sack beside Ari's belongings and took a position beside the fire, her gaze lingering on Kati taking up his protective stance beside Kata. She smiled before turning away, still concerned, but satisfied her pets would be fine through the evening and night.

She still found it difficult to accept they'd slept most of the day away. The gods had surely protected them, for even though their camp was away from the main path and surrounded by trees, the danger of travelers, or worse, outlaws, remained a worry.

"What troubles you?" Ari didn't look up while he poked at the flames, stirring the kindling so the fire crackled and the flames flared. Juices from the cooking birds sizzled and spit, the smoky aroma making Thora's mouth water.

"I was just thinking how odd that we slept so late into the day."

He paused and met her stare steadily. A hint of a smile tugged at one corner of his mouth. "We may do so again tomorrow."

Thora gaped at him, his laughter echoing in the still forest. "Are you a fool? Do you know the danger we could have found ourselves in, caught asleep like that?"

"I don't know why you worry. This glen is secluded enough and difficult to simply stumble upon."

"Yes, but to be taken by surprise leaves us both most likely dead."

"Don't you think your wolves would have given us notice long before anyone neared?"

She didn't answer, disgusted at her pitiful arguments. Odin's teeth, of course the animals would have alerted them to any intruders.

"You know what I think, Thora? I think you are trying to avoid the coming night."

Heat flooded her cheeks when he winked. He read her well. Too well. While part of her looked forward to more of the delight he'd bestowed upon her, part of her remained guarded against any dangerous intentions he may have. When he kissed her, she lost all sensible thought, her only focus on their lovemaking. She risked more than her life. Sometime in the last hours, she'd come to the realization she likely also risked her heart. Perhaps that frightened her most of all.

She liked him too much. Only one day and one glorious night and she had already become ensnared by his wit and charm, and the intensity of his attentions.

He'd saved her, and truthfully, her gratitude for that was likely the foundation for her dreamy notions. His taking of her innocence had been more than a means to thwart her father, it had been a sheer delight she had to admit she looked forward to repeating.

"Is that true, Thora? Are you trying to avoid laying with me again?"

The husk of his voice shivered along her spine and drew her from the troublesome thoughts.

"I will not resist, if that's what you're asking."

"Not exactly, but I'm glad to know that. But why do I have the feeling you would rather we didn't…"

She shrugged, searching for a witty retort. None came to mind.

"I know you liked it. And I know you want more."

"I shouldn't."

His eyes darkened to a strange shade of blue, the smile slowly fading. "Don't be afraid. I won't hurt you." His lips quirked. "Well, maybe a little, but I promise you'll like it."

Once more fire scorched her face. "You were sent by Hel herself to torment me!"

"And you like that, too, *ástin minn*."

"Can you not understand the costs of what I've done? I have given up my innocence."

For a moment, she swore regret flashed in his stare. "You regret that?"

"It does make certain things… difficult for me."

His shoulders lifted, the harsh rasp of his inhalation echoing in dusky air. "I understand."

Behind him, the sizzle of the birds grew louder. With a shake of his head, he turned. Why did the loss of his gaze leave her with a chill that had nothing to do with the mild temperature?

"Our meal is ready. We'll discuss this later."

The idea of talking about the coming night left her with little appetite. She hated how he forced her to admit her enjoyment of his wickedness. Seemingly unaware of the turmoil twisting her insides, Ari used the dagger in his belt to carve one of the grouse. She accepted the offered leg and focused on the meat. The first bite restored her appetite and she savored the hearty taste of the fowl. A few more bites and her head seemed to stop spinning with inane worries. When she finished the leg, she paused to lick her fingers. Her eye caught Ari's gaze and she froze at the feral gleam in his eyes.

"What?"

He said nothing, merely bit into his meal and chewed slowly, a contemplative expression lining his face. When he slowly licked the juices from his fingers, she suddenly understood the hunger still glowing in his eyes.

"You are a wicked man." Was that hoarse tremor her voice? The way this man affected her left her senses reeling. She didn't like it. *Oh yes, you do.* Why didn't the voice in her head stop?

"You have no idea just how wicked I can be."

Pressing her thighs together in an attempt to assuage the ache growing in her sex, she lifted her chin, holding his stare despite the ferocious need to look away.

"You take advantage of my worries. There is no skill in that!"

He threw his head back and laughed. When he stopped, yet still chuckling, he grabbed her arm and drew her near.

"Do you challenge me?"

Freyja, help me now. "Perhaps."

"I accept. You will be screaming my name soon, this I promise."

He leaned in for a brief, yet possessive, kiss, his tongue sliding along her lips in a tantalizing tease before he drew away. He stood, reached for another one of the grouse and cut a piece off. He chewed noisily, laughing again when she fixed a disgusted sneer on him.

Thankfully, he said nothing more while they ate. Reaching for a handful of the berries, Thora kept watch over her wolves, but they seemed content. Kata once more slept, still weak. Thora estimated at least another three or four days before the wolf could comfortably travel modest distances. Three or four more days with Ari. Surely by then, he would be tired of her. The thought was accompanied by another uncomfortable twinge she found difficult to understand or ignore.

He stood, drawing her from her reverie. Her entire body tensed, wondering if he planned to seduce her now.

"I go to the stream to bathe. When I come back, you had better be ready for me."

He turned and stalked into the forest, and the tightness in her muscles eased. Be ready? Ha! She would set her pallet near the wolves. Falling asleep before he returned posed a very different dilemma.

***

Ari reached the stream quickly, needing the cool water to calm his raging desire. His plan for tonight depended on his ability to retain control. In this state, it would be over before he even had a chance to begin digging to uncover the true depths of her passion. Anger at his weakness roiled through him, making it easier to subdue the hunger.

Stripping off his tunic and hose, strode straight into the stream, diving when the water grew a little deeper. The coolness surrounded him and he floated for a few moments, savoring a return to sanity.

Which wouldn't remain once he returned to camp, and Thora. What was it about this woman that had him so bewitched? He sighed, turning and stroking his arms against the current. The brief activity also served to expend some of the intense energy keeping him on edge. When he rose out of the water, his thoughts ran clearer.

Now calm once more, he shook his head, shedding much of the water from his hair.

He reached for the cloth from his pack and quickly dried off. The last of Sol's chariot had winked out on the horizon some time ago. The fact they had lost so much of the day in slumber also troubled him, but he wouldn't let Thora know that. While true her wolves would have alerted them to intruders, the heavy sated slumber could turn out deadly for a warrior. He must find a way to contain this lust that overtook him every time he was near her. Hel, he didn't even have to be near her. Just the thought of her had his cock poised on full hardness.

He'd never met a woman like her before. At times, she seemed lost and afraid, and the urge to protect her, care for her, surged through him. But when she showed her fiery temper, she set him alight. He sensed she'd been quite troublesome as a child. Clearly much of that still guided her actions.

The image of her dark eyes, wide in passionate wonderment as he'd brought her to climax left him breathless and aching to have her now. She waited for him, had she obeyed his instruction? A smile pulled at his mouth. Probably not. *Good.*

He tugged his trousers on but didn't bother with the tunic, needing the cool evening air on his skin. With his pack slung over his shoulder, he turned toward the camp.

As he'd suspected, she lay on a fur near her wolves, still fully clothed. He grinned. Stepping slowly and quietly toward her, he studied her supposedly sleeping form, her back to him. Her long dark hair cascaded across the fur and he fought the urge to bend and gather the tresses in his fingers. Not yet.

Instead, he dropped his pack noisily near her head. She jerked, but didn't rise.

"I know you are awake. And you disobeyed my order."

Her shoulders went rigid and he almost laughed

imagining how hard it was for her to restrain her response. He crouched behind her. Reining in the impulse to haul her up and against him took a few moments. He leaned in close to her ear, taking another couple of seconds to linger, savoring her sweet and musky scent. The slightest tremor passed over her and he smiled. He kept his voice low.

"We had an agreement and you keep trying to break it. I won't allow it."

She moved so fast, he had to jerk out of the way to avoid being bashed in the head.

"Who in Odin's name do you think you are? You cannot allow or disallow me anything!"

He laughed, knowing the coming hours would be even more powerful than last night.

"You owe me." Another laugh punctuated his taunt.

"You oafish bastard!" She punctuated each word with another jab of her finger into his chest. "Yes, I do owe you. However, I have already given you what you want."

"Again, you seek to twist the terms. There is much more that I want from you."

Her lips pressed together and he fought the need to kiss her into compliance.

"Why must you torment me so?"

The softening of her voice, the hint of desperation, startled him. Again, the contradictions that made up Thora left his head spinning.

"You enjoyed it. I know you did."

She lowered her head. "It's... very intense."

"Yes, I agree."

She lifted her head, her dark eyes holding myriad emotions, many of which he found himself unable to name.

"What we... when you... it frightens me."

With a groan, he pulled her close. The impulse to protect her, take care of her, overwhelmed him. The feel of her trembling form in his arms roused a maelstrom of feelings he didn't recognize, or perhaps he didn't want to. A twinge of anger lingered as well, for his own weakness. If he continued to put her needs before his, the goals he'd set for himself might never be accomplished.

After several minutes, her trembling eased and Ari reluctantly released her. The crackling of the fire filled the heavy silence with an intensity that spurred his hunger for her.

"Come." He took her hand and pulled her to the other side of the fire, where he'd earlier arranged the furs. He paused and indicated she should remove her dress. She hesitated but a moment before obeying. He folded his arms while she removed the *smokkr* then slid the undershift down, baring her delicious body. She held her head high, but the sight of her lower lip caught between her teeth revealed her anxiety.

"Turn," he said.

Her brow furrowed, confusion creeping into her eyes. "Why?"

"You have a beautiful body, Thora. I simply wish to look upon it."

Pink crept up her chest to her neck and into her cheeks before she slowly obeyed. The line of her back, the flare of her hips and the enticing swell of her buttocks had him once more near the breaking point. Without any word to indicate his actions, he stepped closer, nearly touching her back and resting his hands on her hips. A sharply inhaled breath shuddered through her when he curled his fingers tighter and drew her against him.

He caught one hand in her hair, pulling her head back toward him. The curve of her neck drew his focus and he skimmed his mouth along the tender skin. A low moan escaped her when he grazed her with his teeth, his tongue soothing the sharpness while allowing him to savor her tantalizing sweet taste.

The hand remaining on her hip slid around to her

belly and the muscles there twitched. He smiled. She was ticklish. He would find ways to exploit that. Not yet. Now he wanted to be inside her, his cock near splitting his pants open. He released her just long enough to strip out of his clothes, ignoring her frustrated whimper. He resumed his former position, guiding them both to their knees, bracing her against his chest.

"I can't wait to hear you beg."

Her sudden stiffening encouraged him to tighten his embrace. As an added restraint, he slid one hand to her pussy, fingers giving teasing strokes that soon had her trembling and languid in his arms once more.

His mouth found her ear and he breathed heavily. "I want to hear you tell me exactly what you want."

She struggled in his embrace, tilting her head to the side to look at him.

"Why must you torment me so?"

"It gives me pleasure. As it does you."

Again, that enchanting blush crept into her cheeks. Her contradictory reactions thickened the haze of lust surrounding him. He kept his fingers gently moving along her sweet cleft, once more drawing those soft hoarse cries from her throat.

When he stopped, she gave a slight whine of frustration. He ignored it, taking her hands and guiding them to the ground, so she knelt on hands and knees before him. She tried to straighten, but he held her there, pressing against her back to keep her in his chosen position.

"Don't move. That is an order."

Her only response was a sharp inhalation. He leaned back. Her skin gleamed in the firelight and each breath brought a quiver to her body. Her bountiful breasts hung enticingly and he reached under her to cup them. Thora turned to face him, a hint of bewilderment dancing in her eyes.

"You are cruel, putting me in such a degrading

position."

He shook his head. "I think you will like this very much."

He barely forced the words from his parched throat. He moved behind her once more, grabbing her hips and pulling her towards him. His cock slid against her pussy, wet and inviting, tempting him to drive right into her waiting body. But he held himself back. Sliding one hand under her once more, he caressed her breast, even as the tip of his cock nudged against her sex.

"Oh! What... Oh!"

He chuckled at the garbled words escaping her, continuing his dual torment, his cock pausing every so often as if he might enter her. The way her body jerked toward his at those moments nearly had him exploding. He tightened one hand on her hip, stilling her.

"You will wait until I am ready." Forcing command into his voice nearly used all of his control. He rolled his shoulders and gritted his teeth, forcing his release back until it no longer threatened.

Thora gave a jumbled slew of words, but Ari barely understood any of them. But the frantic frustration in her tone told him all he needed. He grinned, his cock once more nudging at the entrance to her body. A tightening swept over her, clearly part of her struggle to obey his order. He wondered at her acquiescence, half-expecting her to resist again. Was he disappointed when she didn't? The urge to compel her to do so gave him the strength and control he needed to continue tormenting her.

Rolling her pebbled nipple in his fingers, he gave a gentle squeeze and a low, keening wail erupted. He slid his hand from her hip to her pussy, his fingers moving in rhythm with his cock along her slick flesh.

"Ari!"

He smiled at the note of frustration engulfing his name. With continued deliberate movements, he teased and caressed her, noting the way her arms and legs trembled while she fought to remain in position. The tempo of his fingers and cock kept her quivering and gasping, half-uttered protests echoing around him. The scent of her desire grew ever stronger, surrounded him, spurring his need. He had to have her. Now.

He paused in his movements, smiling at her unfulfilled growl. Using his hand to hold her sex open, he slowly eased the tip of his dick into her. Her protests turned to soft mutterings of thanks, but he remained motionless, barely breaching her sheath. Grumbling replaced her appreciation. He lifted his hand and gave her a sharp slap to the ass. Her entire body stiffened and she turned to face him, eyes blazing with seething anger that might have reduced him to ash had there been real flames.

"Bastard! Why must you tease this way?"

"Because I know you like it, despite what you say."

Her eyes narrowed then, her lips pressed together in a tight line. "If I had my axe –"

"You don't. So stop complaining and heed my orders."

"I am, you oafish ass!"

She near snarled the words and he rewarded her with another strike to her bottom.

"Insulting me will not work in your favor," he warned with another blow. Her body jerked under him, nearly dislodging him before he pulled her further onto his cock. Yet again, her words and tone changed and he slowly inched into her, landing another slap on her pinkened flesh. This time, her need-filled cry exploded around them, sending any remaining birds in the surrounding trees into flight.

Finally, with his cock seated fully inside her, Ari stilled again. Beneath his hands, Thora quivered and shook, nearly undoing his hard-fought control. He slid his fingers around the soft flesh of her pussy, loving the way she clenched on him with each light caress. Finding her clit, he slowly circled it, and she tightened again. How did he resist the urge to plunge into her hard and fast?

"Ari, please!"

"What is it, Thora? What do you want?"

She hesitated, her heavy breathing rasping through her. "I... I want you to move!"

He smiled. "Did I not promise you would tell me all you wanted?"

"Bastard!"

"I think you screamed my name before as well."

What she said after that, he wasn't quite sure, but he did recognize a threat to unman him. He laughed and slowly slid inside her, reducing her warning to babbling moans and cries of delight.

The feel of her hot wet flesh surrounding him, tightening fiercely on him with each glide in and out of her body, drove him beyond the boundaries of pleasure. When he flicked at her clit, her entire body jolted, nearly sending him into his release. He wasn't quite ready yet, clenching his jaw in the effort to hold back.

Her skin shone bright in the firelight, a tempting lure he had no power to resist. He lowered his mouth to her back, trailing a line of kisses along her spine, using his teeth to scrape her skin and draw the most enticing moans and wails. When he latched onto the back of her neck, she tossed her head back, her sharp cries filling the glen. He couldn't wait any longer and finally loosed the reins of the command over his body, his cock erupting with such force, it near blinded him.

He gave Thora's clit a squeeze and she screamed his name, or at least he thought that was what he heard. Her body rocked under his as if she sought to draw him still deeper inside. The feel of her pussy tightening around him drew out his own release and he rode the tide with her, the bucks of her body corresponding with each pulse of bliss racing through him.

The tumult seemed to last hours before finally quieting, Thora's warm body now trembling continuously. With a heavy regret, he pulled his softening cock from her pussy, holding back a chuckle at the moan she gave, laced heavily with disappointment.

Slow movements eased her up and he turned her to face him, pulling her close to nestle her against his chest. The urge to hold her like this all night overcame him. He gently lowered them both to the furs, spreading her now-drowsy body across him. Taking up the other fur, he pulled it over them and tucked it around Thora's shoulders. She snuggled closer.

"I think you liked that." His voice was heavy with satiation and weariness. Thora said nothing, her only response a brief tightening of her shoulders. He chuckled.

Sliding his fingers along her back, he pressed a kiss to her forehead. How odd that he should feel so content. Every now and then, a tremor swept over Thora. An echo of the pleasure they'd just shared? Ari wondered how long it would take the ferocity to fade for both of them.

CHAPTER SEVEN

Thora woke with a start, tense against the robust hold of Ari's embrace, though her tentative glance told her he still slept. She remained still, knowing the slightest movement would wake him. After what had passed between them this night, she needed some time to think, without his intense stare focused on her, distracting her, as if he saw into her very soul.

A sudden fear took hold, a fear that Ari had found a place inside her she hadn't even known existed and used it against her. Was she weak for wanting the alluring and decadent delight he gave her? Or was he in league with the gods in an effort to test her?

Last night had gone beyond anything she'd ever imagined passed between a woman and a man. When he had positioned her on her hands and knees she'd thought he meant to degrade her. He hadn't. Instead, he'd shown her how wild and tempestuous lovemaking could be and damn her soul to Hel, she wanted more of that incredible sensual carnality. He'd woken her two more times, each coupling fiercer than the last.

That she still owed a debt seemed a cruel taunt. Surely he would see she had given in to his debauched demands with little resistance. Would it be enough that he might release her from her obligation? Even as the thought arose, she dismissed it. Ari had made it clear he intended to control and dominate her in every way until he was ready to be finished. She hated admitting part of her reveled in his attentions. The idea of him leaving her seemed suddenly unthinkable. No, she could not stay with him forever, much as the idea enticed. She mustn't let these traitorous thoughts take solid root or she would be doomed. She clung to her plans to find a way free of him.

At least they hadn't slept the day away this time. She

lifted her head from the pillow of Ari's shoulder to see how Kata and Kati had fared through the night. Did Kata still sleep? Kati sat up, alert and watching her, waiting for her command. She smiled.

"You want to tend them?"

With a start, Thora met Ari's sleep-clouded gaze, laced with an affectionate longing. The sight sent her heart to racing once more. Throat suddenly dry, she merely nodded.

He gave her a smile that brightened his eyes and again sparked that fluttery feeling in her belly. He tangled his hand in her hair and tilted her head back, taking her lips in a bruising kiss that soon had her aching for his touch once again. Abruptly, he released her.

"Go. I will see about our morning meal."

Once disentangled from Ari's embrace, Thora reached for her undershift to cover herself and hopefully chase some of the chill. Aware of Ari watching her every move, she rose gracefully and strode over to her pets, chin high. Did he chuckle? At least with her back to him, he couldn't see the heat scorching her cheeks.

She knelt beside Kata, a gentle hand along her head. The she-wolf opened her eyes. No sign of fever. Relief trembled through her and she put her arm around Kati and kissed the top of his head.

"She will be fine, Kati. Maybe in only a few more days." She ruffled the wolf's fur. "Go fetch food for you both."

Kati licked her cheek and trotted into the forest. Thora once more checked Kata's bandage and gave the pet a gentle caress. "He'll bring you a meal, Kata. Soon you will be well and we will be on our way."

"Yes, we will."

Ari's voice behind her made her spin about. She hadn't even heard him approach. He'd donned his trousers, but remained without his tunic. The dappled sunlight danced on his shoulders, making it appear as if stars surrounded him. The sight enticed her more than she cared to admit and flashes of recollection from the night before slammed into her thoughts, leaving her sex slick and hot, her her breasts tight and hard.

"I'll see if I can catch some fish this morning."

She nodded. "I will tend the fire and change Kata's bandages. Do you have more of the salve?"

"Yes, right here." Holding out the small jar, he crouched down before her, his heady male scent swarming her senses. She clenched her fingers to keep from reaching for him. He said nothing, and she couldn't look away from the greenish-blue gaze studying her.

"Is there something else you need to tell me?" She held back her pleased smile at the strength of her voice.

His lips curled into a small smile. "You amuse me, Thora. I am enjoying your company."

With that, he stood and walked away, pulling his tunic over his head before bending to pick up one of his packs. Thora stared after him for a few moments then shook her head and looked away, out past the small grove of trees in the direction Kati had gone. Yet her thoughts remained firmly on Ari, his kiss, his wicked touch, the way he filled her completely. The recollections left her more off-balance than ever and it seemed she could think of nothing else. At times, she swore he read her exact thoughts, but she never seemed to get a grip on understanding his.

She walked to her pack, her thoughts awhirl. Almost absently, she removed the additional strips Ari had made from his tunic yesterday. When she returned to Kata's side and gently untied the bandage around the injury, she forced herself to focus on applying more of the healing salve then wrapping new strips of cloth around the wound. She was pleased to note that the wolf had not bled any further, a sign that Ari's skill in sealing the gash had worked.

Once more her focus returned to her mysterious

savior. A thrill passed over her as she imagined him returning and drawing her into his embrace, sealing his mouth against hers in a kiss that would reduce her to cinders.

She shook her head. What trick did the gods play on her to leave her so addled by the mere kiss and touch of a man she barely knew? She'd used him for her own intents as well, but knew he surely didn't feel this continually growing feeling of vulnerability. Fear and anticipation battled to be heard, combining in a strange anticipation that threatened to sap her will and willingly give herself to Ari for as long as he wanted her.

Why did she look forward to surrendering?

***

Ari strode toward Gyllir, forcing himself not to take another look back at Thora. He enjoyed watching the bewilderment creep into her eyes. Dark and expressive, they told him exactly what feelings and sensations she possessed at any given moment. He especially liked the way they glazed over with passion. Passion that he caused. His grinned, proud of how easily he made her succumb to his touch.

After tending to his saddle and pack, he mounted the stallion and guided him toward the stream. When he reached the bank, he dismounted, yet held tight to the reins. He pulled Gyllir around to face him, staring right into the tall animal's dark eyes.

"I won't have you chasing all the fish again today." He led the animal to a patch of sweet grass and tethered him to a nearby tree. The steed could reach the stream to drink, but not go all the way in. Satisfied with Gyllir's security, Ari took his pack from the saddle.

He pulled out a hook attached to a short rope and moved closer to the riverbank. Many decent sized fish swam in the clear running water, for the moment unaware of the intruders on the bank. Not for the first time, he wished for a harpoon, for his aim was excellent with the tool, but carrying such an implement had early on proved difficult. Not that he lacked skill using the line, for he'd often dined on fish, catching plenty for both his immediate and future needs. But the extra time involved in using the hook had always left him uneasy and on edge. Perhaps because he so wanted to end his journey. This time, however, he felt no such agitation. Because his justice was close at hand? He refused to consider any other reason.

He crouched and dug into the muddy dirt of the stream bed, turning over a large handful. Several worms squirmed and he caught one and quickly jammed it onto the hook. He flung the baited rope into the water, holding tight to the end. It didn't take long before a tug forced him to tighten his grip and he pulled the rope back in, pleased with the size of his catch. The fish flopped wildly on the bank for a few moments.

Ari laughed. "Look Gyllir! Thora and I will feast on the fat fish in this stream!"

He removed the hook from the fish's mouth and secured the creature in a pouch on his pack. Bending to grab another worm, he repeated the process, several times, until a half dozen fish filled the bag.

While he fished, his thoughts veered toward The Thing. In a few short weeks, he would finally have his reparation, his name once again honorable. The runes carved into the daggers and pieces of tree bark in his pack contained testimony from the men who would not meet him in Tingwalla. Those who agreed to attend would verify all of Hersir's foul deeds and the way he had set Ari up for banishment. Ari imagined the surprise on his brother's face when he and his fellow witnesses stood before the high council and presented the facts. He would be reunited with his clan, his mother and sister, and Hersir would face justice for his crimes.

It seemed he'd waited his entire life for the day of reckoning. The last three years had stretched out endlessly, one lonely day after another. He'd been welcomed in several towns, taken his pleasure here and there, but he longed to be back among friends and family. In his imaginings, an additional person remained near. Thora.

Now why would he think she might want to stay with him? And why did he find the idea of her doing so more than appealing? He'd known her two days, had shared two incredibly passionate nights, incomparable to anything he'd experienced before. Surely it was only the lust she inspired, with her delectable curves and passionate responses. The idea of taking his pleasure with her for years to come grew stronger. What would she look like, large with his child? With silver streaking her dark hair? With crinkles of laughter around her mouth and eyes?

"Bah! I am a fool, these wishes are nothing more than bards' nonsense!"

Gyllir whinnied, almost as if he laughed at Ari. Ari scowled.

"Silly beast, mocking me will not get you any treats." Again he had the sense the horse found his concerns humorous. "Be careful, or I'll let Thora's wolves have you."

Gyllir shook his head and Ari's chuckle burst free. Truthfully, he would never endanger Gyllir in such a way. The steed had been his only companion for all of his travels, and the animal showed more loyalty than some of Ari's friends.

Catching one more fish, he put the flopping creature into the sack and sealed it. Striding to Gyllir, he mounted and guided the horse back into the forest. Again his thoughts focused on Thora, waiting for his return. A smile formed as he recalled her passionate responses to everything that passed between them last night. She'd seemed stunned at the way he'd positioned her the first time he took her. But soon her passion had taken over. When he'd woken to take her again, he'd bound her, stretching her arms up over her head, allowing him to explore every inch of her trembling body. The thought of her stretched out beneath him, helpless to his whims, hardened his cock faster than when he'd first touched her. He shifted in the saddle, the glaring sun dimming as he rode into the forest and headed toward their small camp. He looked forward to another night of similar pleasures.

He leaned over and patted Gyllir, hoping to stem the never-ending tide of recollection. Her needy pleas had spurred him, savoring the way she'd called his name, begged him to bring her completion. Only once he was deep inside her had he allowed that, rewarded with the blissful sound of her screams of completion. Those he heard most clearly, as if she shouted now, crying his name while caught in the throes of her climax. Instantly he knew it wasn't just his imagination. Those shouts were real!

Thora.

He cursed loudly, hating how easily, and not for the first time, the recollection of her passion distracted him, made him careless. He kicked the horse into a lope, ducking to avoid low-lying branches, desperate to get to her.

Why did the sound of her shriek spur such a fierce and desperate need to protect her, almost to the point that he disregarded the goal he been striving for these last three years? How had his priority fallen to the wayside? He'd think on it later. No time now to focus on his own plans. At the moment, he had only one goal.

To save Thora.

CHAPTER EIGHT

"Well, well, well. If it isn't the runaway daughter of our esteemed jarl."

Thora's hands froze where she stroked Kata's head. She turned, her stomach rolling. Muli, a member of her clan. One of her father's adversaries. While Muli always managed to avoid being banished for his dishonorable deeds, he'd always sworn to exact revenge from Kori Thorfinsson. Thora had heard only hints of what had caused the animosity between the two men, and it had started around the time Kori had claimed Thora's stepmother, Geira.

She momentarily raised her eyes toward the heavens, thanking the gods she'd dressed once Ari had left the camp. With a hand resting on the axe in her belt, she rose.

"I don't care that you've found me. I'm not returning home."

Lips pulled back in a feral grin, he chuckled. Beside her, Kati gave a low growl. Some of the amusement left Muli's gaunt features. He spit on the ground and sneered at Thora and her wolves.

"I have no intention of returning you to Grindafell. Not yet, anyway. You are the key to my vengeance."

Dread formed an icy shell around her heart. She pulled the axe free. Though she shouted the command to attack several times, Kati responded at the first, leaping toward Muli, teeth bared and snarling in warning. The tall man had barely seconds to react, not even enough time to draw his own weapon before he turned to run. The wolf latched onto his shoulder, the momentum of the animal's attack driving him to the ground. Agonized screams echoed around her, accompanied by Muli's desperate attempts to free himself from Kati's mauling.

Thora shouted encouragement to the wolf, falling into a momentarily stunned silence when Kata appeared beside her, half-standing and leaning against Thora's legs. The she-wolf gave a menacing growl. Only Thora's hand on her neck stopped the wounded yet determined animal from the frail attempt to leap into the fray.

Hoofbeats thundered behind her. She turned at the moment Ari reined in his steed and leapt from the animal's back. He rushed to her side, sword drawn and ready. He skidded in the dirt, stopping short to watch the wolf's attack.

"I heard you scream."

He never looked at her, focused on the wolf and man engaged in battle. Thora turned back just at the moment Muli finally yanked free of Kati's jaws and ran, pleading with the gods to call off the beast. Kati chased for a few yards, barking and growling. Once he stopped, Muli slowed as well and turned.

"I'll find you again, bitch and I'll kill your mangy dogs!"

He turned, his bellowed threat fading along with him when he disappeared into the trees. The excitement from the encounter left Thora's legs weak and wobbly when she turned to Ari. He met her stare with amusement twinkling in his eyes. Despite the scare of moments ago, she found herself smiling, then a giggle escaped. When Kati trotted over to them, she knelt before him and ran her hands affectionately in his fur, allowing him to lick her chin.

"You are a good boy, Kati. Thank you for chasing Muli away."

She stood and faced Ari once more. The humor had fled, replaced with an intensity she found both alarming and intriguing.

"You know him?" Ari asked.

She nodded. "He is from my village. He hates my father, though I've only heard the stories secondhand.

But if he's been searching for me, then so have others."

She turned away and began to pace. Time and again, her gaze fell to Kata. While the wolf healed nicely, she was still unable to travel any great distances. But there was no choice. She spun about to pierce Ari with a determined stare.

"We have to leave."

"But your wolf –"

"I know. But I can't take the chance he will bring others back here. At the very least, we must leave the immediate vicinity."

He gave her a brief nod. "I've caught more fish, I think we have time to eat before we find a new place to settle."

At the mention of eating, Thora's stomach reminded her of her hunger. Ari chuckled, the lines in his face once again softening. Why did she find all of his expressions so enticing? A different hunger rose, and she clenched her fists in annoyance.

After easing Kata back to her resting spot, she helped Ari prepare the fish and stirred the fire before placing the skewered portions over the flames. The fish would cook quickly. She dug the last of her flatbread from her sack and returned to sit beside Ari. Breaking the bread, she handed him a piece and accepted a portion of the savory perch. Silence hung heavily between them.

"Tell me more of this Muli. He intends you harm."

It wasn't a question, but Thora nodded anyway. "I don't know all of it. My father told me Muli has resented him for a very long time. Something happened during the raid when my father… met his new wife."

How would Ari react to know that her stepmother had come into her life as a lowly slave? She eyed him cautiously then decided to share some of her past. She sat up straight, a deep breath lifting her shoulders.

"My father took his wife as a slave at first, in revenge against the man who murdered my mother."

"I see." He bit into the fish in his hand, seemingly uninterested.

"I would have been his next victim if my uncle hadn't saved me. I was barely twelve summers yet."

She dared a glance at him. After his unconcerned manner of moments ago, the fury tightening his face surprised her. Why? He'd proven himself capable of cruelty, yet knowing he possessed anger for what she suffered oddly eased some of the concern she held about his honor.

"I assume he is now dead."

"Yes." Thora held his stare. "My father killed him. Not only to avenge my mother and me, but also to ensure my stepmother, Geira, didn't fall into his clutches again. In taking her as his slave, he saved her."

"And Muli was involved in this somehow?"

"Only as one of the warriors who went on the raid. My father never told me directly, but I learned Geira punched Muli during the journey."

Ari chuckled. "It seems Muli is not a very strong warrior."

Thora smiled. "No, he's a coward who preys on those weaker than him. Muli bought a slave from my uncle, then ended up beating her to death."

She shuddered as she recalled the sight of the badly disfigured body of the woman who had betrayed Geira when they'd both been taken during the raid all those years ago. Muli had battered her beyond recognition.

"Only a coward beats a woman."

Thora nodded. "Yes, though I've heard at one time he was quite a fierce warrior in battle."

"I find that difficult to believe."

Thora shrugged. "I only know what I've heard. But whatever happened on that journey left Muli and my father enemies. He's lucky he hasn't been cast out."

"Your stepmother must be an impressive woman."

"What do you mean?" While Thora agreed, there

was a time when she'd disliked Geira immensely and had treated her very badly. She found herself unwilling to share that with Ari. Shame over her selfish and cruel behavior still tasted bitter on her tongue, despite the sacrifices she'd made to win back Odin's favor in the past few years.

"She was taken as a slave, yet is now your father's wife."

"Yes. She is a brave woman." Especially after the way she'd saved Thora from a deadly wolf attack. The very wolf who had birthed her beloved pets.

"Like you."

Thora gaped at him. "What do you mean?"

"You stood up to two outlaws and then again to me, and today to this Muli. You are brave."

"I have my wolves to protect me."

"True, but you still were ready to fight if necessary."

Thora narrowed her eyes. "You said I couldn't defend myself."

"Not against two, but today you could have."

Did he truly believe that, or did he taunt her again? He seemed sincere and delight shimmered through her to think he thought her capable. Why should she care? She owed him only the debt for saving her life.

In an attempt to dislodge the troubling thoughts, she bit into her food, the flaky moist fish satisfying her hunger as well. The rest of the meal passed in companionable silence. With a start, Thora realized how at ease she felt beside him. She frowned. She shouldn't be comfortable with him, she needed to focus on getting free from him her debt.

When they finished eating, Thora carefully wrapped the remaining portions of fish for later. She stood and turned to resume her packing. Ari's hand on her arm stopped her.

"There is no need to panic."

She wanted to believe him, but knew Muli to be a

cruel man, yet one who somehow still maintained, no, enjoyed, several allies in the clan. If any of those warriors had traveled with him, they could be upon them soon. She refused to speak aloud the depth of her worry, for fear of making it real.

"I am not panicking. But it's no longer safe here. I want to leave."

"Soon. But not now."

"Yes, now."

He tilted his head and considered her. "Why?"

She hesitated before answering. The men who would accompany Muli were vicious and cruel. She didn't want to tell Ari about the terrifying images her mind insisted on rousing. Damn his insistence on keeping her, for those situations might truly occur. If Muli had indeed convinced others to join him in searching for her, Ari would be outnumbered. The very thought sent a chill along her spine that left her breathless with fear.

Why should she care? She wanted to be free of him, didn't she? Yet, the idea of Muli and his collaborators harming Ari, or worse, left a lump that threatened to expel her meal.

"Thora? Why do you insist we leave this very moment?"

She sighed. "Because Muli may have others with him. We cannot hope to repel them all should he decide to attack."

A smile slowly curled Ari's lips. "Are you worried for me?"

She fought the urge to slap the smug grin from his face, though she suspected part of her annoyance came from the fact he'd echoed her very thoughts.

"No, but I will not be responsible for your… possible death. Now that I think on it, it would be best if you were to go on your way and leave me to my journey."

He chuckled and stepped closer with a slow shake of his head. "Your debt is not fully repaid, and you know this. And I have no fear of Muli."

"But –"

"We will be gone before he can return, if that is indeed his intention."

"Yes, but only if we leave now!" Why didn't he worry Muli could return at any moment? His arrogance could mean both of their deaths. Her fingers curled and uncurled, an attempt to keep from striking some sense into him.

"Thora, he had no horse. If he has others aiding him, we would know by now if they lingered nearby. Tend your wolf and I will see to the packing. Trust me."

He said the last with a solemnity that brought reassurance, even as she wanted to resist. Realizing she had no chance of convincing him to flee this tiny glen immediately, she gave him a curt nod. She turned toward her wolves, but before she took one step, Ari again grabbed her, pulling her near.

"I will keep you safe. I promise you this."

His mouth was on hers before she realized his intention. Heat slithered through her veins, her heart thudding like a drum in her chest. His lips and tongue sparked a hazy passion that soon had her forgetting the potential looming danger. Her fingers tightened in his tunic, needing to hold on tight lest the passion his kisses aroused rendered her incoherent. When his hand slid across the swell of her breasts, her knees trembled. She leaned heavily into him, no longer able to hold herself upright, wanting only to drown herself in the delight of passion.

As always, his abrupt release left her shivering with confusion and a need that demanded more of his wicked seduction. Why did he do that? Heavy breaths rasped through her, gaping after him when he turned his attention to gathering their belongings. She pressed trembling fingers to her hot and swollen lips, his heady taste lingering. If only she didn't want to savor it.

***

Ari utilized every ounce of his determination to avoid looking at Thora. Allowing her to see how deeply her physical response to the slightest touch affected him left a weak point she might exploit. She was a smart young woman and kept him on alert. How easily the sight and feel of her, her taste and scent, made him forget his goals and how close he was to achieving them.

He stalked to the furs and blankets that made up their bed, annoyance rising tight in his chest. Or was it lust demanding fulfillment that left his head pounding nearly as fiercely as his cock? He didn't like feeling this uneven and off-balance.

He made short work of their bedding and stuffed it into one of his saddle bags. After that, he ensured the fire was completely out and gathered up the rest of his belongings. Mixed in with his soiled clothing was Thora's undershift. Instead of putting it aside for her, he folded it and put it with his own belongings. He much preferred less clothing on her anyway, should he decide to avail himself of her body. He smiled, imagining her protests. He'd silence them quickly enough.

When he was sure all had been packed and the fire truly extinguished, he turned toward where Thora tended her wolves. Surprisingly, the wounded animal stood beside her, the only indication of an injury the bandages wrapped around the furry body. The healthy wolf stood on her other side.

Ari's cock surged once more, the sight of Thora flanked by the beasts strangely arousing. She eyed him steadily, yet her dark eyes held uncertainty and wariness. For a moment, he thought she might say something, but she remained silent. He walked over, stopping mere inches away, close enough to hear the rasp of her uneven breathing.

"Is something wrong?" he asked.

"Well, it appears Kata is better able to travel now after all." She glanced down at the wolf on her right. "I never thought she'd heal so quickly."

"The cauterization helped. As did the salve."

Thora nodded. "Which means I will be able to resume my own journey."

A hint of hope crept into her gaze, but Ari recognized sadness as well. Interesting. Did this mean she didn't truly want to leave despite her latest attempt to end their agreement? Didn't matter whether she did or not, he wasn't ready to declare her debt paid just yet. He shook his head, sliding his hand against her soft cheek.

"I admire your determination, but no. How many times must I tell you I decide when your debt is paid?"

Was that relief softening her eyes? Had the encounter with Muli frightened her enough that she wanted to stay with Ari, even if it was only for her safety? He didn't care, he only knew the delight sparking in his veins almost made him lower her to the ground then and there.

"Yes, but –"

He covered her lips with a finger. "And I say again, you belong to me, Thora. For now and for as long as I deem it necessary. Do you understand?"

Her eyes narrowed, but there was no anger. She nodded.

"Good. Now finish gathering your belongings, we will search for a new place to camp until your wolf is completely healed."

He resisted the urge to draw her close for another kiss and turned to Gyllir. His horse stood quietly, but Ari noticed the way the animal kept a wary gaze upon the wolves. Still, his steed now seemed less concerned than he had before. He patted the horse's neck.

"Believe me now, Gyllir, that they won't hurt you?" The horse looked him in the eye and Ari swore to himself the animal understood perfectly. "Thora will ride with me, but the wolves will be close."

"Do you always talk to your horse as if he's a person?"

Ari turned to find Thora standing a couple of paces away, her filled sack held tightly in her hands. He winked and grinned.

"Do you not speak to your wolves the same way?"

A blush pinkened her cheeks and she looked away for a moment before meeting his gaze once more. "I suppose you are right. I just… I've never had a horse of my own, though my father owns many."

Ari patted the horse's neck once more. The steed had accompanied him through some of the most difficult and the most promising moments of his life. "Gyllir and I have been mostly alone the last few years."

A curious look crept into Thora's eyes. "You've been traveling a long time."

He nodded, though her words were not a question. "I have. My journey nears its end."

"Why?"

He knew what she asked, but pretended not to. "Why what?"

"Why have you been traveling?"

"I've been on a quest of sorts."

"What sort of quest?"

He wasn't about to tell her he was named an outlaw by his own clan. "Just an adventure. Which will soon be over."

"When you go to Tingwalla."

He nodded, taking her sack and attaching it to his saddle. "I hope to settle somewhere near one of the northern fishing villages after The Thing is over."

Another lie, but one he had no choice but to tell. If he told her of his family, his clan, she would soon figure out he was not who he appeared to be.

"Are you in some kind of trouble?"

Did she notice his brief hesitation when securing her belongings? He hoped not, but she was smart and perceptive. When she said nothing, he released the breath he hadn't even realized he'd held.

"No." More lies. He longed for the day when he could finally tell her the entire truth. How would she react? His stomach knotted at the possibilities.

CHAPTER NINE

Thora said nothing as Ari readied their possessions. He kept secrets and she grew ever more determined to uncover them. She'd told him about the reasons for her own journey, but why wouldn't he tell her his? Was he some sort of outlaw?

A moment's panic stole her breath. He had been noble in saving her, but his wicked sexual games and insistence on possessing her as if she were little more than a slave hinted at a darker side. She'd best remember to keep her wits sharp about him.

She stifled a bitter laugh. The moment he kissed her again, no doubt her wits would scatter on the wind. His slightest touch roused a passion she'd often doubted was real. Now, she knew it was. Just thinking about his kiss, or the way he'd claimed her body, or even the way he'd spanked her sent her thoughts skittering in all directions. Barely suppressing a shiver of excitement, she forced herself to calm, clenching her fingers to stop the trembling of her hands.

Finally, all was packed into the pouches attached to Ari's saddle. With an almost indifferent manner, he withdrew a dagger and used the blade to scrape dirt from his tunic. Then his intense gaze settled on her. Time seemed to slow, his stare pinning her in place. Several times, she thought he meant to say something, but his silence hung heavily, muting even the sounds of the forest creatures. Even Kata and Kati seemed to be silent, though Thora knew it was just an odd power he possessed, to drown out their surroundings when he looked at her. Had the gods given him this gift? If so, she had no means to resist.

"Your wolf cannot travel long distances."

His words snapped her focus back to the hindrance

to their need to relocate. She nodded. How did he manage to create then break such an enticing lure? In one moment, she thought for sure she'd be reduced to ash; in the next, frozen for all eternity. This strange hither and fro war of her feelings ended now. She forced herself to focus on those who truly mattered in her life. Her wolves.

She studied the beasts, disheartened to see Kata had once again resumed her prone position. The she-wolf remained too weak to walk more than a few steps at a time. "You are right. She must be carried somehow."

Ari seemed to consider her words, then gave a curt nod. "We will fashion a *pulka*."

That he offered to create a sled for his horse to pull her pet splintered her resolve, and roused other strange emotions, ones she didn't want to acknowledge. Doing so meant she gave up her freedom; end up forced into a life she didn't want. Still, she really had no choice but to express her gratitude.

"Thank you."

"Thora, understand this – while you have a duty to obey me as payment for your debt, I have a duty to protect you. That includes your wolves. This is the best way for them." He paused, a leering smile tugging at his lips. "And for me."

She tilted her head. "Why you?"

"Because you will be riding before me."

A heartbeat later, Thora realized his intentions. A healthy portion of apprehension accompanied the flash of heat billowing along her spine. She should be angry at the way he intimated he would so casually use her, and yet, she found herself wanting his touch, no matter how it came.

While her anger easily roused, it remained tempered by the desire that hummed through her veins. Knowing he possessed many secrets made it impossible to trust him completely, yet she knew without a doubt he would protect her. Damn him, or no, perhaps damn her, for wanting that. Near as much as she wanted the pleasure he gave.

Hel should drag him to her realm for causing such turmoil in Thora's mind and body. A sacrifice might help, but how would she find the time and means to offer one?

"Thora? Are you listening?"

She shook her head, realizing how deep in thought she'd been not to hear the rumble of his voice. Her vision cleared and she lifted her chin.

"I was considering Kati." Would he believe the lie?

His brow furrowed, giving him an untamed appearance that only set her heart to racing once more. "What do you mean?"

"Of course he will want to stay beside his sister, but he is loyal to me and will want to protect me as well."

"He knows I will protect you, just as you do."

She had no answer and looked away to hide her annoyance. Certain she appeared aloof and uncaring once again, she faced him. "What will you have me do?"

He hesitated, a strange look creeping over his face, a mixture of knowledge and curiosity. She lifted her chin. He grinned.

"Very well. I want you to find me several long sticks. They should be at least as long as I am." He held up one hand, palm facing down, even with the top of his head.

Thora nodded and turned to her wolves. She stroked Kati's head. "I will be back soon. Then we will leave this place and find someplace new to rest until Kata is healed."

Kati licked her chin and gave a little whine, as if he understood. With a smile, Thora stood and began her search for the long sticks Ari would need; not only to fashion a small sled, but to create the saddle harness that would hold the *pulka*. She dared a look back. He didn't notice her watching, intent on the ropes and furs in front of him, so she took the opportunity to study the strong hands and long fingers working on the harness for the sled. The recollection of those hands on her, those fingers *in* her, set off a wild trembling. Breathing grew difficult. When had his hands stopped working the leather and furs? She lifted her gaze, catching his knowing stare. The hint of a smile hovering on his full lips sucked the air right from her lungs.

She narrowed her eyes and turned away with a snap of her head. Damn the man to Helheim for being able to read her so easily! She lifted her gaze to the sky. Had Freyja and Freyr conspired to toy with her this way? Was it some test? What sort of sacrifice would appease them? She must figure that out, and quickly. She wanted her debt paid, her wolf healed and to be on her way.

Why did the thought of traveling on without Ari spark a strange melancholy? With a huff, she forced her focus back to her task, scanning the forest floor for the branches she needed. The answers would come. She only feared they wouldn't come soon enough.

***

Ari chuckled and returned to constructing the harness and furs for the sled. When Thora returned with the sticks, he'd attach them to the harness then secure the fur pelts across the frame. When fastened to his saddle, Gyllir would easily carry him and Thora and pull the wounded wolf.

Setting aside the ropes, he walked over to the wolves. The injured female did seem to be greatly improving, but was in no condition to walk more than a few minutes at a time. The male wolf stood before the female, but made no threatening moves or sound. Ari slowly reached out a hand, allowing the creature to sniff him. After several minutes, he was rewarded with a rub of the animal's head. Grinning, Ari knelt and playfully petted the wolf, noting how the furry tail wagged furiously.

"Your mistress won't be pleased that you like me."

Kati gave a little whine and licked Ari's face. He laughed and patted him heartily on his side.

"We'll protect them both, eh?"

Kati yipped in response, and for a moment, Ari could swear the wolf smiled at him. With a shake of his head, he returned to the harness. Where was she? He scanned the surrounding forest, but didn't see her. A hint of worry poked at him, worry for her safety. Surely she didn't flee him, she would never desert her wolves. What if Muli was still nearby?

Anger and fear twisted painfully in his gut. He set off in the direction of the last place he had seen her, staring at him with passion clouding her eyes. Damn! He should have watched her more closely.

He stalked through a group of small trees. As he came out of the other side, he collided with someone. Thora. He caught her arms to steady them both, a rush of relief shaking through him.

"What's wrong?" she asked.

He inhaled sharply, composing himself and forcing what he hoped was an imposing expression on his face.

"I thought you were trying to flee."

The curious way she stared at him, a mix of wariness and amusement, threatened his hard-fought calm.

"You know I would never leave them." She nodded in the direction of the camp. "Perhaps you were worried I'd gotten lost."

He clenched his jaw for a moment then nodded. "I considered it."

"I see." A smirk danced at the edges of her mouth. He tightened his grip on her arm.

"Have you done as I asked?"

She rolled her eyes. "If you'd let go of me, you'd see."

Impertinent minx! Still, he did release her, holding back a groan of chagrin to see three sturdy branches in her arms, as tall as he, just as he'd instructed.

"Very well. We'll need at least one more."

She pointed past him. "I was about to retrieve that one when you rammed into me."

Her gaze sparkled with renewed amusement. The urge to kiss her nearly overtook him. Somehow, he refrained, knowing it would reveal his weakness and vowing she would pay later for mocking him. His cock hardened at the thought of holding her across his lap, reddening her ass while she squirmed against him. He turned, seeing the branch she indicated. Without another word, he strode over and picked it up. With the four, a simple *pulka* could be quickly fashioned. The reality of the slower pace of their journey rankled, but Ari knew he had no choice, if he intended to keep Thora for more than a few more days.

He stalked back to her, taking her arm and pulling her beside him. He wanted to be on their way, anxious to have her in his arms while they rode, so he might indulge some of his lust-filled desires. Spying yet another branch that met his requirements for the *pulka*, he bent and picked it up, glad to have his thoughts focus, however briefly, on his task, rather than the recollection of Thora's warm body against his. Still, he never released his hold on her, ignoring the protests she muttered underneath her breath. Soon enough, they reached camp and Ari set about securing the branches to Gyllir's saddle, whispering quiet words to the animal to keep him calm. Aware that Thora sat between her two wolves, her gaze on him as if it were a tangible caress, brought an odd shake to his fingers. He clenched his fists for a moment, pleased when they steadied and he could resume.

A short time later, Ari secured the furs and harness across the branches and stood back to admire the sled. Kata would rest comfortably there, and Gyllir, while each hour growing calmer about the beasts, would likely keep up a quick pace, knowing the wolves were behind him. He tied the lead poles of the sled to his saddle, ensuring they would hold firmly within their bindings.

He turned to Thora. "It's ready."

She gave a nod, a flush creeping into her cheeks. He suspected he knew why, judging from the heat in her eyes. He recalled how he'd caught her watching him earlier. Knowing that she wanted him, as he wanted her, brought a vehement satisfaction. Clearly, she anticipated the coming journey with eagerness as well. He gave her a lazy smile and sauntered over to her.

"Come, let's get your wolf onto the *pulka*."

He noted the way her fingers tightened in each of the wolves' fur. The male turned and licked her cheek and the action seemed to stir her from the worry that held her motionless. She stood and turned to the female. Ari hurried over, pushing her aside to scoop the injured animal into his arms.

"Be careful she might…"

Her words trailed off when she saw how Kata rested her head against Ari's shoulder. He held back a smug smile and carried the animal to the *pulka*, laying her upon it. Kati trotted beside him, darting in and around him, as if trying to guide him and offer assistance. Ari longed to see Thora's reaction, but by the time he turned to face her, she possessed a bland expression, which told him nothing.

Again, he smiled. Chances are she forced that visage, to persuade him she cared nothing that her wolves treated him as friend. That the creatures were so at ease around him told him much about how she had raised them. Their natural instincts assured them he was not their enemy, even if Thora wanted to believe he was hers. He recalled the way Kati had attacked Muli, how both animals had attacked the outlaws moments before he'd come upon them. Not once had they made any attempt to turn on him.

He shook his head. Odd how the men who had

known him his whole life, some even having helped train and raise him, had believed him capable of treachery and murder, and these two wolves intuitively knew Ari was no threat.

Now to convince their mistress.

CHAPTER TEN

Thora hoped her trembling didn't show. In a few moments, she would be atop the steed, with Ari behind her, his arms around her. The flames dancing in his dark eyes hinted at how he intended to pass the time. How she wanted him to.

She knelt beside the wolves and gave them each a long stroke on their heads. Kata turned and licked her hand. Her golden eyes once more held a sparkle. Had it only been two days since the animal been wounded? Kati inched closer, leaning his weight against Thora's side. She grinned and ruffled his fur.

"Jealous of all the attention she's getting, eh?" She gave a giggle when he butted his head against hers. She recalled how they'd slept most nights before the attack, with Kati resting in front of her, Kata along her back. Their protection and warmth had kept her feeling safe. Now she found she wanted the safety of Ari's embrace.

As if her thoughts made him appear before her, his shadow loomed over them. Thora looked up, sucking in a shuddering breath when he held his hand to her. Clenching her fingers to stop their shaking, she placed her hand in his.

He pulled her up and against him, but instead of kissing her as she'd expected – and hoped – he turned and led her to Gyllir's side. Still silent, he easily lifted her and placed her in the simple wooden saddle, encouraging her to settle astride before climbing up behind her. The low pommel kept her from sliding forward, her dress bunched up around her thighs. Ari's left arm reached forward for the reins, the other slid around her waist and pulled her tightly to him. He leaned close to her ear.

"This will be a most enjoyable ride."

The husk in his voice sent a shiver whisking along

her spine, the movement drawing a thick chuckle from Ari, which only deepened the quiver. The heat of his tongue slid along the curve of her ear, and she bit her lip to keep from crying out at the fire it left in its wake.

Her thighs held open by sitting astride seemed to intensify the warmth oozing from her sex. When the hand on her waist slid slowly up to cup her breast, she gasped sharply, her heart racing, her breathing skittering into panting. His caress was gentle at first, but even through her clothing, she felt as if he seared her bare flesh. She clutched his wrist then gasped at the sharp sting on her ear where Ari nipped her.

"Do not refuse me."

His voice, thick with lust, sent a shiver along her spine, despite her attempts to suppress it. His low laugh brought a similar response.

"Who knows how long it will take before we find a suitable location to camp."

Thora just barely managed to understand his words, for he once again cupped her breast, fingers flicking at the tip. The barrier of her clothing seemed to somehow intensify the heat building within. If only she'd been able to find her undershift, to give her additional protection against the spark of his touch.

The scrape of Ari's teeth along the side of her neck left her shaking with a mad swirl of desire and confusion. The delight he roused made her want to forget everything else but the decadent pleasure. Her rational side continued to poke at her, reminding her of the very real danger he posed to her safety. And her heart.

While he'd been typically dismissive of her abilities, just like almost every man in her clan, including her father, every now and then, a glimmer of admiration glinted in his eyes. The recollection of his statement that she would have ably defended herself against Muli warmed her. And reminded her of the many facets of the stone Ari had been carved from.

The arm around her waist pressed her tighter still to him, the hard ridge of his cock poking at her bottom. Her body took over her thinking and she let her head fall back against his shoulder. A moment later, his mouth devoured hers, sending the longing into heights she both craved and feared. Surely the gods had given him this ability to create a hazy, passionate fog, one that clouded her wits, made her care for nothing but the fiery desire dancing between them.

He drew away and she opened her eyes to find him watching her with the now-familiar heated intensity that sent delightful flashes skittering along her spine. A moment later, he gave the signal to the horse to move and their journey began. Thora turned to watch the forest before them, occasionally twisting around to see how the wolves fared. Kati walked beside the sled holding Kata, the slow pace necessary to keep from upsetting the she-wolf too much.

A moment later, her thoughts scattered on the breeze when Ari caressed her breasts once more. She really should insist he not toy with her this way, but she found no words to dissuade him when his fingers slid up to the brooches holding the upper part of her dress. It took barely a moment before he released the clips and the *smokkr* fell. The feel of the cool morning air caressing her heated flesh, now bared for Ari's touch, jolted her from the haze of lust.

"Stop." The word came out on a hoarse whisper.

"You refuse?"

There was a hint of annoyance in his tone, but it mixed with a sliver of amusement.

"Anyone could come by and see."

He didn't answer, merely caught her nipple in his fingers and gave it a tug. Fire erupted in her core, a violent quivering overtaking her from head to toe.

"Please, Ari." Desire gave her voice a sharp pitch, revealing her mingled desperation and lust.

Another tug and she bit her lip to keep from crying out. Damn him to Hel, why did his touch have to be so delicious? A half-breath later, he released her, lifting her dress to cover her once more. Her shaky fingers took longer than normal to refasten the brooches.

"Thank you." The words barely passed between her dry lips.

"You will repay that favor when we make camp."

She gave a nod, still trying to clear the haze in her thoughts. But when his hand crept lower, she shifted, moving the dress in an attempt to protect her sex from the lusty assault he intended. Clarity would likely elude her for some time to come.

***

Ari breathed deeply, savoring the musky yet sweet scent that was Thora. It only spurred his desire, and the need to make her beg for his touch, either over her clothes or naked, and he found himself eager to explore her and uncover more of her sensual secrets.

He'd never met a woman who could climax just from having her breasts touched. He recalled the way her body had rippled beneath his when he had feasted on her soft flesh the night before. Already, his cock strained against his trousers. This was going to be a long ride. He intended to make it as enjoyable as possible. For both of them.

He slid his hand to the heat between her legs, held open by the position on the saddle. He held back his grin at the way she used her dress in an attempt to conceal her sex. A soft whimper escaped when he cupped her pussy in his hand, scorching even through the barrier of fabric that, for the moment, he allowed her to hold in place. She shuddered, the movement bringing her right up against his cock. He held back a groan, not wanting to reveal just how deeply the feel of her stirred his passion. If he wasn't careful, he might halt their journey and throw her to the ground, take her and slake this fiery need deep in the wet heat of her body.

Instead, he focused on teasing Thora, savoring the way her fingers clenched on his arm, her nails bringing a tiny bite to his skin. He leaned over and slid his mouth along the curve of her neck, rewarded by her low, yet heated sigh.

"What is it, Thora? What do you want?"

She didn't answer so he pressed harder against her sex. A strange squeak escaped her, drawing a chuckle.

"I've never met a woman with such passion before."

"It's you who's done this to me. What sacrifice did you make to Freyr to give you such wicked skill?"

He laughed again, pressing his cock against her ass. She sucked in a deep breath, the sound echoing in the quiet of the forest like a shout.

"It's you who does this to me." He nipped at her neck, eliciting another delightful quiver.

"I think the gods are toying with us both."

He shrugged. "Perhaps. Perhaps we should simply make the best of it."

A quick flick of his fingers quickly removed the last impediment of fabric, and he pushed the rest of her dress up past her thighs to her hips, giving him unhindered access to her sex. Her grip on his wrist tightened, but she made no real attempt to stop him from sliding his fingers along her inner thighs, damp with her juices. As he drew closer to her pussy, her body tightened further. In anticipation? He grinned.

Finally, his fingers slid through the curls covering her charms, to the slick hot flesh beneath. Thora's head fell back, and the sight of her closed eyes and parted lips sent another jolt of hunger to his cock. A gentle caress of her swollen pussy drew a keening wail. He avoided her clit, knowing she would explode the moment he touched it. No, he wanted her trembling and pleading for release. He didn't realize until that moment just how much he enjoyed her hoarse cries and pleas.

Her body trembled in an erotic dance as he stroked her, slowly, then hard, each touch changing the tenor of her gasps and moans. Each sound vibrated through him, sending his own need to dangerous heights.

Catching the curve of her neck between his teeth, he bit lightly at the same moment he plunged a finger inside her, slowly imitating what he truly wanted to do. A fierce tremor shook her, a short sharp scream erupting before she cut it off. He halted his rough movements within her sex.

"I want to hear you, Thora."

A shuddering breath racked her shoulders and she gave a low moan. The need in the sound jolted his cock. He resumed his torment of her sex and sucked hard on her neck. Her cries came continuously now, and with great reluctance, he withdrew his finger and pulled his mouth from her throat.

"Wh-what? Ari…?"

The confusion in her hoarse voice added another layer of hunger to his desire. Still, if he wanted to hear her beg, he had to maintain his control, no matter how tenuous his hold.

He rested his hand against her sex, not stroking, not penetrating. A few moments later, Thora began to thrust her hips, pushing her groin into his hand, as if trying to spur him to continue. Her sharp, frustrated gasps drew a smile.

"What is it, Thora? What do you want?"

She gave a low groan of frustration. "You're heartless. How can you… do such things and then stop?"

"Tell me what you want."

She stiffened against him. He sensed the clearing of her desire. He would give her a moment or two of clarity before sending her into that lustful state once more.

"I know what you want *me* to do." Her voice grew stronger, and a little colder.

He held back a grin, forcing his expression to sober

when she twisted around to meet his gaze.

"I will not beg."

Her declaration rang out among the trees around them. At that moment, he once more slipped inside her, this time with two fingers. She wiggled against him, her eyes widening before hazing over with desire once more.

"Won't you? You want this, Thora, don't you? Me touching you, making you feel things you never knew before. Things only I can make you feel."

Passion and anger warred in her gaze. He let his thumb brush against her clit for the barest moment. Her mouth fell open and she sucked in a deep gulp of air. Once again, he ghosted over the hard bundle of nerves and her head fell back, a long low moan echoing around him.

"You like that, don't you?" He didn't do it again, just kept his fingers sliding gently inside her.

She remained silent, her body still. He sensed the struggle within her, her pride refusing to give in to his demands, her lust screaming to yield. She didn't push him away, despite her hands maintaining their ever-tightening grip on his arm.

He gave her clit another stroke and her fingers clenched again, yet she still made no effort to fend him off. He continued the steady rhythm inside her, gently pushing her against his needy cock. Soon her hips began to undulate against his hand, now her grasp on his arm changing, this time to aid his efforts. He once more lowered his mouth to her neck, giving her a little nip and caressing her clit again.

He forced himself to focus entirely on pleasuring Thora, in an attempt to ignore his own desperate need. Each movement sent her rubbing against his cock and he offered a small prayer of thanks to Odin that the trousers muted some of the fiery desire her motions spurred. He'd never known such wanting, such need. It threatened to overpower him until another soft cry from Thora drew his attention back to her.

He ground his teeth to force his yearning back. For a few moments, he succeeded in ignoring his lust. The tempo of her cries sent birds rushing from the trees. Ari barely noticed, too caught up in the taste and feel of her, savoring each sound she make as he waited for the words he wanted to hear. He teased her clit again, then once more before sliding his fingers from her pussy.

"No!"

Her voice, filled with frustrated anguish, accompanied more thrusting against his now motionless hand. Her eyes shone with tears. The sight roused all sorts of emotions he didn't recognize. Or perhaps he chose not to.

"Damn you, Ari! Why did you stop?"

He chuckled. "What do you want Thora?"

He held her gaze, daring her to refuse him again. To his surprise, and also his delight, she actually did, giving him a short shake of her head. He studied her, trying to discern what he read in those dark eyes. Did she actually enjoy the way he tormented her? So be it.

He leaned over and devoured her mouth, sweeping his tongue deep inside. Her moans echoed into him, sending his passion even higher. He forced it back. She wanted this, he would give it to her. Later, she would repay him in the most delightful ways, over and over.

He didn't want to relinquish her sweet mouth, but he needed to concentrate both on their journey and making Thora beg. For she would, he had no doubt.

Several moments passed before he made another attempt to touch her pussy. The moment his fingers slid along her moist flesh, the mad quivering began anew. This time, he kept his touch light and teasing, avoiding her clit entirely. The music of Thora's cries urged him to keep up the torment, giving her a respite only after she'd called his name.

Close to what he wanted to hear. Soon.

Without any warning, he plunged his fingers into her tight sheath, extracting the most delightful squeal that evolved into a breathy moan. He continued to thrust harshly into her for a little longer, then withdrew. This time, anger intensified her shout.

"Damn you! I call upon Odin to strike you down for this!"

The laugh escaped before he thought to contain it. "Odin would do the same, if he had you in his arms."

This time, she did attempt to dislodge his hand, but he held fast. She was strong, but he was stronger.

He bit her earlobe. "Stop fighting. I will bind you if I must."

"Filthy mule!"

He laughed and bit her lobe once more, scraping his teeth against the soft flesh. A moment later, his fingers once more slid deep into her, the barest brush of contact against her clit at the same time. She fell back against him, once more meeting his rhythm. When he stilled inside her, she let loose a sob of frustration.

"Tell me what you want, Thora." He crooned the words softly into her ear, drawing another tremor.

"I want more."

"More what?"

Several panting breaths later, she opened her lust-glazed eyes. "More of you. More of what you were doing."

"You want me to make you come?"

Her cheeks reddened, but she held his stare and gave him a single nod.

"Then tell me."

A deep breath shuddered through her. "I want you to make me come."

He arched an eyebrow. He wanted her to say more, and from her expression, she knew it as well. Her lids lowered briefly before she stared almost defiantly at him once more.

"Make me, come. Please. Ari, please make me come."

The husk of her plea undid the hold he had on his body and he drove his fingers into her again, this time using his thumb to firmly caress the hardened bud of flesh, taking her mouth in a bruising kiss at the same time.

It seemed as if she screamed into him, her body bucking furiously beneath him, her long-denied release rolling through her with a force he'd never witnessed. Her juices flowed over his fingers, and he had to tighten his hold, lest she fall from the horse, such was the violence of her release. He kept up his steady movement in her pussy, drawing out each ripple that drove her against his cock.

After what seemed hours, Thora finally quieted in his arms. He pulled his mouth from hers and she leaned her head weakly against his shoulder. He gently slid his hand from her sex, drawing another round of gentle trembling, echoes of her climax.

He lowered her dress, succeeding in only arranging the wool around her hips and upper thighs. With a hand under her arse, he lifted her, carefully sweeping the back of her dress under her bottom. When he settled her back down, he shifted her so she nestled snugly against his chest, her head cradled in the crook of his arm. He lifted his other hand to his mouth at the same moment her eyes fluttered open. Hesitating only an instant, he licked his fingers, tasting her musky sweetness. For a moment, her eyes widened, then darkened with passion once more.

"You will be very busy tonight."

She said nothing, but the delightful way her body tensed then eased sent another shard of fire to his cock.

"You begged, didn't you?"

More silence. He laughed, a brittle sound forced out between clenched teeth when she shifted against his excruciatingly hard shaft. Several moments passed before he breathed steady once more, the painful need settling back to a dull throb.

"I liked hearing it." He whispered the words beside her ear, causing another tremor, igniting his lust to the earlier pitch.

Finally she lifted her gaze, annoyance sparking in her eyes. "You are cruel, but I am too tired to punch you as you deserve."

He chuckled. "Then rest up, Thora. We have a long way to go before we make camp."

She remained silent, but little quivers still passed over her, remnants of the ferocious orgasm he'd drawn from her. When she quieted for the last time, leaning heavily against him, a heavy sigh of satisfaction escaped her. Resting his chin atop her head, he smiled. Holding her as she snuggled against him was as close to Valhalla he'd ever gotten here on Midgard. He anticipated the coming days with eagerness.

***

Thora opened her eyes, the gait of the horse jolting her from the warmth of sleep. The feel of Ari's hard chest supporting her soothed her momentary disorientation. His arms around her, holding her near, the steady thump of his heartbeat, brought a comfort and sense of belonging she hadn't felt since fleeing her village. She could barely recall the time when Ari hadn't been a part of her journey.

A moment later, the memory of the pleasure he'd given her before she'd drifted into sated slumber slithered heatedly along her veins. Already, her breasts ached with the need to be touched once more. What had she done to anger the gods that they would torment her this way, just as Ari did, to make her crave such passion? Her sex clenched, the recollection of his hands sliding within her rising through the cacophony of memories.

"Did you sleep well?"

His low voice rumbled through her, adding to the

tumult in her senses. At this rate, she feared she'd never gather her wits again. She forced her arms to move and shifted away from his embrace, stretching in a way she hoped appeared casual.

"I've had better rest while laying on rocks."

His bark of laughter exploded around her. "Why must you always be so stubborn? There is no shame in admitting you are comfortable with me."

She remained silent, holding herself away from him. She didn't want to admit his embrace felt more right than it should. Odin must have given him the power to ensorcel her, leaving her helpless against his passionate assault, rendering her normally sharp faculties dull and confusing.

"We'll stop to rest soon. I must tend Gyllir."

Good. She needed to be off this horse, away from him, so she could regather her wits. She must keep her guard up around him. In an effort to focus on anything but the heat simmering under her skin, she looked down at the steed beneath her.

"He is a fine animal. How long have you had him?"

"I raised him from a foal."

She wondered what he was like as a child. Here was a way to learn more about him, perhaps gain some insight on how to use him to her advantage. He'd taken her innocence, no, she'd given it to him, and that worked to lessen the success of her father's plan. Having Ari with her as she traveled also offered an additional protection, though once Kata healed completely, she knew her wolves would keep her safe.

She leaned over and patted Gyllir's neck. "Where were you raised, Ari?" She bit her lip, keeping her face turned away, hoping she sounded casual.

Several moments passed before he shifted behind her. He gave a heavy sigh.

"North. Though my mother has family near Uppraka."

"You are very far from your home."

"It's not my home. I have no home."

What did he mean by that? "Why not?"

"It's a complicated tale."

Warnings that he might be more dangerous than she'd first imagined rose again in her thoughts. Even so, more questions formed, ones she wanted answers to.

"Tell me. We have plenty of time."

"No. It's not your concern."

"Yes, it is. I am indebted to you. I'd like to know more about the man who holds my fate in his hands. Are you an outcast?"

Several heavy moments passed in silence before he answered.

"In a way, yes. But I won't be for long."

His vague answers roused her frustration.

"Why is that?" Somehow, her voice sounded calm and even, casually curious. She raised her eyes to the skies in a silent show of thanks to the gods for the strength.

"Not for you to worry about. Just know I will keep you safe."

"After what we've… shared, I want to know more about you. You know my reasons for traveling alone. I still don't know yours."

The arm around her waist tightened, as did his entire body. What was so terrible he couldn't tell her?

"When the time is right, Thora, you will know everything."

A healthy portion of doubt reigned in her thoughts. When would that right time be?

CHAPTER ELEVEN

Sol's chariot had raced more than halfway across the sky, seemingly faster than Ari could remember and he reined Gyllir to a halt. The animal needed to rest, and he needed to stretch his legs. More importantly, he needed to be away from Thora's tempting form for a few minutes. Holding her, teasing her and bringing her to climax had taken a toll on his control. If he didn't take some time to gather his senses, he just might give in and take her then and there. But he had plans for later and doing so would ruin them.

He shifted her away from him, urging her without words to lift her leg over the saddle so she could slide down. She turned and gave him a questioning look but obeyed without voicing her concerns. Without the warmth of her body a shiver passed along Ari's spine. He suppressed it and took a deep breath, carefully dismounting. His cock, still hard with need, finally started to calm. He walked a few paces, ignoring the way Thora stared at him. For a moment, he thought she might ask what troubled him, but thankfully, she turned her attention to her wolves.

He tethered Gyllir to a nearby tree and made sure the animal had something to eat before walking further into the forest. The sound of water indicated they path had been fairly straight along the nearby stream. He should bring Gyllir over now, but needed more time to cool the heat still engulfing him. When they resumed their ride, he would follow the flow, and hopefully find a suitable place to make camp near the water.

When he turned, his gaze immediately settled upon Thora as she sat beside the *pulka*, the male wolf on her other side. One hand slid along the she-wolf's head, but Thora's stare focused firmly on Ari. He found breathing difficult at the inviting desire he found in the depths of her dark eyes. Fingers tightened on the hilt of his sword and he deliberately looked away. Reminding himself of the need to find the fresh water, he once again strode away from her. Her allure tempted him nearly beyond his endurance. If she knew just how she affected him, she would take advantage, of that he possessed no doubt. Better he appeared cold and uncaring. Refusing to answer her questions had been a good start to maintaining his aloof demeanor. He'd almost answered them automatically before realizing he didn't want her to know everything yet. Once he'd shared his past with her, she would hate him. Admitting that the notion bothered him more than a little came hard. Was that why had he been reluctant to push her to that point? She was only a part of his vengeance, he reminded himself. Then why did he care so much?

Because he wasn't ready to give up her passion. She had more fire than any woman he'd ever encountered and he wanted to enjoy it as long as possible, keep her as long as he could. Eventually, the time would come she wouldn't watch him with such hope. When she realized he intended to compel her to attend The Thing, it might hurt her less.

He slammed his fist against his thigh, frustrated at again worrying so much for her tender feelings, when she said so often she wanted to be out of his debt. But he knew the lies she spoke. They were the same ones he told himself. The ones he told her were so much worse. What might she do if she learned the brute she was promised to, despite her objections, was the very same brother upon whom he'd sworn vengeance?

And that she would ultimately be part of that vengeance?

***

Thora watched Ari as he paced a few yards away. Her questions clearly unnerved him. And so did her nearness. She'd felt his hard cock against her bottom, had been aware of it from the first moment he'd settled behind her in the saddle. Even through his tempestuous assault on her body and senses, she'd known he'd been as lust-filled as she. She smiled. This was a way to get him to lower his guard, trust her enough to tell her what she wanted to know.

No sense denying the enjoyment of their shared passion. Perhaps this was Freyja's way of easing the difficulty of her predicament. She was indebted to a powerful and attractive warrior, and for the foreseeable future, she had to stay with him. Making the journey gratifying was her reward for enduring. But she didn't endure. She reveled in the passion her stirred, the way he made her body sing with delight.

She stroked Kati's head and leaned in close to the wolf's ear. "Go find food for you and Kata."

"I must unfasten the *pulka* to take Gyllir to water. When I do, your wolf may accompany me."

Thora turned to see Ari standing behind her. She hadn't even heard him approach.

"All right. I will remain until you return."

Something about the way he stared at her set off a delicious flurry of heat through her veins. Despite the pleasure he stirred, she must remember to focus on a way to be cleared of her debt so she could go on to live her life the way she chose.

"Will you?"

She almost laughed at his obvious concern she might flee. Only knowing that she eventually would confirm his suspicions when she ventured off on own journey kept the mirth from escaping.

"I can't very well leave my wolf, now can I?" She placed a hand on Kati's head. "Go. I will stay with Kata."

The wolf licked her cheek then trotted to stand at the horse's head. Ari continued to study her, then with a nod, turned his attention to the sled. Within moments, he'd unfastened it and led Gyllir away, Kati at his side. She realized her own thirst. Surely Kata must need water. She stood.

"Ari!"

He turned and she shivered under the intensity of his gaze.

"Kata needs water too."

He gave her another nod and indicated his pack then resumed walking. The questions to which she wanted answers loomed larger than ever. How long had he been wandering? And why? She needed to know, to understand what had made him into the man he was. Was his journey a test of the gods? She'd known of many warriors from her clan who had quested on the gods' whims and come back stronger and with many blessings. Was this what drove Ari?

Or did something more sinister in his past haunt him? Something that might come back and harm her as well? Her gut knotted. She'd questioned him about being an outlaw, but he hadn't denied it outright.

"Oh, Kata, how could I be so foolish? I was too quick to trust him, wasn't I?" She stroked the wolf's fur. The animal moved closer to her touch. The apparent understanding of the she-wolf warmed the suddenly cold edges of Thora's heart. She'd made a huge error in allowing herself to be caught in Ari's snare, rescue or not.

She sighed. In the last two days, she'd been caught up in the tempest of a passion so tantalizing, she'd tossed off her caution like letting a handful of flowers be swept off in a gusty wind. After all that had passed between them, this time alone with her thoughts ran rampant, wild and uncontrollable. Just like her body felt when he touched her. The images in her head both terrified and excited. Somehow, she knew she'd never taste passion like that with anyone else. What she feared most was the power Ari possessed to utterly destroy her.

She needed guidance from the gods. A sacrifice would ensure an answer, maybe not the one she truly wanted, but at least she would have some idea of how to deal with Ari. No time now. The sound of Ari returning with Gyllir and Kati reached her and she turned.

Why was there no food? Water? The hollowness of her stomach reminded her how long it had been since they'd eaten. Her thirst seemed to suddenly build until her mouth seemed dry as sand.

The smile Ari gave when he neared nearly stole the breath from her lungs, chasing her growing annoyance. At moments like this, her worries were forgotten and his handsome visage toyed with her senses. The recollection of his kiss, his touch, set off more of those delicious tingles that danced along her skin. She shook her head, trying to grab hold of the alarm from moments ago. It had vanished.

Odin, give me the strength and wisdom to know what to do. Standing, she straightened her kirtle and lifted her chin, forcing a bland expression. Cowering before him, or revealing the frightening worries assailing her moments ago must remain hidden. She'd not give him any additional power over her. If he knew of her concerns, he would surely exploit them, leaving her more helpless and dependent on him than before. The taunting idea of just how he might manipulate her set her core to tightening, heat and wetness threatening to rob her of her calm demeanor. She clenched her fingers, willing Ari to hold her gaze. He did.

His approach seemed to take hours, until finally he stood right before her. "I've found a place where we can settle for the next few days."

"Where? Are you sure it's safe?"

He gave a half-scowl, his brow furrowed in

annoyance. "You question me?"

She shrugged, hoping her uneasiness didn't show. "I just want to make sure we won't be fighting off any other outlaws."

She near bit her cheek to keep from admitting she feared he posed a greater danger to her than anyone or anything else.

He heaved deep breath and gave a shake of his head. "If it will make you feel better, I assure you the location is secluded."

"Explain to me how." She lifted her shoulders, the sight of his rolling eyes rousing a small delight. His exasperation amused her, even as she knew she played a dangerous game that could easily turn back upon her.

"If you must know, there's a mountain at the edge of the forest and a stream runs beside it as far as I can see. There's a formation of rocks leading to a small cave."

"Have you inspected the cave to ensure there are no animals that could harm us?"

His muffled groan nearly drew a laugh. The sobriety in his dark gaze when he took a step closer stifled the urge.

"Thora, you will trust me!"

"As you must trust me."

His head tilted, and he bore an expression similar to the one Kati gave when he didn't understand her command. If only Ari shared the same eagerness to obey her as the male wolf did.

"When you don't share information, I think you have a motive that could pose a danger to me."

The corner of his mouth quirked and he gave the faintest of nods. "Very well. You have made your point."

"So?"

"So...?" Confusion twisted the handsome planes of his face.

"Tell me of this cave."

The lines of puzzlement faded and he smiled, giving a small chuckle. "It's situated higher than the stream, in such a way that we can see any who approach us, though they will not know we are there until they round another cluster of rocks and trees that block the path to the cave. And that is only if I allow us to be seen. The cave will conceal us for as long as necessary."

"Very well. Thank you."

She hoped she didn't reveal the relief that left her knees trembling at his knowledge and understanding of how to use his surroundings to his benefit and safety. Her worries for her protection from outlaws lessened, though she must still remain guarded. Against Ari.

A moment later, the question of why it was so important to him to know how to stay hidden spiked into her thoughts. Forgetting he held secrets, possibly treacherous ones, of his own could be disastrous.

More than ever, she must never forget to follow her plan to be agreeable. She had to convince Ari she followed his command willingly, even as she searched for a way to unearth his secrets, learn everything about him that he seemed to want to keep secret. He gave her a curious look, but she ignored it.

"The fish are plentiful as are the other forest creatures. Come, help me secure the *pulka* and soon we can settle for the night."

A hint of innuendo laced his words. Thora did her best to disregard it, though her fingers suddenly seemed unwilling to obey when she set about assisting him. When the sled had once again been fastened to the saddle, she turned to face her companion. As always, he watched her intently. And as always, her heart raced and her palms grew damp. She pressed them against her dress and turned to the stallion, waiting for Ari to help her up. He did so silently and once more mounted behind her. Senses assaulted by the recollection of the earlier ride, she forced herself to look straight ahead. She must keep her wits in order to ensure her own well-being. Ignoring the warmth of his nearness, however, made achieving that goal much more difficult.

***

Ari sensed a new uneasiness in Thora that hadn't emerged before now. What had happened in the short time he had wandered away? The need to know grew swiftly, and he nearly blurted the question.

She wouldn't tell him, not now, with tension stiffening her entire body. Her fingers remained clenched into fists. He wanted to know, with a fierceness he hadn't felt since he'd been cast out and struggled to understand why. Realizing his attention to Thora, her safety, her happiness, her every need, was attended to had muddled his focus roused a pang of annoyance. He wouldn't let her get away with making him appear less than the warrior he was. He'd spent three years gathering the proof he needed for justice and to clear his name. Her presence would not interfere. He wouldn't allow it.

Still, a part of him warned he risked her hatred if he treated her poorly, as though she were an *ambátt*, a female slave, worthy only of his attention when her service was needed. He wanted her affection and loyalty, not her hatred. Keeping her after his quest ended depended upon her willingness.

He smiled. He knew just how to ensure that.

Knowing how easily he could rouse her passion near guaranteed his success in making her want to stay with him. A few caresses would have her willing to perform any task he wanted. At the moment, only one rose in his thoughts. Would the gods look favorably upon his plan and gift him with that delectable pleasure?

Would she resist? Part of him wanted her to, wanted to bend her to his will. The other part wanted her to offer herself to whatever he wished of her.

Which he preferred, he couldn't say.

The trees thinned as they grew closer to the stream. Once again, he studied the area, satisfied he had found the perfect location for their camp. He looked forward to the time spent in the tucked away cave, knowing he still had at least a few more days before the she-wolf was ready to travel any distance on her own. Days in which he could convince Thora staying with him was best. Id if she still insisted on leaving, he had other ways to prevent that until he was ready to release her.

He reined Gyllir to a halt and once again helped Thora to dismount before following her to the ground. He kept his focus on her while he unfastened the *pulka* and pulled the saddle from Gyllir's back. For a moment, she looked wary and unsure. A second later, her chin lifted. Ari concealed a smile at the way she recovered her determination, and patted Gyllir's neck. Though he'd watered the animal a little while ago, he gave the stallion the freedom to once more return to the stream and drink.

Thora had made her way to Kata's side and now busied herself checking the animal's wound. To Ari, it seemed as if she deliberately avoided looking at him. He remained where he was, content to just watch her for a few moments. An echo of her body in his arms still clung to him and he savored it, knowing she would soon be there again. He strode over to her, waiting until she lifted her face to his. Her eyes danced with a strange trail of emotions. His own gut tightened when he recognized desire for a moment, before she once again concealed it with her cool, aloof expression. He found himself impatient to watch her face dissolve into passion again. He forced the thoughts aside and held out his hand.

"Come, let me show you the cave."

She hesitated but a moment before her warm fingers slid into his palm. Even that simple touch had him near ready to toss her to the forest floor and take her there at that moment. Teasing her this morning had ended up more of a torture to himself. He gave a tug and she stood before him. He liked that the top of her head came to his chin, though he admitted to some relief that he was still taller than she, a sure sign of his greater strength and power over her.

Silently, he led her along the inclined path leading to the cave's opening. At the edge, Thora pulled against him, making him stop. He faced her with curiosity.

"What's wrong?"

"It's dark. How well did you inspect it?"

Her brow furrowed and she stared into the darkness.

"Well enough."

"We need a torch. How far back does it go? The wolves must stay inside with me."

"Aye, Thora. I would not expect you to leave them unprotected outside. We will light a fire and then you will see there is ample room and no danger from within."

She pulled her hand free of his and the loss left a momentary chill. "I will gather kindling."

He nodded, allowing her to tend her task. He set about gathering rocks and placing them in a circle near the mouth of the cave. Though enough daylight remained before Sol's chariot reached the end of her flight, the fire would provide warmth and light and not fill the cave with smoke. When she returned, he fished his fire-steel and striking stone from the pouch on his belt. A handful of touchwood ensured a quick light, with only a couple of strikes needed to spark the fire. He fanned the growing flames and Thora added more twigs, until the flames grew stronger, the heavy scent of the smoke mingling with the earthen aroma of the cave. Finally, Thora laid a thick log upon the small fire and the flickers flared into a full blaze. He stood, once more taking Thora's hand and leading her deeper into the cave. The now-prosperous fire gave plenty of light.

"See? This is all of it. We will be quite comfortable here."

He waved one arm around the expansive cavern, the stone and earth forming the ceiling laced with a thick netting of roots from trees and plants above, adding to the structure's strength. The soft dirt of the floor could be quickly manipulated to their comfort. Ari had learned over the last years to find his small luxuries in many different ways. This cave was one of the most secure he'd encountered. Judging from the way her mouth twisted and her eyes narrowed in skepticism, Thora didn't agree.

"Are you sure it won't fall in on us?"

The need to reassure her rose swiftly and unfamiliar on his tongue. "Don't worry, Thora, I am familiar with caves such as these. We will be safe here."

The uneasiness never left her eyes but she nodded anyway, saying nothing. He led her back toward the mouth of the cave.

"I'll help you bring the female inside."

She remained silent and Ari swore he could almost hear the riot racing in her thoughts. Still, she allowed him to lead her to where Kata rested on the *pulka*. When they approached, the wolf pushed herself to a sitting position, tail wagging. Thora pulled free of his grip and hurried to the animal's side, a joyful cry echoing in the forest. Ari found himself enthralled watching her kneel beside her pet, accepting the she-wolf's licks and laughing when the male forced his way into her embrace.

"You're getting well so fast, Kata."

The delighted excitement in Thora's voice sent a sizzle of lust straight to Ari's cock. He ground his teeth and forced the surge of lust back, knowing he must still wait before he could slake his desires. He slowly walked over to where she knelt, willing his cock to calm. His success was minimal. Thora looked up at him and the grin on her face slowly faded.

"What's wrong?" she asked.

"Nothing. Come, let's get her into the cave."

Thora nodded and stood. "Can you walk a little,

Kata?"

The wolf actually seemed to nod and gingerly raised herself onto all four legs. Thora clapped her hands, her grin returning. Despite his discomfort, Ari found himself caught up in her enthusiasm.

"Look, she's standing." Thora once again ruffled the wolf's fur and walked beside the animal as she took several limping steps toward the cave. Ari followed a pace or two behind, and Kati ran and jumped in excited circles around them, yipping happily. An odd sense of peace settled around Ari. He shook his head to clear the muddled thoughts. Once again, Thora and her wolves had nearly made him forget his goals. She was the reason he acted like a lovestruck lad. He didn't like this unsteady sensation assailing him. There must be some way to make her pay for leaving him feeling unfocused and confused.

A grim smile curled his mouth.

CHAPTER TWELVE

Thora noted that after only a few unsteady steps, Kata slowed. The wolf tired and would need to be carried the last distance to the cave. She turned to Ari. As always, a shiver passed along her spine when their eyes met. She ignored it. Or tried to.

"Can you carry her now?"

He nodded curtly and bent to scoop the animal into his arms.

"Careful, her wound –"

"I know."

His cold tone left her confused. His gaze still held the usual heat and intensity but something seemed more ominous than before. Her heart seemed to skip a beat. What could possibly have angered him now?

"I'll set some furs for her to lay on."

She turned to the packs beside the *pulka* and pulled out two furs. She darted into the cave just before Ari, quickly spreading the pelts along one wall of the cave. Ari elbowed her away and slowly lowered the wolf to the pallet, Kati at his side. Once again, Thora found herself wondering how he had earned her wolf's loyalty so quickly. Had it really only been three days since Ari had saved her? It seemed an eternity, as if she'd never known a time without him.

That feeling could not be good.

When he turned to face her, she had the strange urge to look away. She didn't. "Thank you."

"You'll thank me properly later, *ástin minn*."

His low husked words once again stirred a shiver Thora fought to suppress. When would the fierce need for him wane? She turned away, kneeling beside Kata. She stroked the animal's fur, pleased when the she-wolf turned to lick her hand.

"I'll send Kati to hunt for you."

"I'll take him with me."

Ari's voice shattered the semblance of calm she'd managed to summon. Her fingers tightened in the wolf's fur, but Kata gave no protest. Resting her head briefly against her pet's, Thora forced her grip to loosen and turned. She gave a prayer of thanks to Freyr for leaving her with enough wits to stifle her surprised gasp.

Ari stood over her, silhouetted by the light of the now blazing fire behind him. She couldn't see his eyes, but the sense of being a hare cornered by her wolves drew a shudder she had no hope of suppressing. Despite her shaky knees, she stood, letting loose a sigh of relief as she faced him on more even footing.

"Where will you go?" She forced a layer of ice into her tone, oddly delighted at the way one of his eyebrows arched, his eyes a sparkling blue laced with humor. A hint of a smile tugged at the corner of his mouth. She sensed he mocked her attempt to appear uninterested in his plans and though she should be angry, she detected no malice. Or did she only try to convince herself?

"Where I need to. I won't be gone long."

A heavy silence hung between them, the only sound from the crackling flames that nearly echoed like thunder in the cave. A half-breath later, his mouth crashed onto hers, devouring her with lips and tongue. She leaned into him, fingers curling into his tunic, the heat of passion making it almost impossible to retain her stance. His arms came around her, hauling her tight against his chest. Already her sex ached for him, wanting to be filled. Slick fire coated her insides and she responded eagerly to his demanding kiss.

Just as suddenly as it began, Ari broke the kiss and let her go. She swayed for a moment, stunned by his abrupt release, before composing herself. She smoothed her shaking hands against her dress.

"Don't take too long. I will prepare to cook your catch."

Again, he looked as if he might smile, but the twitch of his lips went no further. Instead he turned, snapping his fingers toward Kati, who fell into step beside him. Together they left the cave and vanished into the forest.

Thora looked down at the she-wolf resting on her bed. "They have banded against us, Kata. We must protect ourselves."

The wolf leaned up and licked Thora's hand. She smiled then forced the last remnants of hazy desire from her thoughts. She had much to do.

She stepped out of the cave, searching the ground. There, a cluster of fallen branches looked to have what she needed. She selected three of the sturdiest, all about the same size and returned to their packs. It took her three trips to haul Ari's large pouches and the branches into the cave, but finally all their belongings were safe inside.

e had chosen well, much as she hated to admit it, even to herself. She sighed and opened one of his pouches. It didn't take long before she found some rope and a small iron pot. As she rummaged further, she found more necessary tools, including a large wooden spoon. Once more, she wondered why he traveled so long and alone. He'd equipped himself with the needs of a man on a quest. Again she wondered what sort of quest. If only he would answer her questions.

Those answers would come, she vowed. In the meantime, she had to continue to earn his trust so he would be more likely to reveal his secrets. Determined not to let thoughts of him consume her entire focus, she turned her attention to the three branches. In minutes, using the rope she'd taken from his pack, she'd made a secure brace that fit over the stones encircling the fire and would hold the iron pot. Once more rummaging through Ari's pack, she pulled out a small bucket.

Water from the stream soon filled the bucket and Thora poured it into the pot. Keeping her concentration on the fire, she picked up a smaller stick and poked at the flames. As the kindling and wood broke apart, the fire settled. Perfect. She carefully arranged the tripod around the stone circle and then hooked the pot to the dangling rope.

Giving Kata a glance to ensure the animal's safety, Thora once more stepped outside the cave and searched. There, just what she needed. Both wild onions and angelica grew in a cluster near a gathering of trees beside the stream. She knelt beside the fluted stems with its curled leaves and studied the greenery. She knew enough of plants, having been taught by the women of her clan after her mother's death, to recognize this was safe to eat. If Ari caught some fish she could boil the leaves with it. She gathered several onions and a clump of the angelica and returned to the cave to prepare them.

She pulled one of the knives from her pack. How easily the handle of the blade twisted in her hand and she savored the feel of the weapon. Since Ari had forbidden her this morning to wear the knife on her belt, she'd missed the comfort of the blade. It had offered a sense of protection and she sorely needed that, though no knife would protect her from the danger Ari posed.

Focusing on her task, she soon readied the angelica and onions. The water in the pot began to bubble. How long had Ari been gone? The last of the daylight had faded some time ago. Shouldn't he have returned by now?

"Damn his soul, Kata, he wants me to worry."

Thora paced along the edge of the cave's entrance, watching for any sign of Ari or Kati in the trees. She turned her attention to another section of forest, wishing one or both would soon show themselves.

The realization she didn't know who she wanted to see more left her stomach churning.

A rustle in the nearby brush drew her attention. Kati? With caution as her guide, she stepped toward the cluster of bushes at the edge of the stream. Her attention also remained on the opposite bank, knowing any sort of creature might linger within the thick growth of underbrush.

A moment later, Kati bounded out of the bushes and to her side. A surge of relief that a wild animal didn't attack left her knees shaking, and she sank to the ground, wrapping her arms around her pet.

"He's quite a hunter."

Ari's voice drew her gaze to him as he walked alongside the stream. On his belt hung several hares. Thora stood, enthralled once again by the heat in his stare.

"Kati caught all those?'

"He caught the first four. The other four are mine. He flushed them all out, made it easy for me."

"We'll feast tonight."

Ari nodded and unhooked the hares from the belt, handing them to her. She took them and headed toward the cave. Kati immediately went to Kata's side. Aware of Ari standing nearby, Thora forced her focus on skinning the hares and preparing them to cook.

"Will you fetch me sticks to roast them with, please?"

She kept her tone cool, yet with a hint of command. After several moments of silence passed, she looked up from her work. Once again, Ari's sea-colored gaze held a hint of anger and despite her efforts to suppress it, she shivered.

"Are you giving me orders?"

So that was his problem. How she resisted the urge to throw a rock at his head, she might never know.

"Must I do everything? Am I a slave?"

He shook his head. "No, but you are the one indebted to me, remember?"

"I do, since you remind me of it at every opportunity. However, if you wish to eat, I need sticks to spit the hares. If you cannot assist, you will starve."

He chuckled. "I do like your spirit, Thora. More than I probably should. Very well, I will be back in a few minutes."

He turned and strode out of the cave. Thora held back the need to release a cry of vexation. She looked over at the wolves, both now settled on the furs.

"He's insufferable," she said. Did she imagine it, or did Kata nod? "He's lucky I don't have corncockle, or I'd poison his meal."

She had just finished skinning the fourth hare when Ari returned with several long, thin sticks. Maintaining her silence, she continued to work until all four of the hares had been readied and spitted on the sticks. She laid the animals across the fire and checked the pot. The onions and angelica boiled at a rapid pace, filling the cave with an enticing aroma. Soon the scent of the cooking meat mingled and Thora realized just how very hungry she was. She gathered the remaining four hares and carried them over to her pets. She gave each animal a gentle stroke on their heads. Returning to the fire, she turned the meat, their juices sizzling and crackling in flames. Sensing Ari's stare on her once more, she met his gaze.

"Why do you always watch me?"

He shrugged, that hint of a smile once again tugging at the corners of his mouth. "I enjoy watching you, *ástin minn*. You are very pretty."

The compliment shouldn't spark that fluttery feeling in her belly. Giving in to his pretty words, the flattery, that somehow made her feel as giddy as a child receiving Jul gifts, seemed a betrayal to her sense of self. Yet, heat scorched her cheeks and it wasn't caused by the fire.

"Thank you." Thankfully her voice held steadier than her trembling fingers. She picked up a stick and poked at the flames then turned the hares. She met his gaze once more.

"What is it?"

"I need a spoon. Can you fetch my pack?'

His eyes widened and she clenched her jaw to keep from chuckling at his bemusement. Clearly, he'd expected her to say something else.

"You're becoming quite demanding."

He rose, giving her a pointed stare before heading toward their packs. When he returned and handed the pouch to her, he didn't release it right away.

"I will have demands of my own after dinner."

She swallowed, her mouth suddenly dry as a summer wind. When he let go of her pouch, she focused on withdrawing a wooden spoon and tending the meal.

***

Ari smiled at the sudden nervousness Thora displayed. The blush still clung enchantingly to her cheeks and the slight tremor in her hands belied her uneven thoughts. Good. He wanted her off-balance, not expecting what he would ask of her.

He resumed his seat against the wall, resting his arm on his raised knee, content to continue watching Thora work. She'd make a fine wife. Wait. No, why did he think of her in such a way? Because she'd crafted a strong tripod to hold the pot she'd obviously found in his packs? What else had she found?

Nothing of import, of that he was sure. If she'd found the weapons and seen the messages their marks carried, she'd surely ask about it. While he knew her attraction for him was as fierce as his for her, he was also well aware she didn't fully trust him. He preferred it that way.

He could hardly contain his excitement for the coming night. His imaginings kept him half-hard. With a heavy sigh, knowing he still had some time to wait, he eyed the cooking meat, willing it to be done. The gamy aroma filled the cave, reminding him of the many hours since he'd eaten last. It seemed the gods still toyed with him, ensuring all his hungers remained at fever pitch. What must he do to earn their favor, the restoration of his name and his keeping of Thora?

"Ari?"

Her voice jolted him from his thoughts and he looked up. Thora held out a leg from one of the now-cooked hares. How long had he daydreamed with silly nonsensical ideas? Rubbing his eyes to clear his thoughts, he accepted the offered food. Thora resumed her seat beside the fire, watching him with curious eyes.

He took a bite from the leg and the hot juices exploded on his tongue, the meat tender and flavorful. When he finished, he moved to sit beside Thora, reaching for another piece of hare. She said nothing, merely used the spoon to scoop out an onion. She handed him the spoon and he purposely brushed his fingers over hers, tightening his grip when she would have moved away.

"You've done well."

Again, a blush darkened her cheeks. "Thank you."

He released her and raised the spoon to his mouth. The onion, soft and sweet, melted in his mouth.

"You are a fine cook, Thora." He liked saying her name, the way it felt rolling across his tongue. He especially liked the way her eyes gave a momentary flare when he did.

"I… thank you."

The contradiction between the sassy hellion and the demure shy maiden only made her more intriguing. And made him more determined to bind her to him, however he could, and despite her wishes.

The rest of the meal passed in silence, the only sound the sizzle and pop of the fire. Ari stood and stretched, his hunger appeased. He strode across the cave to his packs and retrieved the water skin. He'd filled it earlier, but when he lifted the spout to his mouth, the water was still cool and refreshing. After taking a long drink he handed it to Thora.

She accepted with a hesitant smile. Soon she would

be screaming his name, he vowed. Very soon.

He resumed his position against the wall and watched as she stored the remaining meat, placing it carefully in the pouch with the fish he'd caught this morning before leaving their camp. How long ago that seemed. Had he really only saved Thora three days ago? He felt as if he'd never known a time without her. Had she ensorceled him somehow? Had the gods sent her to him to torment him? For she certainly did that, in so many ways. Time for him to repay her for that.

CHAPTER THIRTEEN

Thora held Ari's stare. She recognized that look too well now. Part of her anticipated the coming hours, while another part of her felt afraid. Very afraid.

What had he said earlier, during the tormenting ride of this morning? That she would repay him for the pleasure he'd bestowed upon her. What would he ask of her?

He suddenly stood before her, forcing her to tilt her head way back to hold his stare. In silence, he held out a hand. She took it, willing the trembling to stop. When his fingers closed around hers, he tugged until she stood before him. She had barely a moment to breathe when his mouth descended roughly on hers, his tongue sweeping her lips apart. The heat weakened her knees and she leaned heavily into him, already the passion rising with such force it tore the breath from her lungs.

He drew away, breathing as heavily as she. The flames in his eyes scorched her soul and her fingers curled in his shirt.

"Remove your dress."

She should have been annoyed at his sudden command, but the husk in his voice overrode her displeasure, instead sending those delightful tingles whisking across her skin. She stepped out of his embrace and reached for the brooches, keeping her eyes on his. His gaze lingered on her hands as she freed the *smokkr*, letting it slide from her shoulders. His breath hitched, echoing over the crackling fire. She held back her smile, enjoying the ability to tease him for a bit, as he did her, though not quite in the same manner. She reached behind her neck to unfasten the laces holding her tunic closed.

Lust tightened the planes of Ari's face, his eyes alight with desire. Knowing she caused this reaction in him intensified her own passion. The earlier fear had vanished, completely overtaken by eagerness.

She wiggled her hips so the *smokkr* fell further down, allowing her to slide the tunic from her shoulders, slowly baring her breasts. Another sharply inhaled breath signaled Ari's growing yearning. She held back a smile and let the tunic and *smokkr* drift down over her hips. Without her undershift, she soon stood naked before him, the fabric piled at her feet. She stepped out of the clothing and took two steps closer.

"Your turn," she said.

He grinned, and now it was she who watched with eagerness when he reached for the laces of his shirt. Soon his chest, burnished in the firelight, was bared to her hungry gaze. Her fingers itched to slide along his shoulders and chest, feel the softness of the dark hair dusting his skin. She fisted her hands to control the urge.

His hands went to his belt, his fingers fumbling in his haste. A moment later, he slid the leather from his trousers and shoved them down. Thora's gaze was drawn immediately to his cock, standing hard and erect. Soon, he would fill her with his flesh. Her mouth watered in anticipation, as did her sex.

She took another step, now mere inches away. Her gaze once more locking onto his, she lifted her mouth to his, savoring the way he briefly froze, apparently surprised by her boldness. Using her tongue the way he did, she teased his lips apart, slipping inside to stroke along his. The feel of his hands tightening on her shoulders added to the tumult assailing her senses.

Giving in to her earlier urge, she placed her hands on his chest, loving the way his skin heated under her touch. She took her time exploring the muscled flesh, noting from time to time how he groaned. Still kissing him, she raked her nails along his nipples and she swore he growled. She dared to reach lower, sliding along his abdomen to the curls at the base of his shaft. His entire body went rigid. She took the opportunity to trail her fingers along the length of his cock. That time he definitely did growl.

Abruptly, she found herself pushed away, though he still held his grip on her shoulders.

"What's wrong?" Freyja's blood, was that hoarse croak her voice?

"Nothing. On your knees."

She blinked. What did he mean?

"Must I repeat myself?"

The hint of frustration in his voice told her how her brief touch had affected him. She tilted her head and studied him.

"Yes."

"Yes, what?"

"Yes, you must repeat yourself." She stifled a laugh at the way his brow furrowed.

"You test my patience in so many ways." His husky words sent the familiar shivers along her spine. "I said, on your knees."

"Why?"

"Do not question me further. Just obey."

She shrugged, hoping she appeared casual and unaffected. Doing as he told, she lowered herself to her knees, wincing as tiny pebbles bit into her skin. Ari bent and lifted his tunic, folding it and offering it to her. After she placed the fabric under her knees and straightened, she found herself face to face with his cock. Suspicion rose as to what he intended. Uneasiness mingled with her desire.

"Thora, touch me."

For that, she needed no further encouragement, reaching up to encircle his cock with her fingers. Hard and at the same time soft, his hot flesh quivered under her hand. She stroked slowly, noting with interest how he seemed to grow even thicker under her ministrations. The ridges along his flesh scorched her hand. His fingers slid into her hair, a gentle caress that encouraged her to stroke more firmly. A wild quiver overtook him, his fingers tightening in her hair almost painfully. She released her grip, trailing her nails along his length. A hoarse groan shook him again and she looked into his face. Her heart raced at the sight.

Eyes closed, the lines of his face melted in pleasure, his lips parted as he sucked in deep breaths. Once more, she tightened her grip and stroked faster, until his hand covered hers, stilling her motions.

"Stop, lest this is over before it's begun."

She didn't understand his meaning, but allowed him to uncurl her fingers. He held her stare, and she sensed a question he didn't voice. Several moments passed in heated silence. The feeling of vulnerability caused by kneeling at his feet roused a strange intoxication that left her shuddering in excitement.

His hand cupping her cheek in another gentle caress stirred yet more tingling delight. He ran his thumb along her lips, and she sucked in a breath, her core tightening.

"Suck me, Thora."

For a moment, she wasn't sure she'd heard him correctly. His chuckle told her the surprise registered clearly on her face.

"What? You want me to…?"

"Yes. Take me in your mouth and suck me."

The idea left her shocked, yet strangely giddy at the same time. Her gaze fell once more to his hard cock, inches from her face. His heady, musky scent surrounded her, leaving her with the sensation she'd just drank several horns of ale.

With a deep breath, she once more enclosed his shaft in her hand, leaning forward, now eager to please him. Eager to learn his taste. The wanton feelings added to the chaos in her body, and her apprehension vanished on a wisp. Closing her eyes, she darted her tongue out, lightly licking the tip of his cock. A low moan echoed around her. His sound of delight intensified her lust and she found his earthy flavor almost enjoyable. She parted her lips and slid her mouth around his tip. His fingers once again fisted in her hair, urging her to take him further in. She obliged, finding the hot flesh filling her with a strangely wicked delight. Using her tongue to slide along his length, she sucked hard, rewarded with his harsh shout. His cock thickened still more. She gave another pull, using her fingers to cup and stroke his balls. A violent quiver swept over him and Thora found her pussy slickened and heated even more with the knowledge that she had brought him to this state. She continued to stroke and suck, finding a rhythm that kept him trembling and groaning under her touch.

Another shout and he erupted in her mouth, Taken by surprise, she attempted to pull away, but Ari held her firmly in place. She swallowed, his salty seed almost filling her mouth faster than she could keep up. When he finally stopped, breathing heavily, his shaft softening in her mouth, he released his hold on her head. She pulled back, licking her lips and shivering at the echo of his taste on her tongue.

"You are a delight, Thora."

His hands curled around her upper arms, hauling her up and against him, devouring her mouth with a bruising kiss. The cave seemed to spin, her fingers curling into his shoulders, looking for something with which to steady herself. Didn't matter. The tempest engulfed her and her awareness narrowed to his mouth on hers and the corresponding throb in her sex.

Finally, Ari broke the kiss and Thora sucked in several heavy breaths, still leaning heavily against him. His musky scent teased her nose, intensifying the trace of the flavor of his seed on her tongue. She forced her eyes to open, only to find him studying her as usual.

"Come."

He turned her and for the first time she noted the furs

spread across the cave floor along the wall. When had he done that? She gave a glance to where the wolves lay, both clearly asleep. Her awareness returned to focus on Ari as he guided her to the bed he'd prepared. She slid into the soft pelts, turning to her side to watch as he followed. Her entire body seemed to ache with need.

He raised himself up on one arm, reaching out to cup her cheek with his other hand. Just that simple contact intensified the longing. Judging from the gleam in his eye, he intended that reaction. A moment later, he pulled her across his chest, his arms encircling her, holding her tight against him. He buried his face into her hair, inhaling sharply. The feel of his body engulfing hers left her senses in disarray. The contradiction between his intentional coldness and warm moments like these left her confused, yet fully aware of the ferocity of his need. For her. She knew it instinctively, for it matched her own yearning.

What had happened in only a mere handful of days that she wanted to give herself over to the control of a man, to let him lead her on a journey that only they two would understand? She'd fled her home to avoid an unwanted marriage and now here she was, wanting to stay with this man forever, even after only knowing him a few short days. No, not short days. Long days that took over all sense of her past, as if she'd never known a time without him. How could this be? She didn't want to be beholden to any man. Yes, she owed Ari a debt, and yes, she knew very well how his claims of repayment went far beyond acceptable. That she allowed him to take advantage gave her the satisfaction of knowing she maintained control as well, and perhaps better than he did. Without her virginity, she had no value her father could place on her, and she now held the right to make her own life decisions.

Still, the desire to let Ari make those decisions grew ever stronger and troubled her more than she cared to admit. The constant to and fro of her wants and needs left her head near spinning. She needed to stop dwelling on her dilemma. Her head ached at the thought of trying to decipher what the gods meant when she knew they would reveal all to her when it was time for her to know. Still, she longed for the chance to plead for relief from the tempest that refused to give her true peace. Would a sacrifice such as she might be capable of making be enough to sway their compassion?

She frowned. Likely not.

The troubling thoughts scattered like ashes on the wind when Ari rose above her, spreading her thighs, his cock once again hard and straight.

***

Ari woke with a start, the haunting tendrils of a frightening dream leaving him gasping for breath. Little of the dream remained, but instinct told him it related to his upcoming victory. In his now tight embrace, Thora protested and squirmed. He let loose a deep heaving breath, her warmth soothing, even as he sought to recall his dream.

Nothing came clear, except a shadowy image. A woman. Thora? The vision was cloaked in a thick grey fog. Somehow, though he couldn't be sure exactly he how, he knew her time walking Midgard approached its end. Once more he hugged Thora tighter. He wouldn't allow that. Surely there was more to his dream, something to confirm or deny his fears.

The shift of her head against his shoulder drew his gaze to hers, open wide and intent on him. Heat slithered over his skin, the simmering fire having little to do with the rapid increase of temperature. She slid her tongue along her lower lip and the half-rational thoughts baffling him vanished as desire took control.

A deep groan shook from him the moment before he took her mouth, sliding his tongue deep, as if somehow claiming her as his. Her fingers dug into his arms, the sharp prick of her nails another torment to his lust-clouded thoughts. The brief suspicion she was sent from Loki to trick him into some ill-fated turn skittered away as he tore his mouth from hers and slid his mouth along her cheek to the underside of her jaw.

The high-pitched sounds escaping her told him how his touch excited her and thrilled him further, his cock hard and hot and seeking her cleft, only inches away. Somehow, he pulled hard on the reins of his desire, knowing he wanted to savor her, taste her, in every way possible.

With a quick flip so she lay beneath him, he meandered his way along her throat, nipping and licking as she arched her head back, her fingers now tightening in his hair. He welcomed the way the tug brought his awareness to greater heights, still, he wanted her helpless and pleading beneath him. With a deep breath, he pulled himself away and reached for his belt.

The firelight revealed both disbelief and excitement to her dark eyes. "Why?"

"Because I would not have your touch distract me."

Her eyes widened and she sucked in a breath. "Not fair! You claim I owe you a debt, yet you won't let me repay it."

He paused, staring hard at her, then grabbed her wrists and held them together with one hand, wrapping the leather around them. She tugged, but the effort seemed half-hearted. He suspected she liked being under his control, much as her fiery nature might protest. He pulled her face close to his.

"You are repaying it. On my terms. Not yours."

"The day will come when you will repay me. On my terms."

He grinned. "I look forward to that day, *ástin minn,* though if it ever comes, will be a long time away."

Her eyes narrowed and instinct screamed a moment before she struck, driving her head against his. He easily evaded the move and laughed out loud, suspecting she had fought back simply to draw his ire. And his punishment.

He stretched her arms over her head. He reached for the dagger still resting beside their pallet and used it to stake her bonds to the earthen floor of the cave. She tugged, but the position gave her little leverage. Once he resumed his torment, he doubted she'd be capable of gathering the strength needed to free herself.

He knelt with one leg between hers. With slow, deliberate movements, he placed his hands on her hips and slowly slid them up her sides, his fingers stroking across her belly.

"What are you doing?"

He didn't answer, just continued his journey along her heated skin, noting the way her breathing came heavier, and the tips of her breasts hardened, drawing his gaze. Sensing she wanted him to touch them, he didn't, instead tracing his fingers along the underside of her arm, drawing breathy giggles that rang through him like sunshine and fed the fire licking at his insides. His cock throbbed, yet somehow he managed to resist the need to rise up and fill her.

"Damn you, Ari! I won't tolerate your cruel games anymore!" Her words devolved into a laughing shriek as he once again tickled the sensitive skin under her arm. She lurched against her bonds, but they held fast, keeping her vulnerable to his whims.

"How will you stop me, *ástin minn*?" Another flicking of his fingers had her biting her lip. A moment's pause and he ran his thumb along her lip, pulling it free.

"You will tolerate everything I choose to do to you." He leaned closer to her ear, letting his tongue slide along the soft flesh before catching it between his teeth in a gentle nip. "And you will like it."

Before allowing her to respond, he slid his mouth to hers, muffling her cries. Yet, she responded in a way that left his head spinning, her tongue dueling his, as if she hoped to spur him into intensifying his attentions.

He refused to be rushed, taking his time devouring her, his hands sliding along the sensuous curves of her body. Blood roared in his ears while he meandered along her skin, following the trail his hands blazed with hot wet slides of his tongue and lips. The only sounds Thora gave now were cries of delight, rising higher in pitch as he continued, pausing to fondle her breasts. Gripping each lightly, he lowered his mouth to one hardened tip, circling it with his tongue. She gave a little shriek and a violent quivering almost dislodged his hold. He chuckled, daring a glance at her.

She'd lifted her head and watched him, her eyes glazed with arousal, sharp pants of air escaping her lips. With a wink and a grin, he gently sucked her tight nipple into his mouth. Her eyes rolled back and she flopped back to the furs, her entire body shaking. He scraped his teeth along the pebbled flesh and a strangled wail echoed in the cave. He turned his attention to her other breast, drawing that into a tight peak as well. He drew away and blew on her nipples before returning to his earlier journey.

Sliding down across her belly, he savored the slow ripple, using slow and gentle movements to tease her. Her frantic moans and gasps filled the air and several times, after he'd let his tongue glide along the skin at the top of her mound, he swore she pleaded to Odin himself for release from the bane that was Ari. This time, he let loose his laugh, before positioning himself between her spread legs.

The movement of her head coming up drew his attention. He gave her another wink.

"What are you doing?"

He shrugged, saying nothing, using his fingers to poke through the soft hair covering her pussy. A moment later, a howl of delight filled the cave when his fingers glided along her hot slick flesh. Her hips undulated wildly, her legs wrapping around his shoulders. He continued the maddening caresses while parting her sex, holding her wide.

Without hesitation, he used his tongue to caress her. Her entire body went rigid, her heels digging his back. When he repeated the motion, she gave a keening wail and fell back onto the furs. Her wild rasping breaths urged him on and he held her open, driving deep and savoring the honey of her juices. When he pulled away, her moan of frustration turned to exultation when he caught the tight nub of her clit between his lips. Giving a gentle suck, he stroked it with his tongue. A sudden tensing warned him he drove her too far, too fast, so he gently eased away, using his fingers in soothing motions as he released her and rose up on his elbows.

"Ari, stop this torment!" Her voice was scratchy and cracked, her eyes heavy-lidded and filled with frustration.

"You will beg me for more."

Her gaze snapped to his, frustration mingled with passion in the dark depths of her eyes. "Why must you do this?"

The plea in her voice sent his lust surging more forcefully through him. He leaned his forehead against hers.

"Tell me the truth. You are enjoying this."

She nodded, catching her lower lip briefly in her teeth again. "You shame me like this, treat me as no more than a possession. That my desires don't matter."

He slid his fingers along her cheek, a strange pang tapping at his heart. The need to reassure her, to make her understand why he did what he did, how deep the pleasure it gave him, overtook him.

"You owe me, remember? You are my possession."

Her eyes developed a sheen. Tears, he realized. Why did regret nearly cool his desire?

"I do this for your pleasure as well. Don't you find the... result enjoyable?"

Again, she nodded. "I do, but damn you, Ari, it's almost painful when you tease this way. Why will you not let me share this with you?"

He studied her closely, trying to understand what he read in her eyes. From the first, she had always wanted to be treated equally, despite her debt. Perhaps this once, he could forget the debt she owed. He reached up and withdrew the dagger from the ground, pulling it free and loosening her bonds. She held his stare, confusion now lining her face in the most enchanting way. A moment later, she had wrapped herself around him, clinging tightly, her lips melded tight against his. The momentum sent him tumbling backwards, clinging tightly to prevent her from being hurt in the fall. After a few moments, her frantic assault slowed. Hands on her waist, he eased her from him, chuckling.

"Easy Thora, I won't be rushed."

"You have done this to me. I won't wait any longer. You tease and deny me every time. Not this time."

She held his stare, daring him to refuse. Instead he grinned. She continued to surprise him.

"Very well. Not this time." But he'd sleep with a crone before he gave her control. Wrapping his arms tight around her, he once more positioned her so she lay beneath him. Her embrace never loosened and when he slid his cock along the hot soaked folds of her sex, she jerked upward, trying to force him into her. A hand on her hip halted her motion.

"Patience," he warned, even as he nudged the tip of his cock toward her entrance. Once again, she tried to gain control, but his grip prevented most of her movement. Her eyes narrowed.

"You are still being cruel."

"I must be ready, silly girl."

"Well get ready!" Her fingers dug into his shoulders

and he savored the tiny sting for it gave him control over his desire once more. Satisfied he wouldn't explode the moment he entered her, he gently eased himself into her, groaning at the way her slick tight sheath gripped him. He paused, then drove a little deeper, his fingers tight on her hips to hold her still.

With each forward glide, Thora's cries came closer together until he had finally filled her. For several moments, he remained engulfed in her warm body, her lips rising to meet his in a fiery kiss that left his head spinning.

Daring to move, he eased his hold on Thora and she met his gentle rhythm. A few moments of this delightful glory intensified when she quickened her movements, forcing him to move faster as well. Soon, he thrust hard and rough into her, her hips rising to meet each drive. Her nails scored his back and shoulders, her tongue dueling frantically with his, her cries reverberating through his body.

Lust hazed every one of his senses, Thora's scent surrounding him like the sweet aroma of ambrosia. Her feel and taste both around and within him drove him higher than ever before. A moment later, she pulled her mouth from his, a piercing howl near shattering his ears. Beneath him, her entire body bucked furiously and the feel of her sex tightening around him was enough to send him over the edge. He tumbled into the abyss, surrounded by her in ways he'd never thought possible. The pulsing, blinding lights of bliss seemed to last hours, his own hoarse shouts driven out by the force of the pleasure consuming him.

What seemed hours later, the roar in his head receded and his body calmed. Beneath him, Thora continued to periodically quiver, her pussy squeezing him again, gently this time. Almost soothing. Careful to remain joined with her, he eased himself to his back, arranging her carefully atop his chest.

Brushing her dark hair from her face, she lifted her head and met his stare. Softened by her climax, her eyes were dark and luminous, glowing in the firelight. Her tangy scent clung to him and he inhaled sharply, to take her essence in deep.

"Thank you. That was..."

He smiled and caught her chin in his fingers. "It was." He pulled her close and pressed a soft kiss to her lips. When he drew away, she snuggled against him.

"But you still owe me."

She stiffened and once more raised her head, her eyes now blazing with anger. The anger faded when he laughed.

"You are a vile beast!" But her usual sword-sharp tone was missing. In its place, he detected a hint of amusement tinged with sated weariness.

"Go to sleep, Thora." He pushed her head back to his chest. His soft cock remained only barely inside her. When she shifted against him, nudging him free, a strange sense of loss mingled into his fulfilled fatigue.

CHAPTER FOURTEEN

The thumping rhythm of hooves cut into Ari's slumber. He opened his eyes and blinked several times. Dawn pinkened the sky. He glanced down at Thora, nestled against him. While holding her, he'd once again slept deeper than he had in years. The thought roused alarm. These last days spent with her in easygoing camaraderie, and passion, had made him too comfortable, leading to carelessness. The consequences of that slammed into him.

His distraction endangered not only his life, but that of the woman sleeping against him. It threatened his chances of clearing his name, raising a very real fear he might be prevented from entering Valhalla when the time came to cross into the next life. He took a small measure of ease in the fact that surely the gods were well aware of how he had been blamed for another's deeds. That concern could wait, in light of approaching people. His gentle shake of Thora's shoulder grew more intense when the earth rumbled even louder. The riders neared faster than he'd first thought.

"Someone comes. Don your dress."

He disentangled himself from her embrace and reached for his trousers and sword. The horses grew closer still. How many? At least three, perhaps more. Travelers to The Thing? Likely, but even so, he'd take no chances and expect whoever approached to be hostile. Thankfully, he and Thora remained out of sight, but if the riders rounded the stand of trees to the left, they'd see Gyllir and know someone lingered nearby. Best be ready. He snapped his fingers toward Kati and the wolf was instantly alert.

"Why does he obey you so easily?"

The annoyance in her voice might normally have

drawn a chuckle, but nothing about the coming moments contained any humor. His attention was torn between the two ways one could approach their cave, thankful the forest concealed it nearly completely from both directions. But it was that last realization that worried Ari. If only he could be sure from which direction the riders approached. If he knew that and how much time before they showed, he might attempt to bring Gyllir into the cave with them. Again, he silently cursed the contentment that appeared to sap his wits as well as his senses.

The rustling of the brush grew louder to his left and he turned. There they were, four men on horseback quickly approaching the cave. Though his vantage point of being higher off the forest floor made it easy to see further as well, ensuring the four were the only ones, he couldn't make out their faces, even though something seemed familiar about the leader poked at him, raising his alarm. For the moment, he and Thora, and their refuge, remained unseen, but he knew that wouldn't last much longer. Unlucky for them, the riders approached from the one direction that provided the weakest protection.

"Ari, who is it?"

"I don't know. Just stay back and let me handle it."

"But –"

"Do not argue with me now. Do as I say."

She harrumphed and stomped about. He dared a glance her way, shaking his head.

"Thora." He forced a stern order into her name.

"I'll not hide."

"You will obey my orders!"

Seconds passed as she stared defiantly at him, seconds that drew his attention from the potential impending danger. Damn the woman for being so stubborn!

"You will not distract me. You are safest in the

cave."

Her lips pressed together, as if she attempted to hold back her protests. The pack grew nearer, leaving Ari with no choice but to return his attention to the riders. Surely they'd seen Gyllir by now. He stepped out from his cover and froze when his gaze settled upon the leader. It couldn't be!

His brother? Yes, it was Hersir, and he was accompanied by the jarl's men. Or were they Hersir's men now? Ari realized he had no idea if the jarl still lived.

Mere moments remained before the riders spotted him. He turned to Thora, who had once again come to stand behind him. He pushed her further back into the cave.

"Get inside!"

Her resistance dashed his hope she would obey. Again, he pointed to the back of the cave, dark and hidden from view.

He glanced back over his shoulder. The riders' pace slowed. The way Hersir raised his arm confirmed to Ari he'd been seen. He turned his back to Thora, needing to focus on his brother. The one who had convinced everyone Ari was a killer and a threat to their entire clan. Except Ari now had proof the deeds, both planned and committed, were at Hersir's hands. Was he so close to clearing his name only to be struck down now? Jaw clenched, he raised his weapon, hoping the advantage of his added elevation made him more imposing. He'd not go down without taking his brother with him. At least then, for sure he'd awaken in Valhalla.

Hersir pulled his mount to a stop a few feet from the mouth of the cave, an evil grin adorning his scarred face. The other men remained a pace or two behind him.

"Ho, Ari! I'd not expected to come across you so close to Tingwalla." The grin turned to a sneer.

"I'd not expected you either."

Hersir's gaze darted behind Ari, then back. "And you're not alone."

"She doesn't concern you." He didn't look down when Kati came to stand beside him. He sensed the animal's fur standing on end, his teeth bared. A low growl sounded in the clearing. Surprise cooled the bloodthirsty eagerness in Hersir's eyes. His mount pranced and tried to bolt, taking all of the man's strength to contain the animal.

"Wolves? My how you've changed. You've grown into quite the ...animal."

Once more, Hersir fought to retain control over his horse. The men behind him kept their distance, inching around their leader until they stood on the other side of the cave, clearly positioned to flee. Satisfaction drew a smile. Even one healthy wolf left powerful warriors on edge, particularly since their horses continued to dance about in agitation. Knowing the beast beside him could easily take at least two of the men, should they dare to attack, raised Ari's confidence several more notches.

"Indeed, I have changed. Thanks to you."

The rustling behind him indicated Thora continued to move about, which once again drew his brother's attention. Angry excitement shivered through him, growing stronger. He would not let Thora fall victim to Hersir's evil. The idea that her father could give her to this poor excuse for a warrior knotted Ari's gut. His grip tightened on his sword. He'd kill her and himself before he'd let Hersir anywhere near her.

"Are you daring to go to The Thing?" Hersir asked.

"I am."

"Hersir, it's three years now, isn't it?" asked one of the men. He led the others in positioning themselves near the trail that led out of the forest. Did Hersir realize what cowards he had protecting his back?

The grin he fought to suppress dissolved when a sharp gasp echoed behind him, like a shout in his head.

Damn the fool to Hel for giving away one of the secrets Ari wished to keep.

Thankfully, Thora said nothing. Still, he sensed her anger. If her rage had been a blade, he would be lying helpless, his life's blood seeping from his body. He shoved the realization deep, forcing himself to concentrate on the foe before him. He had plenty of time to deal with Thora.

"I suppose it is. So, brother, you are no longer an outcast. But I doubt you'll be welcomed by the members of our clan." Hersir's smirk grew, even as he fought to maintain his command over his mount.

Another gasp, more like a muffled shout, spurred the desire to charge Hersir. The strength to hold back his need to force the other man into battle could only have come from Odin himself. Beside him, Kati growled again. Hersir's steed gave a half buck, nearly unseating his master, a high-pitched whinny signaling the animal's fear.

Ari savored the satisfaction that arose at seeing his brother's difficulties. "I seek only to return to my life, whether in our clan, or another. And I will succeed."

Finally soothing his horse to an agitated pawing at the earth, Hersir gave another one of his evil grins. "I can't think of any who would have you, but I admire your determination to try. I am on my way to seal the bargain for a bride."

There were more muffled sounds of outrage behind him, though thankfully Thora now had the sense to remain in the shelter. The coming confrontation both excited and worried Ari. But first, he had to chase his brother off.

"Then be on your way. You wouldn't want to risk ruining your alliance."

This time the noises from the cave were a cross between a laugh and a groan. He could only imagine the thoughts rioting in her head. The alliance was already ruined and by the time Hersir knew the truth, it would be too late. All would know exactly who had mastered the plan to murder a jarl.

"I will soon be jarl, and wed to the daughter of another will make me very powerful indeed. You are still an outcast and always will be. Planning to kill a jarl is not easily forgotten." Hersir's gloating words only sent Ari's temper higher.

The musky, yet sweet scent he now knew as Thora's warned Ari she neared. Did she test him, or was she merely being foolish? He didn't dare turn to face her, but kept his stare focused firmly on his brother, disgust rolling in his gut to see the interest in Hersir's eyes when he caught sight of Thora. The man guided his jittery horse up the incline, closing the distance. As long as Ari possessed breath within his body, Hersir would never lay a hand on her.

"Enjoy your slut, then, while you can. I will see you in Tingwalla."

Hersir held tight to the prancing horse's reins and rode past, guiding the animal so close that Ari had to step back into the cave to avoid being trampled by the agitated beast. The wolf beside him gave a snarling howl, the menacing sound sending a shiver along Ari's spine. Hersir's horse reared and bolted, past the other men, and leading the way out of the clearing deeper into the forest.

Ari waited with sword in hand for a time, until ensuring the men had truly left the area. Once again, circumstances forced them to move their camp. This time, in case *his* enemy returned. Finally, he sheathed his sword.

"Liar!" Small fists pounded on his back and shoulders.

Surprised she'd waited this long, Ari turned, catching her wrists.

"Stop!" he shouted.

Still, she struggled in his grip and he ducked to avoid

her head as she aimed at his, screeching curses and spitting. He gathered her hands in one of his and caught her chin, forcing her to be still.

"You bastard! You tricked me!"

He tightened his grip on her jaw, forcing her to silence. "I did not! I merely did not share the truth of the man who would be your husband."

She spit again, and he dodged. The movement was enough for her to jerk free of his grip.

"Why would you not tell me who you were? Unless you are planning to use me as some sort of revenge."

Her eyes widened, clarity sharpening her angry stare. She bent and bit the hand holding hers. Ari let out a shout of surprised pain and released her, stunned by her move. Thora quickly moved out of his reach and waved her fingers toward Kati.

"Take him, Kati!"

The wolf didn't move. For the first time, Thora pulled her furious gaze from Ari to stare in surprise at her pet.

"Kati, now!"

The animal backed away, a soft whine escaping. Thora stomped her foot, then moving with lightning speed, charged Ari, a dagger raised high. He caught her before she could stab him, squeezing her wrist until she cried out and dropped the weapon.

He twisted her arms before her and turned her, yanking her hard against him. She struggled in his grip, but gained no leverage. Her efforts soon eased. Because she tired, or because she thought to trick him? He'd not give her the chance. A shudder ran through her. Was that a sob? He resisted the urge to confirm if she wept.

"Why? When I told you my reasons for leaving my home, you didn't tell me yours. Clearly, I am nothing more than a means to vengeance for you. You are a heartless bastard who tricked me, and you have somehow even cajoled my wolves to be loyal to you."

The break in her voice poked his conscience, his heart aching at the pain in her words. He leaned his cheek against her head, wondering what he could say to convince her she was wrong. None arose, because she was right. The instant he'd learned who she was, he'd plotted to use her in his final revenge.

Yet, despite the remorse over his initial intentions, he now knew he was not ready to let her go, might never be, no matter her wishes. Once he'd tasted the fiery passion dwelling within her, he'd grown addicted, and knew he'd fight like a berserker until he'd slaked his need. How long that might take, he didn't know. And at the moment, he found he didn't care. Thora was his and he had no intentions of letting her go.

Wait! What was he thinking? She was merely a tool to be wielded in his vengeance. The gods had put her in his path to be used. His enjoyment of her was a reward for the last years of hardship. He must remember that, and keep his focus on the real purpose of his journey. The last days had dulled his concentration. No more.

***

Despite the need to break free and escape the lying outlaw, Thora grudgingly admitted the feel of his solid body behind her brought an odd comfort. One she longed to give in to.

No! She struggled anew against the tight grip on her wrists. With her arms caught tightly around her, she had little leverage to fight him off.

"You thieving and lying animal! How dare you treat me as though I'm no more than a piece of property, livestock to be sold on a whim!"

"I assure you, no cow will give the pleasure I get from you."

His low voice in her ear rousing the familiar desire sparked sensations she wanted never to feel again, as far as he was concerned. The knowledge her body reacted to his no matter what she wanted only fueled her fury. She jerked her head back fast and hard, catching Ari square on the nose. He let out an enraged howl, but his grip loosened, giving her enough time to break his hold.

Now free of his dangerous yet enticing embrace, rage took over. She darted down the hill to the forest below, bending to gather a handful of rocks. The crunch of his boot behind her made her stand and whirl about, ready to defend herself. Fury etched into his face, he stalked toward her, ducking the first stone she hurled toward him.

"Kati! Attack!" She screamed at the wolf who stood oddly still, his gold eyes watching both of them. Why didn't he obey? What had Ari done to usurp her command over her pet? She tossed another rock, moving further from the cave that would trap her.

Ari ducked, clearly anticipating her evasive move. "Stop, woman!"

She threw another rock, his bellow of rage accompanying the strike of the stone into the side of his head. The small rock did little to slow him. Daring a glance at the ground as she backed away, a much larger rock caught her attention. She bent and lifted it, the size and heft assuring her this would render him harmless, or at least, slow him so she could put more distance between them. She raised her arm, but before she could hurl the rock, Ari's hand closed around her wrist, stilling her movement.

Caressing the smaller stone in her other hand, she paused, determining her best chance and place to strike. But his quick motions never gave her the chance to execute her move, grabbing her fisted hand in his before she took the opportunity to release the stone. Her frustrated cry echoed in the oddly quiet forest at the moment he once more pulled her tight against him, again leaving her caught.

His grip on her fist shifted to her wrist, squeezing until the pain grew too much and she released the rock still clutched in her fingers. She jerked against his hold, but his hold was relentless. With a choked cry of frustration and anger she slammed her head once more toward his, but this time he anticipated her intention and evaded her. Long fingers caught her chin, stilling her and forcing her to look into his fury-lined face.

"You keep adding to your debt. It would seem you will be in my service for quite some time to come."

His low voice, even and deep, terrified her more than if he had shouted.

"If you live after The Thing. From what I heard, you're an outlaw, and likely to pay for your crimes with your life. "

His eyes narrowed, gaze hardening to coal. Thora resisted the urge to shiver. He'd not see her fear.

"I've committed no crimes, and I will prove it."

The grip on her jaw loosened and the conviction in his voice near convinced her. Yet, plenty of doubt remained. Still, she'd finally seen for herself the man her father intended to give her to. No matter Ari's reasons, instinct warned her best chance for survival remained with him. Even from the shadowy shelter, she'd seen the evil in Ari's brother's eyes. Why hadn't he told her the truth of his identity, his family? Her anger rose once more to nearly choke her.

"You are still a liar! And I will never forgive you for that!"

Silence hung heavily for several moments, then he gave a curt nod.

"Perhaps, from your perspective. But you'll all see I was right. They put their loyalty into the wrong man's hands. The gods are on my side. And you will be too, when I claim you as mine before all witnesses."

Thora's breath eluded her as the implications of his determined words sank into her addled thoughts. Something in his tone hinted he might even dare to declare her his slave before all attending The Thing.

Before the kings seeking alliances and meting out justice. Before her clan. Her throat tightened. Before her father. With every ounce of her will, she drew strength and determination from the knowledge of who would ultimately save her.

"My father will be there. He will fight you."

"When I clear my name and prove the guilt of those who sought to destroy me, I will be granted anything I wish."

"What are you, a jarl's son?"

He stared at her for several moments then released her. "No. I am his savior."

"I deserve an explanation."

He released her abruptly and she stumbled back before righting herself. Ari stared at her, something fierce and angry in his eyes before he closed them and ran a hand through his hair. She folded her arms and waited. Finally, he tuned his gaze to her once more.

"My brother and I were raised by the jarl after our father's death in battle. He was thirteen summers, I was ten. Part of the reason he took us in was because he wanted my mother, though she didn't return his affections."

"Did he attack her?"

He shook his head. "He was, is, a good man, mostly. He could have forced her, I suppose, but he didn't."

"So why did you try to kill him?"

"I didn't. Hersir did."

"I don't believe you."

"No one does. But I have proof and witnesses, and I will present them before the council. My name will be cleared."

She still couldn't trust him. He'd deceived her and she would never forgive him for that. How many times over the last days had she bemoaned the fact that her father had seen her only as a bargaining chip? Not once had Ari said anything to indicate he knew exactly what sort of life she had facing her if she hadn't run away.

"Well, good luck to you, then."

"I don't need luck. I told you, I have the truth and the gods on my side. And everyone will soon know that as well."

She shook her head, still angry over his lie of omission. What else did he lie about? "I've more than repaid my debt."

"I don't consider throwing rocks at my head repayment."

"You deserved it, for lying to me. My wolves and I will go our separate ways, beginning now. Kata is almost healed."

With narrowed eyes and a shake of his head, he reached for her, but she darted back, away from his grasp. Still, he stalked closer, forcing her to retreat. Her foot caught on a root, wrecking her balance and she toppled backward, landing hard on her ass. Before she could rise and evade him once more, his hand landed tightly on her arm. He pulled her up, grabbing her free hand before she could strike.

"Didn't you hear what I said? I am claiming you, Thora, before all gathered at The Thing."

She jerked against his hold, hating the way her heart danced at his words, at the heat in his voice and gaze. Why should she find delight in his wanting to claim her as his own? The heartless beast didn't care for her thoughts and wishes. She tried to ignore the ever-growing pang of hurt squeezing her heart.

"No! You have no right!" She struggled against his grip, but his hands only tightened on her.

"As the first man to lay with you, I most certainly do. I am keeping you, Thora. It's up to you how you want to be kept."

She stilled, clarity at his meaning slicing through her thoughts. She lifted her chin. Making this easy for him was not an option.

"I will not stay willingly."

"So be it."

When he switched both her hands to one of his, she didn't realize what he intended until he pulled a rope from his belt. Though she tried to break free, she wasn't fast enough to keep him from binding her wrists and pulling her against him once again. He caught the trailing end and wrapped it around his hand.

"My father will kill you for this!"

He gave a feral grin that sent gooseflesh rising along her arms and the back of her neck.

"Once my name is cleared, your father will be glad I claimed you instead of my brother."

Damn him to Hel, he was probably right. Stubborn as he was, her father was also honorable, and Hersir's actions would damn him in Kori Thorfinsson's eyes.

"I'll be free of you, you'll see."

"You can try." He stepped back, but still clutched the end of the rope in his hands. "Come, we have to move our camp again."

She shook her head. In another day or so, Kata would be well enough to travel longer distances. The further they rode west along the forest, the closer to Tingwalla they would be. She needed to travel in the other direction.

"It won't be good for Kata to be moved again." The moment she spoke, she knew the excuse sounded weak.

"She'll be fine in the *pulka*, as she was before." He turned toward their shelter, tugging on the rope and forcing her to follow. She looked over at the wolves, who sat quietly, watching all with their golden eyes.

"Traitors," she muttered. As if he understood, Kati whined and walked over to her, nuzzling her leg. She jerked back on the rope to make Ari stop and knelt before the wolf.

"Are you saying you're sorry, boy? Or that your loyalty is now to him?" She jerked her head in Ari's directions, ignoring the responding chuckle. Kati licked her chin and she ruffled the fur behind his ears. "I should be angry with you, but you must keep watch over Kata. Go."

The wolf gave another whine and trotted back to his sister. Thora stood, defiantly meeting Ari's gaze. The warm affection and humor in his glowing eyes threatened to break through her anger.

"You may have won them over, but I am not fooled. And I will be free of you!"

He merely shrugged and gave her rope another pull. She sighed and followed him to their bedding and helped him gather their belongings. All the while, she tried not to think about being in his arms atop his horse once again.

He led her back into the cave and bade her to sit against the far wall, beside Kata. "If I must bind your feet as well, I will."

She said nothing. He turned and continued packing, pausing every now and then to look at her, as if to reassure himself she obeyed. If only she did dare try once again to flee, but not yet. Soon. Caution and concentration must remain her guides, watching and waiting for the right chance to make her move. After the packs had been filled and closed, the last of the fire covered with dirt, he came and knelt before her.

"I must tend Gyllir." He removed another rope from his belt and reached for her ankle.

She kicked his hand away. "Bastard! I didn't try to run!"

"I can't trust you to stay when I am out of sight."

She kicked again, catching him on the shoulder. With a blistering oath that singed her ears, he reached for her ankle again, this time succeeding in capturing it. Though she had little leverage, she raised her free leg, only to find he anticipated her move and caught her. Soon, her legs were bound together. He pulled on the rope trailing from her bound wrists and fed it through the rope around her ankles, securing the knot behind her, where she couldn't reach it.

"Vile, disgusting jackass!"

He stood, his shout of laughter echoing in the cave. "Don't go wandering." He laughed again and strode out of cave. For several moments, Thora stared after him, stunned with the quick way he'd secured her and his callous attitude.

The brush of fur against her cheek drew her attention to Kati. The wolf whined, nudging her head with his. In this bent position, Thora couldn't pet him. Instead, she leaned her forehead against his soft fur.

"Kati, what am I going to do?"

He whined again and lay across her feet. Her fingers curled in his coat, calming her anger, at least a little. Only now, something rose in its place, something that threatened to leave her struggling to breathe.

Pain. Ari had lied to her. Used her. After these last several days where they'd reached an accord, and shared passion surely only the gods had ever tasted, she'd begun to believe he truly cared. The harsh and bitter truth roiled her gut. For a moment, she found herself thankful they'd not yet eaten today, for surely she would expel anything she consumed.

Tears burned her eyes but she refused to let them fall. Clenching her jaw in the effort to hold back the sadness caused by the agony slicing through her heart, she took several large breaths, finally satisfied she had the weak emotion under control.

He'd used her, yes, and now she would use him. She'd occasionally seen a flash of regret in his intense stare. An idea sparked and grew, solidifying. A way to be free of him, using that regret to her advantage. She glanced over at Kata. The she-wolf healed further each day. In two or three more days, her strength should be fully restored as well.

Enduring the coming days would be a true test of Thora's own strength, but she knew the wicked pleasure Ari stirred gave her power over him as well. She'd take everything he gave her and hold the memories for a long time to come. If only he cared for her as more than a means for vengeance, but that was a foolish and dangerous hope. For if he did, she might never have the courage to leave.

Perhaps that frightened her most of all.

CHAPTER FIFTEEN

Long hours of holding Thora before him again left Ari aching with need. He'd refrained from tormenting her as he had the last time they'd ridden like this. He wasn't sure why, his fingers itched to make her writhe against him and beg for her pleasure. But something warned him that her already frayed senses might not withstand any more conflicting emotions. He found himself unwilling to break her, and if he didn't ease up, he surely would.

Yet, when he'd returned to unbind her, the fury in her dark eyes warned he must use caution around her. The trust he'd garnered had been shattered once she'd learned his true identity. Remorse mingled with the need to show he was unmoved by her hurt. He'd kept up a callous expression and mood since they'd set off once more, but maintaining the pretense grew more difficult with each step Gyllir took.

Why did he care? She was meant to be used as a tool in his revenge, but somehow, the feisty wolf mistress had ensnared him in a way that left him doubting himself in so many ways. Was he weak to care so much for her feelings? He'd learned long ago not to trust anyone, yet here he was practically forgetting his goals all so he could slake his desires with the woman before him. A sharp, twisting pinch on his arm drew him from the troubling thoughts and he let out a growl of pain.

"You're squeezing me too tight! I can't breathe!"

With a snap back to clarity, he eased the arm around her waist, but offered no apology, allowing his annoyance to rise again. His behavior was all her fault. At least, he tried to convince himself of that. Several days ago, he hadn't even known her. What would have happened if he hadn't come upon her with those outlaws? His heart squeezed at the possibilities.

Perhaps meeting his brother had contributed to this

uneasiness and fierce need to keep Thora safe. Doing so had been a priority since the day he'd saved her, but only because he wasn't finished claiming the debt she owed. But now... somehow, this need had grown deeper, more intense. As if losing her to his brother would devastate him more than being cast out of his home. When had she become more important than his clan, his reputation? Showing such concern was a weakness, one easily exploited if he didn't control the pandemonium destroying all coherent thought.

He glanced skyward. Soon, Sol's chariot would begin its descent, allowing Máni to rise and resume his flight across the starlit sky. Ari wanted to have their camp made, but so far had seen nothing suitable for their needs.

"There!" Thora sat up, her bound arms outstretched.

Ari reined Gyllir to a halt and peered in the direction she indicated. Sure enough, another cave carved into the side of a mountain lay not more than several paces to their right. Smart girl.

"Thank you. My father taught me well." The pleased note in her tone sent a shiver along Ari's spine. He hadn't realized he'd spoken aloud. And he wasn't sure he regretted it.

He forced himself to ignore her excitement, assuming it meant only that she could be away from him once they camped. He guided Gyllir to the mouth of the cave. Though not as secluded as the other, it still looked to provide adequate shelter for them both and the wolves. For now. His journey must resume in a short time. Not willing to focus on the other factors of his quest at the moment, he dismounted and unsheathed his sword, cautiously daring a few steps into the hole in the mountain. Perhaps slightly larger, the cave appeared very similar to the one they'd fled this morning. He faced Thora.

"I'll inspect it."

"Of course." She grabbed the edge of the saddle with her bound hands and swung her leg over, sliding to the ground before he moved to offer assistance. "Light a torch."

Moving in close, he fixed a stern glare on her at the command in her tone, but said nothing. Did she forget her place? He'd remind her soon enough. A surge of lust speared into his cock but he tamped it down. Grabbing the trailing end of the rope binding her wrists, he pulled her close.

"Can I trust you to wait here while I study the cave?"

Her gaze held his, a steely determination clear in their depths. "As I trusted you when you lied to me?"

"Then you shall come with me."

Reaching into the pouch on his belt, he pulled out the fire stone and turned, stopping short. Thora held out a sturdy stick. He hesitated before accepting the small branch, part of him wondering if she'd intended to strike him with it instead of offering it for use. Her bland expression served to deepen his concern. She hid her fiery nature well when it suited her. However, it didn't suit him. He wanted to tap the full depths of her spirit. Tonight, he vowed, she would bare her entire soul.

He made quick work of setting the branch alight and headed toward the cave. A sharp pull on the rope binding Thora's wrists forced her to fall into step behind him. Her exasperated muttering contained language sure to scorch his mother's ears. Ari was glad she saw only his back and not his grin.

The torch confirmed the cave was shallow. Any fire would have to be lit outside the mouth, increasing the chances of being seen at night. Ari determined they would stay here only this night. Hopefully, the she-wolf had healed enough to be better able to travel on her own for a time, giving the journey a quicker pace.

And justice sooner claimed.

Silently, he led Thora back to Gyllir. "Bring the

packs into the cave, set up a pallet for us and your wolves. Then return to me."

"So now you will treat me as slave."

He found himself longing to kiss the tight line of her lips into surrender. "No, not slave. But I can't do everything."

She continued to glare at him but accepted the packs without complaint. He kept a casual watch over her while she spread the furs out inside the cave. Her bound hands made the task more difficult. Watching her struggle roused the urge to help her, but he forced it aside. Glancing up, he found the sun still high enough in the sky that they didn't need to light a fire just yet. Unhooking the *pulka*, he tethered Gyllir to a tree near the cave entrance. If his judgment and direction were accurate, as they usually were, the same stream should be just beyond the edge of trees. They would follow it out of the low ridge of mountains to some of the more traveled roads. Then Ari would decide which path to take to The Thing.

In the days ahead, he expected his supporters would also arrive or be close to Tingwalla. They were to meet on the night that Máni appeared whole in the sky. With Odin's blessing, on the following day, Ari's opportunity to speak would come, bolstered by the testimony of the others. He would reveal all then, starting with the poison slipped into the jarl's food during a feast. It hadn't killed Drengr, but it had sickened him and left him weak for quite some time.

Hersir had used that time to garner support for becoming the jarl's heir. Feigning concern over Drengr's condition, he'd convinced the sick man to share some of his political plans as well as those for upcoming raids. Hersir had quickly used that information to carry out some of the raids and further cement his position as the next in line to rule their clan.

Months later, one of the clansmen had snuck into the

longhouse and attempted to murder the jarl while he slept. Instead, the attacker had been caught and with his last breath, had named Ari the one who'd ordered the assassination.

Thankfully, Jarl Drengr was not convinced of the accusation, which left Ari merely banished and not dead. While the sentence had devastated him, he'd been grateful for the chance to eventually clear his name, instead of to die in shame, barred from Valhalla.

His time was at hand. The witnesses who were paid by Hersir had also been badly betrayed by him, forcing them and their families from their homes. Every one of the men Ari had searched for and spoken with had said the same thing. They wanted the opportunity to take Hersir down, to make him pay for stripping them of their honor, their homes. Alone, fearing the murder of their families and that they too would face execution rather than the glory of dying in battle, they had remained silent. Now, with a solid plan and the support of each other, their determination had returned. Ari had made many blood and mead sacrifices to Tyr for each successful meeting, knowing the god of war would ensure victory in the upcoming battle. For Ari had no doubt, he would be forced to fight his brother at some point. He intended to be victorious.

Satisfied Gyllir was secure, Ari turned back to the cave. Thora stood with an impatient expression lining her beautiful face. How could the mere sight of her make him forget all he'd been thinking on? She posed a very real danger, one he intended to subdue, for fear it made him weak. Now was not the time to be seen as pathetic and incapable of controlling one small woman. He stalked over to her.

"Call your wolf. She should be able to walk to the cave."

Her eyes widened at his harsh tone, but she obeyed, summoning her pets. Though still weak, the she-wolf followed the male to the cave, her gait a little more sure than it had been even a day ago. After allowing Thora to settle the animals, Ari grabbed the tail of her bonds and pulled her behind him.

"Help me gather kindling."

He didn't dare look at her again, knowing the confusion in her gaze would only make him again forget his true goals. He never expected her to force him to.

***

Thora tugged on the ropes binding her wrists, compelling Ari to stop and turn. She nearly laughed at the surprise and frustration lighting his eyes so they looked as green as the leaves of the trees surrounding them. But her anger easily subdued her mirth.

"How do you expect me to help like this?" She held her bound hands toward him.

"I can't trust you not to flee."

She rolled her eyes. "As much as I would like to be away from you, I will not leave them." She nodded her head toward the cave.

He seemed to ponder her words for a few more moments, then nodded. He stepped closer, his dagger glinting in the dappled sunlight. "Very well. For now, you will remain unbound. But I will not tolerate you running, Thora. You're mine."

Why did it feel as though Sol lit Thora from the inside with joy and excitement? She should hate this man for what he'd done, yet the sound of his deep voice husked with desire, claiming her, undermined her legitimate anger.

"I belong to no one." She lifted her chin, daring him to refute her. Instead, he merely chuckled and sliced through her bonds. Biting her cheek to contain a cry at the feel of sensation returning to her hands, she rubbed them together until the tingling had mostly stopped. Turning her back to Ari, she began her search for kindling and rocks to secure the fire.

The task went quickly, perhaps too quickly. Needing to keep herself busy, rather than give in to the pull of Ari's stare, which she felt on her as if his hands slid along her bare skin, she knelt before her pack. She removed the dried fish and leftover hare from yesterday's meal, keeping the food wrapped in the cloth. She must send Kati to hunt for his and Kata's dinner. Another cloth holding the remainder of her dried berries soon sat beside the others. There wasn't a lot of food here. Ari would have to hunt or fish again. Finally, she turned. He leaned against the wall, near the mouth of the cave, illuminated by the late afternoon sunlight breaking through the leaves. Her breath hitched before she steadied herself, his image seared forever into her memory.

"We'll need more food for our meal." Thankfully, she succeeded in injecting a commanding tone into her words.

The corners of his mouth twitched and she found her gaze locked there, recalling the heat of his kisses. She blinked, wishing he didn't have such a physical pull on her. Surely exhaustion made her susceptible to these errant thoughts.

"Yes, I thought to find more fish in the stream. You will accompany me."

"But I can't leave them alone!" She nodded toward where the wolves lay on their pallet of furs.

"They will be fine for a short time."

"But –"

"Would you rather I bound you again?"

She narrowed her eyes. Damn his soul! He'd given her an impossible choice and he knew it.

"Fine. But I've not much skill at catching fish."

A lie. Her father and uncle had taught her well how to catch fish with a hook, spear or net, but Ari didn't need to know that. Let him do the work. She'd not make his life easy. Maybe he'd even think her a burden and agree to let her go before they reached Tingwalla. The thought evaporated as soon as it arose. She'd worked too hard to prove to him she *was* capable of taking care of herself. Surely he'd see through the ruse.

"I will catch the fish. But I'll keep you where I can watch you."

She frowned. How long before he let his guard down again? Clearly, she had much work to do in order to get him to trust she wouldn't flee. Once he believed she had given up that hope, she'd take her chance.

She stood and followed him out of the cave. The stream was not far from the cave and soon she sat on the bank, watching in silence as Ari cast his line and pulled in several fishes. Once the pouch was filled, he motioned her to join him when he turned back toward the forest.

With the pouch of fish slung over one shoulder, he slipped his free arm about her waist, holding her near as they walked. Did he do it apurpose, knowing the heat from his nearness wreaked havoc on her senses? After the last days of shared passion, he knew very well how his touch affected her. Even now, his hand resting casually on her hip, set her entire body to trembling, anticipating a more intimate touch.

He leaned close to her ear. "After *náttmál*, I am looking forward to the night."

She didn't answer, working too hard to suppress the quiver of delight sliding along her spine. Despite her lingering anger, her body responded, her sex slickening, her breasts tightening to hard points that ached to be touched. She clenched her fingers to stop their shaking.

"I am very tired. I have no wish to lie with you tonight."

He chuckled, the sound like a caress against her ear and neck. She gulped.

"You will change your mind."

"You are very sure of yourself."

"I am sure of your desire. Try as you may, you cannot hide it. I can smell your passion, Thora. It is as intense as my own. I will prove it to you."

Why did she look forward to his keeping that promise?

When they reached the cave, Ari handed her the pouch of fish and turned his attention to lighting the fire. Without his nearness, Thora found breathing came much easier and she set about scaling, cleaning and spitting the fish. By the time she finished, the flames crackled noisily and she laid the skewered fish across the fire. She took a seat opposite Ari, unwilling to be near him again. Her wits needed to be sharp if she intended to hold him at bay.

Ha! Who did she try to fool? Herself? She knew damn well that once he touched her, kissed her, her desire would surely rise and she would be helpless to resist. The wicked pleasure he bestowed on her always left her forgetting anything but being in his arms. Somehow, she had to find a way to break the spell the gods had surely cast upon her, leaving her weak under his passionate assault. What had she done to displease them so? Perhaps a small sacrifice might go a way toward easing their discontent. How she might manage such a feat depended on Ari. If she didn't find some way out from under his watchful eyes, the chance might never come.

Aware he watched her over the flames, she ignored him and turned the fish to cook evenly. Satisfied, she turned to the wolves. Kata slept, the steady rise and fall of her belly assuring Thora she continued to heal. She knelt beside Kati and stroked his head while he licked her chin.

"Go and hunt, boy. When Kata wakes, she will be hungry."

He gave her another lick then trotted out of the cave. Thora resumed her seat beside the fire. The aroma of the cooking fish teased her nose. A fierce hunger overtook her, unlike any she'd known before. Had Ari heard the rumble of her belly? She dared a glanced at him, but he seemed to pay her no mind, carving a small branch with his dagger. She longed for her own, and her axe. She doubted he'd let her have them back before reaching The Thing. Once more, the goal of getting him to trust her, leave her unattended and unbound, took hold, stronger than ever. But how?

The questions that had danced on the tip of her tongue since this morning rose again, demanding answers. While she desperately held onto her anger, she had to know.

"Why didn't you tell me who you were?"

He looked up, clearly startled by her question. "I didn't think it important."

"You lie. Your entire journey is about seeking vengeance against your brother, is it not?

A curt nod was her only response. With a sigh of exasperation, she continued.

"So once you knew I was his intended bride, you should have told me."

"And risk you running away?"

She hesitated. "You know I wasn't going anywhere, not with Kata wounded."

He said nothing, but the blue-green gaze, now almost dark as the dusky sky, focused intently on her.

"If you'd been truthful with me, I might have been willing to help you."

His eyebrows shot up. In disbelief? "Would you?"

"I didn't want to marry him, you knew that. I could have been your ally. Instead, now I'm only–"

"Mine."

A lump filled her throat. Why was it that every time he said that, those delightful fluttery feelings in her belly grew stronger?

"I will not be treated as little more a possession. You are no better than my father, selling me off to the man who can give him a strong political alliance!"

"Hersir likely would have used the alliance to attack your clan, eventually."

That silenced her argument. "What?"

"I've been banished for almost three years, so I don't have firsthand knowledge, but I've heard things in my travels."

Her anger at her father had been replaced by worry for his safety. "I demand you tell me."

He smiled, the arch of his eyebrow warning he might make her pay for her attitude later on. At the moment she didn't care, even as wisps of heat seeped through her veins at the idea.

"You are not in any position to make demands. But I will share what I know."

When he hesitated, Thora balled her hands into fists to keep from approaching and shaking him. Her impatience, heavy and thick, threatened to suffocate her.

"Hersir was a master at casting blame on others. The clan had made an alliance with another nearby, in an effort to resist the increasing invasion of those led by Konall, the Jarl of Skapska."

Thora gasped. Many had heard the legends of Konall, who was rumored to have fought giants to claim his lands and title.

"What happened?"

"Hersir betrayed the other clan to Konall. The jarl and his men swept into the village like a flood and left nothing and no one in their wake."

Only the crackling of the fire broke the sudden silence. Thora's thoughts grew into a tangled, chaotic mess. When he looked up from the flames, his eyes dark as the pines in the forest, the breath whooshed from her lungs. He spoke the truth, of that she had no doubt. The sting of his betrayal still remained sore, however, and she vowed to make him pay for that.

"Konall will be at The Thing." It wasn't a question, but Ari nodded in confirmation anyway.

"How many witnesses will you bring?"

"Enough. Those who were betrayed after they helped Hersir betray others. They were lucky to have escaped with their lives and families."

The thought of her father giving her to a man capable of such evil turned Thora's stomach. Surely Kori didn't know of these deeds. But would not knowing make him foolish? Unless something else had happened that she didn't know about.

"Ari, are you sure that is what happened?"

"One of Hersir's closest "friends" told me himself how they had set a trap for the other clan, lulling their leader into thinking they had made a trustworthy alliance that would see them all safe and comfortable. After, when this man, and others close to Hersir began to voice their doubts..."

Ari shrugged. "He threatened them, their wives and children. And like me, they were forced to flee or cast out, though not quite in so grand a manner."

Suddenly, she had to know. Had to learn just what made him the man who sat across from her now. Her pleas to the gods seemed to appear to be finally answered. Still, she must ask to be sure.

"What did they do to you?"

"Nothing, except make claims against me. But not long after they named me murderer, they fled in secrecy, under cover of night. Whether Hersir knew and let them go, thinking they were no threat, or he truly didn't know, I can't say. But I was named an outlaw before the jarl and the elders, declared a criminal in the eyes of all those in my clan."

A full understanding of his determination to get to The Thing settled over her. She had to admire it, even though it led to his callous betrayal. Still, the anger seemed less fierce, the pain a little duller. No! Those thoughts led to forgiveness and she wasn't ready to forgive him. Might never be.

Foolish girl. Of course you'll forgive him. She ignored the taunting voice. She wanted to make her own choices for her life and staying with Ari assured she never would have that chance.

"And when you have cleared your name what will you do?"

"I haven't decided. I'd like to go home, to visit with my mother for a time, but I don't think I will return entirely to my clan."

"Why not?" She shouldn't keep asking questions. The answers she received only softened her resolve to remain detached until she had the chance to flee. Yet, a small part of her wanted to go to Tingwalla with him, just to see what happened when he finally gained his justice.

"I no longer belong there. I've learned many things during my travels, and I am not the same person I was when I was cast out."

She understood that. Her journey so far was much shorter than his and she had changed in so many ways, even before Ari had come into her life. Of course, he had changed her far more than she'd ever imagined possible. For better or not, she still wasn't sure.

"So where will you go? Surely you want to settle down after the last years of traveling."

"I'd thought to go south for a time. Towards Odense."

She stared at him, unsure of how to respond. When she'd first left her village, she'd had the same intention. A person could easily get lost in a city the size of Odense, and that had been her aim. That Ari possessed similar thoughts roused thousands of questions, though none formed completely, more a maelstrom of chaotic half-thoughts.

"It's a big city." Those were the only words she managed to force out.

Ari nodded, his gaze still focused unwaveringly on

her. "It is. Should be an easy matter to find work."

"Before you were cast out, what did you do?" Despite her intention not to ask more questions, the words came out before she'd even realized they'd formed.

"I was a blacksmith."

That explained his fine sword and the craftsmanship of his other tools. Had he made them himself? She forced the additional questions aside and turned her attention to the cooking fish. It was done and she picked up two skewers and handed them to Ari. He took them with a nod of thanks, but said nothing. They ate in silence, Thora's thoughts still a whirlwind. She sensed him watching her, but she deliberately avoided looking at him. It would only make it harder to stay angry with him. Bad enough she was certain what the coming night would bring, she didn't need him playing with her wits. Her body he could have.

But not her heart.

CHAPTER SIXTEEN

The play of emotions on Thora's face told Ari of the chaotic thoughts assailing her. For a moment, he thought about telling her more of his skills and plans, but doubted she would welcome any explanations. Not yet. But he'd seen the compassion in her eyes, even as she'd fought to maintain her angry demeanor.

He couldn't blame her. He had lied, had intended to use her, still did, and understood how she must feel betrayed. His remorse ate at him, likely because his feelings for her had grown. After the confrontation with his brother, the idea of being apart from her, for any reason, had roused a greater pain than the one he'd known when he'd been banished.

Not that he'd tell her that. If she knew what lurked in his heart, if she believed him, it would give her the power to tear him apart in the worst way. He wanted her to stand by him, support his goals, and stay with him once he was again a feared and honorable warrior. Why did he so badly want that to be her choice? Because if he forced her, he would never be sure of her true feelings for him. He held back his roar of frustration, his thoughts veering to the romantic notions of women. Had Thora cast some spell leaving him unsure as an untried boy, or did Odin and the other gods test him in some way?

No matter, he would not reveal such weakness. If Thora, or anyone else, knew how he felt, knew his desperate need to keep her safe, they would use the flaw against him, possibly destroying his chance to be redeemed. No one would keep him from restoring his honor.

Not even Thora.

As he swallowed the last of his fish, he reached for the waterskin at the same time as Thora. Their hands brushed and she snatched her fingers away before he could capture them with his. He wondered if she intended to refuse him tonight. Part of him hoped she would, so he could render her helpless and focus on showing her just how much lay between them. Until he was free to tell her he cared, the only way he could demonstrate what he felt was with his body. He lifted the skin, his gaze holding Thora's as he took a long drink. He handed the skin to her and he noted how careful she was to avoid touching him this time. He let her have the small victory. Later, he'd have her surrender.

"Do you wish to return to the stream to bathe?" he asked, keeping his tone casual.

She nodded. "I would like to. Kati will go with me."

He shook his head. "No, I will go with you."

She scowled, her eyes narrowing. "You think I will flee?"

"I'm not willing to take the risk. I will bathe with you."

Pink bloomed in her cheeks, her dark eyes taking on an eager note. Did she not know how clearly the feelings shone in her every expression? She lowered her head, then turned to her wolves.

"I must check them first."

He said nothing as she rose and walked over to where her pets lay. To his view, the she-wolf seemed almost healed. Part of him wished the animal had been more severely injured. A moment later, he scolded himself for the callous thought. His own selfishness roused that thought. Logic warned he would have had a more difficult time seducing Thora had the wolf been more grievously harmed, at least in the beginning. Besides, the injured animal assured she wouldn't flee, even though he'd declared his doubts about that. The way the anger flashed in her eyes excited him and he couldn't stop himself from taunting her to gain the reaction.

His gaze settled on her back when she knelt beside

the animals, the two wolves well-fed by the male's hunt for meat. He'd brought back several squirrels and a couple of hares. Both wolves had eaten heartily, as well as Ari and Thora had.

Finally, Thora rose, hesitating several moments before turning to face Ari. She held herself straight, chin high.

"I'm ready."

Ari grinned and stood. A wicked notion rose. She would be furious, but he knew just how to turn that anger into scorching desire. He motioned her closer and she obeyed, albeit hesitantly, as if she sensed his intentions. He waited until she'd stepped around the fire to stand right before him. A second later, he'd retrieved the rope from his belt and looped it around her wrists before she realized what he'd done.

She recoiled, her eyes sparking with rage. He pulled on the trailing end of rope, forcing her near.

"Bastard!"

He grinned. "Maybe. Or am I just using caution? You might try to drown me."

He ignored her spluttering reply, turning and leading her out of the cave. She gave a resistant tug, but ultimately fell into step. His ears burned, the curses she flung at him matching those of any warriors he'd known. If the gods honored any of the promises she made to destroy him, he would spend his afterlife in Helheim, rather than Valhalla. When they reached the stream, he sat down on the bank, using the rope to compel Thora to do so as well. He said nothing, merely held his leg out and pointed to his boot.

"Remove your own boots," she snapped. She turned her back toward him, stirring a chuckle.

"I want you to do it." He tugged on the rope, but she refused to face him.

"I can't, not with the way you've bound me."

Another pull on the rope, this one harder, gave her

no choice and he kept pulling until she had turned to him once more.

"Do you remember when you agreed to follow my orders?"

"I never agreed to be treated like a slave."

"You belong to me, and are to heed my very command."

"You're an arrogant pig! I don't know why I –"

The remaining daylight highlighted the delightful blush creeping up her cheeks. What had she been about to say? She pressed her lips tightly together, clearly an effort to keep those words unspoken.

"Why what?"

She refused to answer, her cheeks darkening to scarlet. For a moment, the hope she possessed a real caring for him rose up before he tossed it aside, disgusted in himself for the weak desire. Instead, he focused on the need to assert his dominance, taking another step and quickly cupping the back of her head to draw her toward him. Her resistance started out strong, but he was stronger, and the moment his lips brushed against hers, the defiance faded and she responded to the kiss. In response, he swept into her mouth, gliding along the heated velvet of her tongue in an effort to stake his claim. A tiny moan escaped her. At that moment, she once more tried to pull away, but he tightened his fingers in her hair, holding her close. He should have expected the sharp bite she gave. Despite the sharp discomfort in his tongue, he pulled away chuckling.

"You test my patience. I think you do it on purpose."

She said nothing, her angry eyes narrowed on him, her bound hands held up in front of her as if to ward him off. He leaned close once more, but didn't stop her this time when she backed away.

"You know I will have to punish you for that."

He suspected she tried to hide it, but he noted the tiny shiver that swept over her, the way her breath hitched. So she anticipated his reddening her ass? What would she say when he used that pleasure against her? For tonight, she would be begging him for her pleasure. Before he finished with her, she would promise him anything he desired in order to reach her climax.

He could hardly wait to get back to their shelter.

***

Thora wondered at the devilish glint in Ari's eyes. Thankfully, he'd given up the idea of having her disrobe him, for he tugged his boots off himself before standing and stripping out of his trousers and tunic. He kept his back to her, and despite her intentions to ignore him, her gaze was drawn to his bare shoulders, powerful and broad, down his back to the tight muscles in his ass. She closed her eyes, pleading with Freyja to take pity on her and make her immune to his sensual allure.

When she opened her eyes again, he faced her. She deliberately kept her gaze upon his, knowing if she looked anywhere else, her determination to stand against him would waver. No, not waver. Crumble into dust. She didn't want to let him know how much she wanted his touch, his kiss, his hard shaft filling her. Yet she knew the moment he touched her again, she might very well reveal the depth of her longing.

When he moved to stand right before her, she straightened her spine and lifted her chin. Surrendering was not an option. His devilish grin gave her the idea he knew exactly what thoughts ran through her mind. Still, she held her ground when he reached for her, surprised when he sliced through the ropes holding her wrists together. A moment later, his fingers were on her brooches, loosening them and sliding the *smokkr* off her shoulders. She sucked in a deep breath when he then slid her undertunic down. A cool breeze arose at that moment, sliding across her bared breasts and sending a small shiver through her. Soon, her clothing lay in a pile around her feet. Still silent, he caught her hand and led her to the water's edge. The darkening sky somehow made him seem larger, more overpowering, and at the same time, the now-familiar comfort settled upon her. Knowing she felt safe with him was a dangerous reality to face, but at this moment, there was no ignoring it.

He'd betrayed her, lied to her. Used her. Was still doing so. Well, she would use him too. Use his body to take her own pleasure, even if she had to submit to his wicked demands. After these last weeks, she knew well just how much he wanted her. In the most carnal sense anyway.

He stepped into the water, pulling her with him. She sucked in a breath at the sudden cold of the stream, yet didn't resist when he pulled her shivering body deeper. He stopped, turning to face her, holding out his other hand. A small ball of scented soap made from conkers from the large chestnut tree rested in his palm.

"Wash me."

Her sharply inhaled breath seemed a shout to her ears. Why must he insist on treating her so callously? She jerked her hand from his.

"Wash your own self." She turned away, her body slowly growing accustomed to the chill of the water. He reached to stop her, but she evaded his grasp, moving further downstream.

"Thora!"

His sharp voice rang out and she paused, slowly turning to face him once more. Even in the fading light, she easily read the heat in his eyes and despite her intentions to resist his cold-hearted demands, her body betrayed her. Her sex swelled, heating and slickening, making her sweat despite the cold stream.

"Why must you treat me so badly?"

"What?"

"Yes, I owe you a great debt. But I am not a slave. Yet, you insist on treating me as though I were no more than a mere possession, to be used and discarded, or worse, sold on your whim."

"I would never discard you, Thora."

Sincerity hung heavy in his tone. She wanted to believe him, but forced herself to remember the lies he'd told her. The way he'd betrayed her. She was a means to vengeance, nothing more.

Why did that have to hurt so much?

Her determination to enjoy his attentions, take her own pleasure while shielding her heart, once more weakened. She closed her eyes briefly, then met his stare once more.

"Then show me more respect." She lifted her chin, daring him to mock and refuse her demand.

He smiled, the one that so often left her lips tingling in anticipation of his kiss. She remained still when he moved toward her, finally standing mere inches away. He made no move to touch her. She remained wary, yet still holding on to the foolish hope that he might make some attempt to assure she deserved his esteem.

He cupped her cheek, tilting her head. His gaze roamed her face, warming her wherever it landed. "I will return the favor."

What did he mean? Did he finally intend to treat her as an equal, or was this some ploy to get his way? Once more, he held out the soap. With a scowl, she took it and dipped it into the water, the oils from the conkers making the ball slippery in her hands. Small bubbles formed as she rubbed the soap between her fingers, another rush of annoyance rising when he turned his back to her.

She placed her hands on his shoulders, running the soap over them with one hand, using the other to spread the thin lather. She held back a satisfied chuckle at the way his skin twitched beneath her fingers. Again and again, each time her hand slid across his back and sides, a small tremor vibrated under her touch. If only she didn't enjoy the feel of his wet skin beneath her fingers.

He turned, the heat in his eyes glowing under the last

of the the daylight. She continued her task, though her gaze remained held by his. Across his chest her fingers roamed, leaving a thin trail of fragile bubbles in their wake. His entire body tensed when she slid her fingers along his side, to his hips. Knowing she caused the sudden sharp intake of breath fed her own desire, made her breasts feel heavier, her nipples tight and hard. Somehow, she managed to maintain her focus on her task, hiding a sly smile.

Holding the ball of soap in one hand, she dipped the other beneath the water's surface. Her seeking fingers soon found his shaft, hard and erect. As always, a thrill passed through her to know she affected him near as much as he did her. The pride mingled with her own anticipation of what would come banished her anger. At that moment, she no longer cared, even if it stung that he didn't care for her beyond their shared physical affinity.

The heat in her body made it impossible to think of anything but the man before her. She curled her fingers around his cock, savoring the wild quiver that passed over him. How nice to be the one with the advantage this time. The knowledge left her breathless and giddy. Her slippery finger slid easily along his flesh, drawing a groan. After a moment or two, he caught her wrist and wrenched her away. He slid his arm around her waist, pinning her against him while he stripped the ball of soap from her hand.

"My turn."

The thick husk of his voice sent a jumble of delight coursing through her. He had barely touched her and already her pussy ached for him to fill her. She knew he wouldn't oblige her, he took his pleasure from tormenting her with pleasure. If only he wasn't so skilled at knowing just how to touch her to make her beg for more, for him to take her to that glorious peak he'd introduced her to.

From the moment his fingers danced along her jaw,

down her neck to her chest, she was panting, unable to steady her heart or ease the wild trembling in her limbs. The soap glided over her skin, guided by his heated fingers. A moment later, he dropped the soap into the water.

Before she had the thought to question his devilish smile, he cupped her breast, chasing the words before she uttered them. The barest touch of his wet and slick fingers drew a moan before she even realized it had formed. Her hands rose to his shoulders and she found herself unsure if she meant to push him away or hold on tight.

A soft slide across her tight nipple drove her fingers deep into his shoulders. Hold on. She had to, for the world spun about her. When he pinched the tip of her breast, the sweet burst of pain-pleasure left her quivering. Her release loomed over her, close, yet still out of reach. She recalled their first night, when he'd stirred that magnificent bliss solely by caressing her breasts. Knowing he had such carnal power over her brought a moment's panic, one that was quickly chased by a tight pinch on her other breast. Fire seared her veins and she wanted more. She'd face the consequences later.

"Ari." His name erupted on a hoarse whisper.

"Yes. I know you feel it too, *ástin minn*."

The words to refute him wouldn't form. She clung to his wet flesh while he caressed and patted, stroked and pinched again. Her mind whirled with the dark and decadent pleasure coursing through her, her pussy wet and hot and demanding to be filled.

When he drew away, Thora shivered. The slow current threatened to sweep her away and she tightened her hold. His chuckle sounded like a roar to her dazed senses. He took her hands in his.

"Come." He led her toward the bank. She obeyed without thought. Each step only intensified the longing in her sex. The man had reduced her to a wanton in only a couple of weeks. When the day came to leave him, and it would, eventually, intuition warned she would never know such passion again.

Lost in the chaos of her thoughts, she jerked to full awareness when he let go. Still unable to think of a word to say, she stood silently when he reached for the drying cloth. After running it over his head and shoulders, he reached for her.

She attempted to take the cloth from him, but he pulled it out of her reach. "Stay still."

The rough brush of the cloth on her damp and sensitive skin stoked the flames once more and her breath hitched. He concentrated on his task, running the cloth slowly over her breasts. Lower and lower he moved, slipping it between her legs. He didn't move it then, merely held it against her sex.

"Stop teasing me!"

The words snapped out of her before she even realized they'd formed. His response was a broad grin and a wink.

"You like when I do this."

He pulled the cloth even tighter against her pussy. Another sharp intake of breath, but the mere contact was not enough. And he knew it as well, of that she had no doubt.

"How do you ask me for your pleasure, Thora?"

At any other time, his words might seem a taunt, and perhaps now they were as well. She didn't care. She'd give him what he wanted, so he would do the same for her. She hoped.

"Please, Ari, stop teasing. Take me. Make me come."

The flare of lust in his eyes bored into her. He dropped the cloth, scooping her up against his chest before lowering her to the furs he'd spread on the ground. He loomed over her, but the sight only stirred more excitement. Her breasts tingled, nipples tight and hard, as if reaching for his touch.

He caught her hands, stretching her arms above her head while he settled into the wide welcome of her legs. Pinned and helpless, her excitement soared to even greater heights. His cock brushed her sex and she undulated toward him. He didn't enter her, instead reaching underneath to pinch her ass. Hard. She squealed.

"When *I* am ready."

His words, husked with desire, reminded her he maintained control. She didn't care, only wanted him to hurry before the frustration racing through her stole her wits forever. She gave a whine when he brushed gentle kisses along her cheek, across her nose to the other side, to her ear and down her neck. By the time he reached her chest, she was gasping for air, her fingers clenched, her entire body aquiver. She wrapped her legs around his waist, an effort to urge him into her, but he held back.

He took his time, his tongue and lips a fevered torment she wanted never to end. He transferred her wrists to one hand, and now his fingers added to the sensations he bestowed. When his mouth closed around one taut nipple, she let out a keening wail, half-plea, half-denial. He murmured something against her skin; she couldn't make out the muffled words, but the vibration of his voice sent an arc of fire along her spine.

Her head thrashed against the furs and she bowed against him, an attempt to convey the ferocity of her need. Nothing she did urged him into her and she fell back in surrender, tears of frustration burning her eyes.

As if he sensed her submission, his hand moved between their bodies. She sucked in a breath, held it, holding herself still and praying to Freyja above to take pity on her. The goddess must have heard, for Ari's fingers moved along her sex, seeking and caressing. She arched her head back, stifling a scream when Ari's teeth nipped at her neck, soothing the sting with his tongue while his fingers continued their passionate dance along her pussy. He caught the hard bundle of nerves and gave a gentle pinch. The first rumbling of bliss taunted her when he withdrew, then returned to repeat the motion, his mouth still hot along her throat.

Another squeeze, this one harsher, and Thora's vision went white, the stinging pleasure so intense, her toes curled and her body bucked wildly against his, even though he pinned her securely. Her cries rang through her head, and for a moment, she thought she tumbled through the air, the pulses of delight seeming to last forever. If only. His wicked touch kept her spinning, soaring from one peak to the next.

The suddenness of his cock filling her sent her into another screaming climax. She welcomed his rough and hard pounding; when he released her wrists, she curled her body around his, squeezing him with her sex. He groaned, delivering another harsh pinch to her ass, but she barely noticed, too caught up in the tumult. She latched her mouth onto his neck, sucking and licking, savoring the heady salty taste of his skin. Soon his shouts drowned hers, and the sound of her name torn from his mouth sent more ripples of ecstasy sizzling through her veins.

He slowed his pace, his heavy breaths mingling with her gasps and pants. She fell back to the furs, her fingers still curled in his hair. How did he manage to make each time more intense than the last? He rested his forehead against hers, his gaze locked on hers.

"You amaze me."

Had she truly heard the softly whispered words? She barely had a moment to think on it further when he slid free of her body. She truly disliked the empty feeling, but it was soon chased when he cupped her cheek and pressed a gentle kiss to her lips.

"Come, we must return to our camp."

His words dissipated the lust-filled haze fog still

holding her in its tenacious grip. On shaky legs, she rose and allowed him to help her dress. When their belongings had been gathered, he slid his arm about her shoulders and drew her close. Good thing, for she wasn't sure she had the strength to walk on her own.

But when the bliss slowly faded, the hurt of his betrayal rose again. While their shared passion was like nothing she'd ever known and might ever know again, the truth stung. He didn't care for her, she hadn't touched his heart, not really. Without that, she was doomed to a future of misery.

CHAPTER SEVENTEEN

Three days of traveling had brought them closer to the main roads leading into Tingwalla. There had been a handful of other travelers they'd passed. For a day or more, Thora had feared the reaction to her wolves. While some people had been uneasy, the contact with the few they'd encountered had been brief. Still, Thora couldn't help a sense of foreboding. Something ominous hung in the air, leaving behind an uneasy chill. Ari must have sensed it as well, for his grip around her waist grew tighter. She noted the way his fingers tightened on the reins, causing Gyllir's step to grow more agitated.

"Something is wrong." She kept her voice to a whisper, not exactly sure why. A moment later, Ari's nod of agreement brushed against her hair.

"I want to continue on a little more. How do your pets fare?"

Thora looked down at the wolves next to them. In the past weeks, Gyllir had grown accustomed to their presence and didn't even mind them walking beside him now. Kata, though she tired easily, still looked to have the strength to travel a little further.

"They are fine for now, but Kata will need to rest soon."

"There is a main road ahead that I wish to reach before we stop."

She didn't voice her opinion that the road could prove more dangerous than their trek through the forest. But there was really little choice. The trees had thinned considerably in the last couple of days, and soon they would be on the lowlands toward Tingwalla. Thora still hoped for an opportunity to flee, but Ari's close watch, as well as the bonds he insisted on keeping around her wrists most of the time, hindered her chances.

They rode on in silence for close to another hour and finally broke out of the forest. Before them, the soft hills and sloping valleys revealed several small groups of people far ahead. No chance of encountering them at the current pace. Thora peered back over Ari's shoulder to see other bands of travelers also emerging from various trails leading out of the thick forest and steep mountains. Her heart pounded. She'd been alone with Ari for so long, the idea of strangers alarmed her. Were any of her family in those groups? What would happen if they found her? She would certainly be free from Ari, but then she would be caught in her father's plans. The two choices battled in her thoughts and combined with the slim chance of fleeing, left her dizzy, her stomach rolling.

"What's wrong?"

Ari's low voice cut into the riot of her thoughts, oddly soothing. She frowned.

"I worry that some from my clan may be traveling this same road."

"Should anyone grow near, we'll find a place to rest where we won't be noticed. I suspect most are not traveling much faster than we are."

She nodded and leaned back against him, trusting he would keep her safe. The warmth of his body surrounding and supporting her further calmed her. She had grown too comfortable with him. The weeks of being alone with him had created a bond she feared would leave her heartbroken in the end. Deep in her soul, the one thing she wished for she knew would never be possible. No matter. When all this was over and she was free of everyone's intentions for her life but her own, she would start over. Eventually, she would marry, have children.

Why was it Ari's face she saw in her visions of the future? That was simply not possible, not when he didn't truly care for her. Admittedly, she now used him as well, taking the physical delights he gave her with no shame or guilt, fully enjoying all that passed between them. But she wanted him to care for her, even if only a little. His passion was just not enough.

You would be satisfied with his passion alone. She ignored the mocking voice, or at least tried to. For in all honesty, she must admit, his desire for her was strong enough that she could almost overlook not touching his heart.

Why couldn't he love her, as she loved him? She sucked in a deep breath. Surely she hadn't just admitted that she... No! She couldn't! Admitting that left her vulnerable to his whims. How could she love a man who didn't love her in return? Would likely never do so, no matter how many pleas and sacrifices she might make to the gods?

The cruelty of Odin and his cohorts sliced deep into her. Had her own past actions of unkindness led her to this point, where the deepest of her desires would be dismissed as a result? To have Ari's love, though she'd buried the longing deep, was more than she'd ever imagined. Now, it was all she wanted.

The sound of rapid hoofbeats coming up fast behind them jolted her from the heart-rending thoughts, and for a moment she thanked the gods for giving her a moment's respite from the agonizing truth. But when his embrace tightened and he guided Gyllir toward a small grove of trees, all nonsensical romantic notions fled as the reality of imminent danger slammed into her. Ari wheeled the horse around. Thora pressed her fingers against her mouth to prevent a scream.

Muli! And he wasn't alone. Three others rode with him and they quickly neared. Thora held her hands up.

"Free me, and give me my axe!"

Ari nodded, slicing the ropes holding her wrists together. A moment later, he slipped her axe from his belt and placed it in her hands, also providing a long dagger. He dismounted, helping her to the ground. Beside them, both Kata and Kati stood in wariness, the fur along their backs standing up, fangs bared and growling. Seeing the she-wolf in such a state convinced her the animal was finally whole again. Ari faced the approaching riders, sword drawn and ready.

Muli and his companions reined in their mounts and the wiry, evil-eyed man leapt to the ground.

"I'll get you now, you bitch!"

Thora's spine stiffened and she lifted her chin. "Don't be stupid, Muli. If you harm me, my father will kill you."

"Not if I do it first," Ari vowed.

A leering smile curled Muli's mouth, drawing a shiver. "If you think you can take all of us, the Valkyries are waiting."

Thora dared a glance toward the other men. They dismounted, axes and swords drawn. Outnumbered. Muli stalked closer, gaze darting between Ari and Thor and the pair of wolves. He waved his sword and Ari shoved Thora behind him. Still she held her dagger and axe at the ready, should Muli succeed in harming Ari.

"Get back," Ari commanded. She heeded his order without hesitation, retreating several paces, Kata and Kati beside her.

She choked on a cry when Muli lunged, but Ari easily blocked the blow. Another lunge, another block, the swords scraping against each other in a loud screech of metal. Thora noted the other men slowly approaching. Her heart slammed against her chest, but she would not make this easy for them. Calmed by the presence of the wolves flanking her, she took another few steps back, her focus darting between the approaching men and Ari in his battle.

Muli jabbed and Ari ducked to avoid the strike. Muli swung his fist around and once again, Ari dodged the blow, landing his own punch hard into Muli's gut, drawing a loud grunt of pain. The other man staggered back a few paces then lifted his sword once again, cursing when he leaped. Ari raised his sword to block his opponent with a shriek of metal against metal, spinning about to free himself of the close fight.

For a moment, Ari and Muli paused in their battle, chests heaving as they stared at each other. In the ensuing silence, the thunder of hooves arose again, growing louder. Thora bit back a fearful cry to see three more riders approaching. With the additional raiders, she and Ari stood little chance of surviving this battle.

"Ho, Ari Hugisson!" The leader waved his hand and reined in his horse, leaping down at the same time with a warrior's grace. A moment later, the others did as well. Thora glanced at Ari, stunned to find him smiling. He knew these men? They neared, withdrawing their weapons.

Moments later, they stood behind Ari, and beside Thora. Muli's men halted in their advance. She imagined this to be some sort of surreal dream, one in which she never imagined saviors to come to their aid. She met Ari's stare, his playful wink rousing all sorts of questions, even as it reassured her.

"In a bit of trouble again, are you, Ari?" the leader of the group asked.

"Not really, though it's good to see you, Karsi. This piece of horse's dung is simply an inconvenience."

At the insulting dismissal, Muli let out a howl of outrage and once more charged. The man named Karsi dragged Thora from the confrontation before she could be trampled by the battling men.

At that moment, Muli's companions jumped into the fray, engaging Karsi and the other two men. Thora ducked behind Gyllir, Kata and Kati beside her, both ready to defend their mistress. She twisted the axe handle in her hand, wondering how she could help, even knowing she was useless in a battle. Still, there must be something. Wincing at the sharp pained scream, she paced between her wolves, grateful to be far enough from the fight to avoid being sprayed by blood. Shouts and insults accompanied the sounds of blades clashing, ringing painfully in her ears. The thud of an axe landing in someone's body left Thora's gut knotted, yet she somehow managed to look and see that Karsi had dispatched his opponent to the next life and turned his attention to aiding one his fellow riders.

Within a few moments, only Ari and Muli still battled, all three of Muli's companions lay either dead or grievously wounded. Thora moved closer to the fighting men, shaking off the restraining hand that attempted to halt her. In her sweaty palms, the dagger slipped and she tightened her grip before dropping it, her gaze riveted to the two men swinging their swords at each other, neither gaining the upper hand until Ari gave an unexpected roll, coming up to stand behind his foe. When Muli turned, Ari landed his fist square in the other man's face.

"I will have my revenge and you will die!" Muli shouted. Blood seeped from his nose, and his free arm dangled at an odd angle. Still, he fought on, lifting his sword once more, though his movements had become more sluggish and sloppy.

Thora studied Ari. He appeared calm and even-winded as he moved about Muli, taunting the wounded man with insults. He didn't need her assistance, yet the urge to be near him while he saved her yet again nearly overpowered her.

"Now who are the Valkyries waiting for?" He mocked Muli with his earlier words and thrust toward his foe again. The injured man somehow managed to block the blow, but in his weakness, he stumbled and fell to his knees. Ari stood over him, sword raised. Why did he hesitate?

"Kill him!" Thora shouted. She noted the way Ari's shoulders stiffened for a moment, then he plunged the sword into Muli's chest. The man gave a gurgling scream at the moment Ari withdrew his sword, before falling to the dirt. Dead.

Thora ran to Ari, dropping her dagger and axe before throwing her arms around him and hugging him tight. His free arm came around her waist, holding her near. Tears streamed down her cheeks, more relief that he had defeated Muli than anything else.

Ari set her away, and his lips curled in a small smile. "You are unhurt?"

She nodded. "Your friends ensured I was safe before they took care of Muli's accomplices."

Ari looked toward the three men gathered a few feet away. He waved them over.

"Karsi, your arrival was indeed a blessing from the gods. We must give thanks!"

"I agree," said Karsi. "We were going to set up camp a bit further. We heard the battle. Wasn't until we got closer that I realized it was you."

"I owe you much. After The Thing, I will be able to repay you properly."

"I just want to return to my home," said Karsi. "As do they."

Ari nodded, his expression sober. "Soon, we will all have justice. Karsi, Leif, Alarr, this is Thora. The man I was fighting is an enemy of her father's."

"So he meant to use you as revenge?" Karsi directed his question to Thora.

"I believe so. It would seem I am quite useful as a tool for vengeance." She gave Ari a pointed stare. When he looked away and shifted uneasily, she gained a small measure of satisfaction at his discomfort. She ignored the curious stares of the other men.

"You are lucky to have someone like Ari to look after you."

Admitting she agreed was not a consideration. She wouldn't give him the satisfaction of knowing how his very presence reassured her. She said nothing, aware of Ari's gaze upon her. When he turned to join his friends in gathering the horses of their enemies, she looked down to see that her wolves had once again taken up their positions on either side of her. This was when she was truly safest, she reminded herself, even if the thought rang slightly untrue.

Her gaze fell upon the horses of their attackers. Would he let her have one, ride alone? A brief sting of disappointment accompanied her answer when the other men took the reins of those horses and led them a short distance away from where their own steeds were tethered. The animals pranced and pawed at the ground, short whinnies of fear piercing the air. Clearly the presence of her wolves frightened the beasts.

"Where did you get the wolves?" Leif asked, once he'd calmed the jittery horse under his control.

"They are Thora's pets. They won't harm the horses, though I expect the animals wouldn't believe it even if Sleipnir galloped down and assured them of their safety."

The men all laughed and even Thora chuckled at the image of Odin's eight-legged horse riding down from the heavens to speak with the horses.

"We can sell the steeds at The Thing. We'll fetch a fine amount in trade for them," said Ari.

"Take their weapons," Thora said.

All of the men paused in their conversation and stared at her.

"They died in battle, and should be allowed to defend themselves on their journey to Valhalla." The confusion in Ari's eyes seemed oddly comical in the heavy moment. Yet, Thora found no humor in the situation.

"Muli is a coward and only dares to attack anyone he sees as weaker than him. He doesn't deserve the glory of celebrating with the gods. If your friends had joined us a day or so earlier, he never would have come after us. He thought to ambush us. Clearly, the gods set things in motion for his defeat. They don't want him there."

She held Ari's stare and noted the recognition in his eyes. Was there a hint of pride there as well? She must have imagined it. He turned back to his friends.

"She's right. He's attacked before, when he thought Thora alone and vulnerable. Just for raiding with him, the others don't deserve the honor."

She held back her words of encouragement, but caught the pleased glimmer in his eyes, making them the blue of the morning sky. He turned away, joining his companions in gathering the fallen men's weapons. Soon the swords, axes and daggers had been placed in a neat pile.

"Put them in my sack."

Ari directed his demand to Thora. For a moment, she thought to resist, then realized she must show his friends she could be trusted. Whatever doubts she still held onto, she mustn't let on. She nodded, taking the offered sack he held out and knelt beside the pile. While she carefully placed each weapon into the pack, she dared a glance at the other men as they spoke with Ari, his back now facing her.

Karsi, his face grizzled and tough like old leather and who seemed the leader, was not the tallest, in fact, he was shortest, but the breadth of his shoulders still gave him a fearsome stature. Leif was the tallest, and the thinnest, but again, Thora sensed a powerful strength under his deceptive appearance. Both men seemed open and genuinely pleased to see Ari.

Alarr gave her pause. Dark and quiet, his height coming somewhere in between his fellow clansmen's, he said little, remaining still and studious. His dark stare met hers and she somehow suppressed an uneasy shiver at the strange light she found in his eyes. Why? He didn't know her, yet, judging from his scowl, he appeared to dislike her. Intensely. He looked away, turning his attention back to the others. Thora released a breath she hadn't even realized she held.

She placed the last axe inside the sack and tied the pack closed around the sword handles. Aware of the conversation halting when she approached, she met Ari's gaze. Silently, she attempted to let Ari know she wanted to speak with him alone, without being detected. Unfortunately, he appeared as oblivious as his friends. She stepped closer, taking up a position behind him, but still with a view of the others. The men continued to discuss their recent journeys, and Karsi and Alarr both spoke of their families, left behind for fear of some deadly retribution.

That should assuage some of Thora's concerns, but she couldn't completely cast off the feeling that Alarr did not fully stand with Ari. That he might in fact be working against him. She needed to convince Ari to speak with her alone, so she could share her suspicions.

Wait. Wasn't she only biding her time for the opportunity to be free of Ari's dangerous possession of her? Shouldn't she let him learn on his own if the man he called friend was truly his enemy? It might give her just the chance she needed. The silent swearing echoed in her head, making her worry the men could actually hear. Faced with the events of the last couple of hours, she had to be honest.

Ari was her greatest chance of surviving this journey. Besides, the thought of anyone wounding or ... She refused to consider anything of the sort. Yes, the gods could be cruel, but surely he had suffered enough over the last years.

This concern for him was truly a curse. Yes, he'd saved her, but he could very well also mean her doom. Once they reached Tingwalla, it was only a matter of time before someone in her clan, or worse, her father, found her. Various scenarios raced through her thoughts, leaving it hard to catch her breath. All of them ended with the loss of someone dear. She didn't know which was worse.

Aware of Ari turning his attention to her, Thora met his gaze. Her heart swelled to read what appeared to be genuine affection in his eyes. For a moment, she allowed the desire to stay with him always rise up, before forcing it back down. There was little to no chance of that being permitted, once Ari had stood before the council, before all those assembled at Tingwalla. Her father might ultimately be glad Ari had prevented the arranged marriage, but she doubted he would forgive what he would surely know had passed between his daughter and her savior.

He might hear your wishes, make a decision based on that.

No! Thora refused to listen to the taunting voice that always seemed to undermine her resolve. The hope was too great to be considered, though perhaps if she made an offering to Freyja, she might stand a better chance.

Again, she rejected the idea. Hope might very well leave her in despair, while facing the reality of her situation gave her the best chance of building a life for herself when this was all over without living in misery. Once her usefulness had ended, Ari would lose any interest he possessed for her. She couldn't bear seeing the heat leave his gaze, have him withhold his touch, his kiss.

Tear burned her eyes, rousing anger that he might see such weakness. She kept her face averted when he took her wrist and pulled her to stand beside him. She curled the fingers of her free hand into a ball in order to resist wiping at the dampness in her lashes.

"Let's make camp. We'll set off again in the morning." Ari faced the other men and waved toward a cluster of trees that offered shelter and obscurity from the road. He twined his fingers with hers and gave a small squeeze. She didn't acknowledge the gesture; instead, she turned toward Kata and Kati, waiting nearby. After a snap of her fingers, they took up positions on either side of Thora and Ari.

She held back a sigh. Her pets had accepted him, shouldn't that be enough for her to do so as well? And fight for a future with him? Even though the hopeful thoughts rose again, she forced them aside. She would not reveal the depth of her longing, not unless she was absolutely sure he felt even a small part of what she did.

"Take Gyllir," he said, gathering up the horse's reins and handing them to her. "I've got to help with the others. Wait over there."

He gave her hand another squeeze before letting go. Thora's heart burst into a crazy, erratic rhythm, one she tried unsuccessfully to ignore. Focusing on her task, her mind awhirl with myriad thoughts of Ari and the men who would stand beside him at Tingwalla, she led Gyllir toward the small grove of trees. She secured his reins to a branch and let him graze on the sweet grass, and sat between Kata and Kati while she waited for the others to join her.

Ari laughed easily with the men, and though they were too far away to be heard, she suspected they spoke of her, judging from the way they kept glancing her way. Once more her gaze settled on Alarr. He spoke easily with the other men, his stance now less rigid, and smiled easily. Perhaps her initial suspicion had been wrong. Still, she wanted to talk to Ari about it. When they reached the shelter of the trees, the men secured the horses. Ari crouched before Thora.

"Gather some kindling. We'll build a shelter for the night, though I may have to hunt again."

"We have plenty of food, Ari," said Leif. "We rode through Manjafell the day before last. They had much bread and pork at their market. With so many traveling to The Thing, they were happy to make a good bargain."

"Then we will feast tonight! Thora here is a fine cook," Ari said. "She and I have eaten well on our travels."

"Where did you find her, Ari?" Karsi asked. "She's a pretty thing."

Ari hesitated, holding Thora's stare for a moment before answering. "We met on the road through the forest. Some outlaws were... harassing her."

"Glad we are to have you join us, Thora," Karsi said. "It's nice to look upon something other than these two ugly faces."

The men all laughed and Thora gave a small chuckle. With a nod to Ari, she turned to tend the task of gathering kindling for the fire. Kati and Kata took up their usual positions beside her while she picked up twigs and small branches. Satisfied she had enough, she straightened, surprised by the sudden alertness of the two wolves. She turned, her heart sinking to her stomach to find Alarr standing a few paces away, his penetrating stare giving him a menacing expression.

"Did Ari send you after me? I was just about to return." She shifted the bundle in her arms.

"I know you."

"Excuse me?"

"You are Kori Thorfinnson's daughter."

She gulped, trying to dislodge the sudden lump in her throat. "Why do you say that?"

"I've traded with your clan. It was a few years ago, but you were there."

"You can't possibly –"

"It was you. How did you join up with Ari?"

"What do you want?"

He took a few more steps closer and Thora was reminded of her wolves stalking prey. Beside her, Kati gave a low warning growl. Alarr glanced at the beast and paused.

"I hear your father has sent parties in search of you. He is paying any who can return you to him with gold."

So that was his game. "If you think to claim his gold, you are mistaken. I am with Ari and if anyone has a right to it, it's him."

"Perhaps. But there is another who will also be interested to know where you are. And who you are with."

"It's none of your concern. Step aside and let me pass."

He didn't move, a slow, leering smile curling his mouth. "You are worth a lot of gold, Thora. A man would be a fool not to attempt to claim it."

"Are you saying you are intending to claim the reward for my return?" Her fingers shook and she tightened them around the sticks she held in an attempt to hide her agitation. Another growl from Kati, accompanied by Kata, echoed around her.

"Perhaps. Unless you wish to offer something else to convince me not to."

Her stomach rolled. Did Ari know the sort of man he called friend? That Alarr would betray Ari roused a rage she barely held in check. She would never give in to his demands. She shook her head.

"It will never happen. Now step aside and let me pass." She repeated the order, forcing venom into her tone.

He still didn't move, just continued to stare at her with that lecherous smile, one hand resting on the handle of the axe in his belt.

"Don't think to try anything. They will attack you and they will kill you."

"I'm not afraid of your wolves."

"Then you should be afraid of me."

Thora's heart leapt with joy when Ari appeared suddenly behind Alarr, who spun about, withdrawing his axe. He lowered it to see Ari's sword raised and ready.

"She is a runaway, Ari. There is a large bounty on her head."

"I know who she is. And I know exactly who else has interest in her. Have you decided to betray me, after all?"

Alarr shook his head, returning the axe to his belt and holding up his hands in surrender.

"I didn't know if you knew. I was just ensuring she meant you no ill will."

"By asking her to lay with you in order to forego the gold she is worth?"

Thora held her breath, willing Ari to look at her, but he kept his stare focused on Alarr. She didn't dare move, waiting for some sign. He finally gave it with a crook of his finger, still watching Alarr.

"I'm sorry, Ari, I didn't mean –"

"I know what you meant." When Thora reached him, he pushed her behind him. "She is mine. And I don't share."

Ari began to pace, muttering under his breath. He paused and faced Alarr. "I should cast you out now. Do you spy for my brother?"

Alarr shook his head. "No! I still want to see Hersir judged for his crimes against all of us. Jarl Drengr will know the truth before Sol's next cycle. I never intended this! I swear!"

Ari gave a curt nod. "Very well. I will consider that. For now, I will have your apology, as will Thora."

"I am sorry. I meant no harm."

Alarr's vow rang through the forest, but the stare he fixed on Thora left her shivering. Only Ari's hand on her hip, where he held her in place behind him, reassured her.

"We need a sacrifice to thank Odin for his blessings. And you'll need to ask forgiveness. Hunt for something worthy. Maybe then I'll believe you."

Ari sheathed his sword and turned to Thora. "Come, we must light the fire."

She hesitated, waiting until Alarr had walked out of earshot. Only then did she step close to Ari. Kata and Kati sat calmly, as if knowing their mistress was safe, now that Ari was beside her.

"I wanted to talk to you about him. I had suspicions, though I didn't expect ..."

"It's not your fault, though I can certainly understand why he would attempt such."

Thora held his stare, confused by the amusement in his eyes. "What do you mean?"

He shook his head, a heavy chuckle escaping his twitching lips. "I've told you many times how beautiful and passionate I find you to be."

He stroked a finger along her cheek, the simple touch sizzling through her. Her breasts tingled, nipples hardening in anticipation of what usually followed. The compliment sank through her dazed thoughts and her heart slammed into her ribs. Did he toy with her, as he often did, just to gain her obedience?

"Thora, I've claimed you, yet you still refuse to believe. I am never letting you go. Ever."

The solemnity in his tone roused the hope she tried to ignore to a pitch she had no chance of resisting. She leaned into him, letting the bundle of sticks in her hands go in a clatter, grabbing onto his arms to steady herself before she locked her lips on his.

Several moments later, she sucked in a deep breath and composed her emotions, tilting her back to study him.

"So you care for me, then, eh?" She wanted to crow with delight at the casual tone of her voice. She didn't, instead continuing to search his eyes for some clue as to his true feelings.

His eyes widened. "You doubt that?"

"Of course! You treat me as little more than a possession, a tool to be wielded in vengeance. You toy with me with little regard for my desires. Once you've regained your honor, you no longer have need of me."

"I will always have need of you, Thora."

She had to admit, she adored the way he always said her name, as if it was another way to claim her. She so badly wanted to be claimed. But only by him.

"You will not cast me aside once you have justice?"

He shook his head, cupping her jaw in his hand. "No. I said I mean to keep you, and I will."

"Why?"

He said nothing for several uneasy moments. She tried to pull free, but his embrace only tightened. His shoulders lifted with a heavy breath and ice crept into her heart. He caught her chin, holding her still and forcing her to look into his penetrating gaze.

"Because I love you, Thora."

She nearly wept, blinding joy suffusing her entire being. It was just what she wanted, had prayed and pleaded to the gods to grant this one wish. Now it was real.

Or was it? This was the second time today she felt as if the events around her were only a dream. Not real.

"Again, you taunt me." She jerked to escape his embrace, but his arm tightened further around her.

Ari shook his head, his eyes glittering with a deep affection she'd never seen before. She stopped resisting, reality seeping through the maelstrom of thoughts, hopes and prayers to bring a sense of peace. The chaotic riot of emotion finally settled on one.

Love.

He loved her! Something deep inside acknowledged that was all she wanted, from the very first moment he'd come into her life. *Saved* her life. From the very first time she laid eyes on him, something primal within her acknowledged the truth.

They were meant to be.

No doubt remained the gods had surely planned this, and despite her momentary annoyance at their games, Thora knew she would endure even more to stay with Ari. As long as he loved her.

Whatever games the gods played, she'd learned at an early age that to appease them ensured a happy and fruitful life. The days ahead would be difficult and the very real threat of losing Ari forever, now that she knew how he truly felt, loomed in the distance, a dark shadow threatening to cast the sunshine from her life.

Now she wondered just how nefarious the gods' games could be.

CHAPTER EIGHTEEN

Ari watched the play of emotions flicker in Thora's eyes, wondering at her thoughts. He'd just confessed his feelings for her and still she said nothing. But her eyes remained locked on his and he read a joy in them he'd not seen before. The sight soothed the growing fear that perhaps she didn't share his feelings.

"Thora?"

She smiled then, her dark gaze shiny with unshed tears. "Do you truly mean it?"

Her voice was a hoarse whisper, much like it was when she was lost in passion. The sound sent a bolt of longing straight to his cock. With a press of his body against hers, he slid his fingers through her hair, holding her still while he lowered his mouth to hers. The heat in her lips surrounded him like a heavy cape, cocooning him in warmth.

He swept deep into her mouth, suddenly desperate with the need to show her how much he wanted her. Needed her. Loved her. She trembled against him, responding eagerly, her fingers digging into his shoulders. When he drew away, he could barely catch his breath.

"Do you believe I meant what I said now?"

She nodded, the tears finally spilling free and sliding down her cheeks. He brushed them away.

"Why do you cry?"

Her sharp intake of breath seemed a shout to his ears. She blinked several times, a broad grin curving her delectable mouth.

"I cry because I am happy."

He rolled his eyes. "I never understood why women weep when they are happy."

She laughed, a melodious tune that hung over them for several moments before fading away. He silently swore. This woman made him think things only a bard should sing in a fantasy tale.

"Ari, I never thought... that is, I had hoped, but I didn't think... I thought I was only a means for vengeance."

"Perhaps at first, you were. But you are much more than that, Thora." He relished the way she gave a little shiver when he said her name. She always did that and he loved seeing it every time.

"I love you, Ari. That you love me as well is more than I ever dreamed."

The last knot of uneasiness loosened. He kissed her again, hard. When he drew away, she murmured a protest, but he finally released his hold on her. When she licked her lips, he almost kissed her again, but somehow refrained.

"We have much to discuss." He caught her hand, her fingers locking with his. "But later."

She nodded. "Your friends are waiting."

"Yes. Come."

She tugged on his hand when he turned to head back to the camp. "The kindling!"

How easily she made him forget where he was and what he was doing. He bent to help her gather the dropped bundle of twigs and sticks and they soon made their way back to the camp, the wolves trotting on either side of them. He smiled, knowing the animals had long ago accepted him and now they protected him as well.

He noted that Karsi and Leif had tended the horses. Ari's gaze settled on Alarr, sitting a short distance away. The rage he'd felt earlier to hear Alarr threaten Thora rose again, but he pushed it back. He didn't need truly Alarr's testimony, there were others he would join with in Tingwalla, and combined with Karsi and Leif's declarations and the runes were more than sufficient to clear his name.

Yet, he didn't want to cast Alarr out, not just yet. The man might be useful in other ways, especially if it turned out he did indeed play them all falsely. He said nothing, but a warning glare drew a curt nod of acknowledgement from the other man.

"Fetch the touchwood from my pack." He released Thora to tend the fire and took a seat beside Karsi.

The other man leaned over. "What happened?"

Ari shrugged. "Alarr recognized Thora."

Karsi and Leif exchanged looks. "From where?"

"He'd had dealings with her clan a few years back." Ari shifted, his gaze drawn to Thora as she set about using the striking stone to light the touchwood and the kindling. "She ran away from her home. Her father planned to wed her to someone not of her choosing.

Karsi chuckled. "And you are going to do so now?"

Again, Ari shrugged. "Perhaps. Once this is all over..."

"It's obvious you are smitten," Leif said with a chuckle.

Ari arched an eyebrow at his friend. "Why do you say that?"

"It's the way you look at her." Karsi nudged him.

Ari grinned. "Yes, I care for her, and I do plan to take her as wife."

Leif gave a knowing nod. "We thought as much. What will her father say? Surely he'll be in Tingwalla. What if he refuses the match?"

"When he learns about Hersir, he will be grateful to have me as son-in-law."

"What do you mean?" Karsi asked.

"The man her father planned to wed her to is Hersir."

A moment of silence erupted into astonished whoops.

"So you will have more vengeance against him! You've stolen his bride!" Leif laughed. "What could be better?"

"She is not just vengeance," Ari insisted.

"We know." Karsi shot him a sly grin before picking up the skin to take a long drink. "I cannot wait to see his face when he learns what you've done."

Certain he had the support of his friends, Ari accepted the skin from Karsi, savoring a heavy swallow of ale before taking another. His gaze settled once again on Thora. The fire now blazed and she sat with her wolves on either side of her as she removed the meager utensils for warming the meal. A few moments later, Leif handed her several cloth-wrapped bundles. She accepted them with a smile and a hearty thanks before setting about heating the meats enclosed in the cloths. Ari decided he rather liked this comfortable feeling, watching Thora as she busied herself, and knowing later she would be in his arms, pressed tight against him.

She loved him! He'd not thought it possible, not after the way he'd lied. But hearing Alarr threaten her had made him realize just how much he needed her beside him. Always. How he'd refrained from striking Alarr down at that moment, he might never know, but he thanked the gods for the strength to do so.

The need to tell Thora how he felt had come upon him with a sudden force he'd had no chance to resist. To assure her she was more than just a means to his vengeance, she had become a part of him that he never wanted to let go. He imagined her large with his son, and couldn't wait to make her his in the eyes of everyone and the gods.

She turned, her gaze settling on his. A flush crept into her cheeks and the warmth and love in her eyes warmed Ari's heart as it had never been before. He anticipated the coming night with great eagerness.

The hours passed quickly. Ari enjoyed the company of his friends, even Alarr, who though he remained mostly quiet, joined in the laughter at some of Karsi's ridiculous tales. Thora sat beside him, snuggled up against his side. Her head rested on his shoulder, and every now and then, he felt her yawn. A few moments later, her body softened as she slipped into slumber. He tightened his arm about her shoulders. Tonight he would be content to simply hold her.

***

Thora jolted awake, gasping for breath, fear gripping her heart in its tight fist. Ari's arms immediately tightened, easing her back against him. The fire had dwindled to a few flickering flames amid a pile of embers, casting a dim light over the camp.

"What's wrong?"

His sleep-heavy whisper against her ear sent a wisp of heat along her spine. She blinked to clear her slumber-dusted thoughts, the panic fading at the reality of the haven of Ari's embrace.

"I... I had a dream. But I can't remember it."

She tried to recall her nightmare, but the images hung just out of clarity's reach. Still, an uneasy chill swept over her.

"It was only a dream. You're safe now. In a few days, we'll be in Tingwalla, and all this will be behind us."

The realization she would soon see her father again roused another shudder of apprehension. Facing him, beside Ari, before all the clans gathered at The Thing, terrified her more than the elusive dream.

"Ari, what if my father... I fear he may try to make me return home."

His lips on her forehead both soothed and stirred her. The soft reassuring caress of his hands along her back chased the fear of the coming days.

"He can try, but you are staying with me."

She wanted to ask him if he meant to wed her, but bit her tongue to keep the words from escaping. He loved her and that was enough, really. Her dreams for the future seemed to be coming true, yet she couldn't help thinking Odin and his cohorts had more tests ahead for them to endure.

"We must make a sacrifice."

"What?"

If she wasn't so worried, she might find the confusion in his voice amusing.

"And it must be more than the meager hares and fowl we've offered. It must be worthy enough to truly assuage the gods, so they will stop playing games with us."

"Thora, the gods are on our side. We've overcome the many trials they set for us, haven't we?"

She pondered his point. Still, the worry would not go away.

"Perhaps. But we must ensure it. What of one of the horses?"

The silence that hung hung between them was broken by a harsh snore from one of the men on the opposite side of the fire. Ari's chuckle rumbled through Thora.

"We can discuss this in the morning," he said. "Go back to sleep."

She leaned her head back into the crook of his shoulder, savoring the warmth of his body against hers, his arms tight about her and holding her near. She yawned, her worry somewhat appeased.

Still, a nagging concern kept her mind racing.

CHAPTER NINETEEN

Ari reined Gyllir in atop the small hill overlooking Tingwalla. Crowds filled the bustling market leading to the massive longhouse near the shore of the river. His redemption lay in that teeming town. Thora's squeak of protest told him his excitement had resulted in a too tight embrace.

"Sorry." He pressed a kiss to the top of her head.

"We can't ride into town," Karsi said. "Should be a stable along the edge of town."

Ari nodded. "It's been a long time since I've been among so many."

"For all of us," Leif replied. "It will be good to return home."

As usual, Alarr remained silent. While he had again apologized most sincerely to both Thora and himself, Ari still wondered at the man's loyalty. Didn't matter. If the others had arrived as planned, he had about a dozen men to swear on his behalf that Hersir had committed the crimes of which Ari and others were accused. The runes on his daggers swore to the fact that Hersir had destroyed more lives in his quest to become jarl. If he succeeded Drengr, he could prove disastrous to all the clans and kingdoms in the country. Once free of the threat of death to their entire families, others would stand up as well, after Ari and his witnesses presented their proof of Hersir's deadly misdeeds.

Ari urged Gyllir into a trot and the others fell into place beside him. When they neared the edge of Tingwalla, they reined in and dismounted. Karsi and Leif held the reins of the horses they planned to sell. Ari helped Thora down and gave her a brief hug before turning to the others.

"After we stable the horses, we'll find the others." Ari patted Gyllir. "King Hemming and the council are likely already meeting. Karsi, you and Alarr find the others. When I last spoke with Gunnar, he said they would gather near the market, close to the council longhouse. Leif, you come with me and Thora. We'll need to form a shelter."

They slowly made their way to the bustling town. Thora's wolves took up the familiar position on either side of him and Thora. Shouts of the traders hawking their wares mingled with laughter and greetings. The smells of food cooking in some of the market stalls filled the smoky air. Thankfully, the gods had seen fit to bless the gathering with mild dry weather. He recalled attending a gathering where it had rained for days. No mud to slog through this time.

A stable had been set up near the edge of the market and once the horses were settled, Ari let the proprietor know that four of the beasts were available for trade or sale. He paid the man with some of the coins he'd saved during the last three years. He and Leif gathered their packs and the group reassembled outside the stable.

"All right, I will meet with you later near the center of town," said Ari. "Tomorrow, we go before the council."

Karsi nodded and he and Alarr disappeared into the crowd. Ari turned to Thora. The tight lines in her face revealed her agitation. Her dark eyes scanned the crowds. Looking for her father, he supposed. He took her hand and pulled her close.

"It will be difficult for any to recognize you in this crowd," he assured her.

"Alarr knew who I was. And with Kata and Kati, word will soon spread and likely reach my father."

Ari shook his head. "Take ease. There are many places to make our camp. By the Máni rises in the sky, all the other witnesses will join us and you will be safe."

She nodded, but he knew she wasn't convinced. He squeezed her hand, not pleased with her pale complexion.

"Come, we have much to do." He led her away from the stables and Leif fell into step beside him. They discussed their plans while they pushed through the crowds toward the part of the town where the temporary shelters had been established. Ari felt more confident than ever that after tomorrow, his honor would be restored.

"Filthy beasts!" The shout came from Ari's left and he turned at the same moment a woman charged toward them, shaking a spear and pointing at the wolves. Thora pulled her hand from Ari's and stepped before her pets. The woman, wild-eyed with disheveled her red hair, waved the point of the spear in Thora's face, yet Thora barely flinched, giving a fierce snarl that sounded almost like her pets.

Dirt stained the screaming woman's *smokkr* and Ari noted her feet were bare.

"Step aside! They killed my goats two days past!

"They did not! They are mine! Not even here two days ago!" Thora shouted.

The crazed woman attempted to dart around Thora. Ari dropped his packs and his hand landed on the hilt of his sword, but before he could step between the women, Thora grabbed the handle of the spear and shoved hard, sending the woman stumbling back several clumsy steps.

"You leave now, or your goats will no longer seem a worry!"

Ari suppressed a grin at Thora's threat. The woman tugged on her spear, but Thora didn't release it. For a few minutes, the two tussled over the weapon, until finally the woman gave up and relinquished the spear. Thora nearly stumbled, but quickly righted herself. She held the lance over her head in a victorious display.

Those who'd gathered to watch the conflict clapped and cheered.

"Get you gone from my sight!" Once more she shook the spear in warning. Finally, the woman shook her head and walked away, mumbling. Every now and then she uttered another threat, but made no attempt to confront Thora once more.

Ari motioned Thora to his side, noting the way her hand shook, forcing her to use both hand to hold the spear. He offered a reassuring smile.

"She was mad. You did well."

A pleasurable light glowed in her dark eyes. "She wanted to kill them. I couldn't let her."

"Of course not. I'd expect no less from you, *ástin minn*."

She smiled again and Ari nearly groaned at the bolt of lust spearing him. It would likely be several days before he could once again indulge himself with her body. A long several days. He turned to the crowd still hovering around them.

"It's over. Go about your business," he declared. People finally returned to their affairs, the confrontation soon forgotten.

"You're quite fierce, Thora," said Leif. "I should not anger you."

Thora gave a light chuckle, the sound filled with as much relief as amusement. Ari wanted nothing more than to take her somewhere far from here. Though his goal was close at hand, he found himself strangely disillusioned with the reality of finally being in Tingwalla. He shook his head. While Thora made him feel stronger than Odin at times, he also recognized she was a weakness he must not allow to unman him. Perhaps it was because the idea of losing her sliced into his heart like a rusty jagged blade.

Or maybe this strange dissatisfaction came from the fact that while they walked to the edge of the city, several paused to stare at them, some actually pointing and whispering to their companions. Suspicion arose, knotting his gut.

"Why do they all look at us like that?" Thor asked, echoing his thoughts.

He shrugged. "Ignore them. We will set up our shelter and then I will go to meet the others at the longhouse."

"I will go with you."

How did he tell her he wanted her to remain out of sight? She'd already drawn notice in the skirmish with the goat woman. Word would spread, but how far? Her worry about her father had now become his. The wolves alone drew attention he could ill afford. Surely her father would soon know Thora had arrived in Tingwalla and seek her out. Ari had no desire to face the man, not until after he had his chance to speak before the council. Nothing he could do about it now.

"You are safer away from the crowds."

He gave her a pointed stare, hoping she understood the message he conveyed. She frowned, shaking her head.

"I am in more danger when I'm not by your side."

Knowing she needed him to feel safe sparked a surge of pride. As much as he feared she made him weak, declarations such as this showed she truly strengthened him.

"You will be safe with Leif and your wolves for protection."

"No, I am not staying behind."

He heaved a deep breath. Truthfully, he didn't want to leave her here, even though he trusted Leif completely. He wanted her beside him when he planned for tomorrow's appearance before the council.

"Very well, but you will obey."

"Of course." A hint of a smile curled her lips.

He narrowed his eyes. The amusement in her eyes told him of her satisfaction in getting her way. He suspected she plotted some other nefarious plan as well. The woman would drive him mad with her defiant nature. Now, however, he suspected she did it on purpose, for he knew she fully enjoyed everything that had passed between them, even his punishments.

She flashed him a devilish grin and sauntered a few paces ahead, her wolves, as always, on either side. Ari's gaze landed on her bottom softly swaying with her step. Yes, Odin had surely given her to him as a test of his limits. Somehow, he no longer minded.

***

Despite Thora's playful attitude with Ari, a large portion of fear and worry still gripped her heart. The confrontation with the crazed woman had drawn more attention to her than she preferred. She'd always known, once she realized she would not avoid coming to The Thing, that her wolves would draw notice. She'd also hoped that notice would soon fade from interest. After the strange altercation, she knew word would eventually make its way to everyone.

She slowed her step to fall back into pace beside Ari, taking his hand. A smile curled her mouth when he wrapped his fingers tight about hers. Kati trotted around to take up a position on the other side of Leif. How easily they'd trusted Ari's friend, and Karsi too. Alarr had been a different matter.

She was glad he was fearful enough of the animals to keep his distance. Despite his apologies, she still didn't trust him, even if he was truly loyal to Ari. His attempt to blackmail her into bedding him had left her sick and almost as frightened as she'd been watching Ari battle Muli and fearing the other man might win.

As they walked further from the center of the city, the bustle and noise of the markets faded. The air cleared and she took a deep breath, grateful to be away from the chaotic commotion. These last weeks alone with Ari had left her unaccustomed to others, and the throngs of people inhabiting Tingwalla overwhelmed her.

She studied their surroundings, not paying attention to Ari's low conversation with Leif. Instead, she made sure to note the markings that differentiated the various parts of town. Finally they reached the edge of the city, where the road led across the increasingly open land. Small clusters of shelters had been fashioned all around, some occupied, some not. Thora kept her face turned away, despite the desperate desire to see if there was any from her own clan camped here.

Ari continued walking until they reached a secluded patch of space near several trees, several paces beyond the nearest group.

"Here," Ari declared. He swept his arm about the small space. "A shelter is easily built among these."

"I will gather branches." She tried to untwist her fingers from his, but his grip tightened. She eyed him curiously. Why did he stop her?

"Stay nearby. No farther away than there." He pointed to another cluster of trees. Thora nodded.

"I have them with me." She nodded toward the wolves. "And you're right here. I am safe."

He nodded, but concern still lit his eyes with a strange glow that left her heart warm and full. Every time she recalled the day he'd declared his love, her insides went soft and her knees trembled. The impulse to kiss him overtook her and she leaned up and pressed her lips to his before turning to tend her task.

By the time she'd brought enough branches, Ari and Leif had already fashioned a lean-to amidst the trees. She handed over what she'd gathered and took a seat at the base of a tree to watch them work to quickly fashion a shelter that would provide privacy for all of the men, once they returned after their meeting at the public longhouse. She stroked Kata's head resting in her lap and slung an arm around Kati sitting beside her. He gave her a few quick affectionate licks and she laughed, rubbing behind his ears.

"So much has changed, hasn't it, boy? And by this time tomorrow, our future will be decided."

The idea both frightened and exhilarated her. How many times had Ari declared his intention to claim her once he'd received his justice? More than she could count. But she still feared her father's reaction. She forced the worry aside, knowing she must trust Ari to resolve what would surely be a bitter dispute.

As if her thoughts had drawn him near, Ari loomed over her, hands on his hips. "Are you sure you won't stay?"

She disentangled herself from her pets and stood. "I am sure. But it's not safe to leave our belongings."

"I will remain here," Leif announced.

"You'll be alone." Ari looked around the area of their camp and then to Leif.

"It's not the first time. Won't be the last. I have food, water and ale. Rest assured, all will be well when you return."

Thora studied Ari. His consideration of his witness' promise showed in the tense lines in his face. He seemed about to say something., but didn't. He merely nodded and turned back toward the crowded town.

With her hand in his, she walked alongside him, a thousand questions running through her mind. She wanted to know all about the others they were about to meet but one glance into Ari's stern expression gave her pause.

"You look troubled," she said.

His fingers tightened on hers. "I'm not. I am close to achieving all I've worked for these last years. Why would I be troubled?"

"Because so much can go wrong."

He stopped, tugging on her hand to bring her close. "That is true, but I refuse to dwell on it."

"Then why do you look angry?"

He heaved a deep breath, closing his eyes briefly. When he opened them, that blue-green stare pinned her in place.

"I worry that something might happen to you. I still think you would be safer with Leif and your wolves back at our shelter."

She shook her head. "I want to be beside you, so that if I am seen by anyone, they will know I stand with you willingly."

"Stubborn girl," he murmured with a soft smile. A quick press of his lips against hers and they were once more on their way.

Once again, Thora was struck by the large crowds of the market. The smell of roasting meat, the sweet scent of tarts, the musky aromas of onions and beets, reminded her she hadn't eaten since they'd broken camp this morning.

"I'm hungry," she said.

Ari chuckled. "As am I. We will eat soon, I promise."

He led her through the maze of stalls. The crowds parted when they walked past, many eyeing the wolves with concern. She tried to ignore the stares and pointing, focusing instead on the wares offered for sale. A vast array of goods lay before them, from fine fabrics and furs, to ornate and colorful pottery and metal ware. The merchants shouted over each other, making it impossible to tell who sold what for how much. Thick smoke from the fires hovered in the air, burning her eyes.

"A brooch for your lady?" a man's voice cut through the din.

Ari stopped and walked over to the metalworker's stall. An array of brooches and hairpins, as well as some lovely pendants, spread across his table. Thora found herself drawn to a dragon head pendant and picked it up to examine the jewelry.

"Do you like it?" Ari asked.

"It's lovely."

"What is the price?"

"Three pieces of hacksilver," the merchant replied, his dark beady eyes moving over Thora. "Not many travel with wolves."

"They are special," said Thora. She didn't like his leering look. When Ari fished a few pieces of metal from the pouch at his waist, her eyes widened and the uncomfortable thoughts of the merchant faded.

He handed the hacksilver to the merchant and took the pendant from Thora's hand. He motioned for her to turn and she did, allowing him to place the long chain around her neck. The feel of his fingers in her hair as he adjusted it sent a delightful shiver along her spine. She turned and wrapped her arms around him.

"Thank you! I shall treasure it always." She stepped back and fingered the dragon, lifting it to scrutinize it more closely.

He gave her another kiss, this time a broad grin brightening his face. "Come." Once more he led her deeper into the city.

"Wait!"

When her hand slipped from his, he turned. She walked to the edge of the market, to an empty space among several of the stalls. She knelt on the ground and her two wolves soon sat before her. She stroked each of their heads, laughing at the lick she received from Kata.

"Go back to Leif. You must hunt for your meal, and I am safe with Ari."

Tails wagging, both Kata and Kati gave little yelps and pranced around their mistress. As always, Ari found himself enthralled by the sight of Thora and her pets. The understanding between the three also roused a hint of jealousy if he were honest with himself. Yet, he knew the animals trusted him, had done so from the very first day. Knowing he had saved their mistress had earned him their loyalty. When Kati trotted over to him and gave his hand a lick and a rub of his head, Ari knew he had truly been accepted. Thora stood watching the beasts until they disappeared from view before she turned to face him. Sadness lined her brow and he drew her near, pressing a kiss to her forehead.

"They will be fine."

She nodded. "I know. It's the first time I've been away from them since they were pups. But it is better for them this way. The crowds are afraid of them, and they draw too much attention."

"Come, the sooner we have our meeting and a meal, the sooner we can return to your pets."

It seemed they walked for hours before reaching the large public longhouse near the center of the town. Behind it sat the private longhouse where the kings and jarls and other nobles resided. Two smaller public houses bordered both.

The crowds grew denser, shouts and laughter and ribald insults rising to a cacophony. Thora resisted the urge to cover her ears. Instead, she hesitantly searched the crowd for familiar faces, torn between wanting to see someone she knew and hoping she found only strangers With more relief than she expected, the only people she recognized were Karsi and Alarr, standing a short distance from the longhouse's entrance. Several other men gathered with them.

Thora pressed close to Ari. Finally, they broke free of the throng and stood before Karsi. The other men greeted Ari warmly and he went to each one in turn, thanking them. When he finished, he motioned to Thora to join him. She did so hesitantly, aware of many gazes upon her, but refusing to meet any of them.

"When this is over, I will be taking Thora as my wife."

Cheers erupted from the men and heat scorched Thora's face at the crude congratulations they offered.

"Ari, she looks to give you a fine ride!"

"He's already claimed her, you fool!"

"How can she bear to look upon your ugly face?"

More laughter rang among them.

"Thora, if he doesn't treat you right, I'll be happy to take his place!"

Ari's arm slid around Thora's shoulders. "You'll have to fight me to the death."

"Ari! Don't encourage them!" she protested

"She's already giving you orders, Ari."

Ari chuckled. "She knows I am the one who gives the orders. And what happens when she doesn't obey."

Once again, fire seared her cheeks at the pointed stare he gave her.

More ribald shouts and laughs filled the air before Ari sobered and drew the men in close. Hearing their tales revealed just how much they had suffered under Hersir's brutal quest to be jarl. She listened closely, knowing that Jarl Drengr's plan to publicly name Hersir as his heir would be destroyed once Ari and the others spoke before the council.

She lifted her eyes heavenward. *Let my father hear and know the truth of the man he would trade me to.*

A few moments later, an odd peace shivered through her, calming her fears. A sign the gods favored her, intended to spare her despair and brutality? Would reward her with a lifetime with Ari? She chose to interpret the sensation that way. Aware of Ari giving her a curious glance, she merely smiled.

"What secrets do you hold now, *ástin minn*?"

She shrugged. "Speaking aloud may work against us. I will share it with you when all is over."

***

Ari stared, wondering what Thora knew and didn't share with him. Later, when they had returned to their small camp, he would ask her what had brought that satisfied expression to her lovely face.

His excitement over finding all of those he'd sought during his exile here in Tingwalla soon had him forgetting what intentions Thora possessed. By this time tomorrow, he would see his brother tried and punished for his crimes. Part of him regretted what was to come. He still held the memories of his childhood, before their father had been slain in battle. Hugi's honor in dying so valiantly had trickled to Ari and his brother, but Hersir had grown vindictive and hateful soon thereafter. If Drengr hadn't taken them in as his own, raised and trained them as their father would have done, Ari feared Hersir would have become even more of an unstable destructive force. Only Drengr had possessed the power to rein in Ari's brother from his cruel desires. But Hersir had fooled the other man, convinced him it was Ari who sought power by whatever means possible. Yet, if Drengr had fully believed, Ari would not be here now, about to reclaim his honor. That knowledge had been the beacon of hope that carried him these past years to this moment. A sacrifice in thanks must be made to the gods.

He leaned in close to Thora. "I will purchase a goat or a hog and we will sacrifice it to Odin tonight."

"Why?"

"To give thanks."

"For the success of your quest?"

Her perception, as always, both surprised and pleased him. She knew him well, these last weeks bonding them in so many ways. Though to Ari, he could no longer clearly remember the time before she'd entered his life. Yes, Odin had blessed him in many ways. One more reason to thank the god who held many a man's fate in his hands.

"Among other things." He slid his lips over hers, drawing away with a smile.

Her dark eyes glittered and he wished they were back at their camp, where he could take her into the forests and claim her in all the ways he now knew she wanted to be claimed. He held back his growl of frustration and faced the men once more.

"Let us find a meal. There is much to discuss for tomorrow."

He led them into the longhouse, where most of the long tables inside were filled with people. Spying a few empty seats along the far wall, he snaked his way through the chaos of benches and people, servants placing platters of food and children running amongst the adults' legs. His grip on Thora's hand never loosened until he had seated her closest to the wall, sliding onto the bench beside her. The other men squeezed into the small space.

Within minutes, large tankards of ale and mead had been placed on the table, accompanied by large wooden trenchers of meat and vegetables, and even fresh bread. He handed Thora a chicken leg and a flagon of mead.

"Thank you." She sipped at the mead. "That is delicious."

He smiled. "Nice not to have to catch and cook our own meal, isn't it?"

She nodded, biting daintily into the chicken. Ari looked over the now nearly two dozen men who stood with him. And with Thora beside him, he truly felt the luckiest man in Midgard.

CHAPTER TWENTY

Weary and sated from the large meal, Thora didn't protest when Ari urged her from the table.

"We'll return to our shelter. All is ready for tomorrow."

By the time they made their way back toward the edge of town, the crowd had thinned, though many people still milled about, fighting, drinking and celebrating. Word had passed that the council would convene at first light and Ari had arranged for his cause to be among the first to be heard. Thora suspected that with so many witnesses to stand beside him, the kings and jarls would easily decide in his favor.

Ari continued to hold her hand, the contact reminding her that as long as he was beside her, she would always be safe. They passed through the market, where several of the vendors still hawked their wares. Thora's gaze landed on a woman bargaining with a fur trader. She stopped short, the long blond hair more than familiar. Two small children stood beside her as she haggled with the man, a dark-haired little girl clutching a small woven doll and a slightly bigger boy, with hair as fair as his mother's. Thora's heart seemed to stop for a moment before resuming a frantic racing beat.

"Ari, we must go another way," she said, her gaze still settled on the woman's back. As long as she didn't turn, there was a chance Thora could avoid being noticed.

"Why?"

"That is my stepmother. And my brother and sister."

"Are you sure?"

She nodded. "This way, please."

She backed away, her stare still focused on Geira, Gunnar and Elin. She couldn't be seen, not now. Not when Ari was so close to achieving his goal, and his public claim on her.

"Thora! Look, Mama, it's Thora!"

Gunnar's voice rang out over the noise of the market. Before Thora could decide which way to flee, the boy ran over and threw his arms around her legs, hugging her tight. Ari's grip loosened and slipped away. She met his gaze, calmed by the reassuring smile he offered.

"We missed you Thora. Why did you go away?"

A moment later, Elin joined her brother in welcoming Thora, her gleeful laughter bringing the sting of tears. She hugged them back, realizing just how much she had missed her younger brother and sister. She squeezed her eyes shut, not releasing them until the threat of sobs had been brought under control. When she straightened, her stepmother stood a few steps away.

"It is you! I'd heard talk of a woman with wolves here in Tingwalla, and I'd hoped..."

Thora found herself encased in another hug. When Geira stepped back, her smile soon faded.

"Your father is sick with worry. He's sent several parties in search of you."

Thora winced at the scolding tone in Geira's voice. "I... had to leave. I couldn't let Father marry me to someone I didn't know."

Geira's stern expression softened. "I understand. But running away was not the answer."

Finally, she turned and focused on Ari. Thora twisted her hands together, trying to stop their shaking while she waited for Geira's reaction.

"Who are you?" the blonde woman asked.

"My name is Ari. Thora has been traveling with me."

Several moments of silence ensued, followed by Geira looking between the two. Her eyes settled and narrowed on Ari.

"What have you done to her?" She took a step toward Ari, her fist raised.

Thora grabbed her stepmother's arm. "Geira, I am with him willingly."

Geira's deep blue eyes widened. "Your father..."

Thora heaved a sigh. "It's a long tale, Geira. Ari saved my life. I... owe him."

Geira shook her head. "What has he done to you? If he's harmed you, there'll be nothing left for your father to kill."

Thora held back her laugh at the surprised rise of Ari's eyebrows. "He hasn't harmed me. He kept me safe. And when Kata was wounded, he helped to heal her."

Geira's lips pressed together and suspicion glowed in her eyes. "You must come with me at once. Your father will want to know you are safe. Well, mostly."

Thora shook her head. "I am staying with Ari." She leaned in close to her stepmother's ear. "I love him. And he loves me. And after tomorrow, when he's cleared his name –"

"He's an outlaw?"

Thora glanced around, hoping no one had heard Geira's outraged cry. Thankfully, none paid them the slightest mind.

"Not anymore," said Ari. "And after tomorrow, I will have justice against the one who falsely accused me."

Thora grabbed Geira's hands. "Please don't tell Father you saw me. Not yet. Tomorrow, when you all hear the truth, you will be glad Ari found me when he did."

Geira hesitated, looking between them both. Thora reached out for Ari's hand, the familiar warmth and safety settling over her when he took it.

"Very well. But I cannot promise the children won't reveal your presence here."

"I won't tell, Mama," Gunnar vowed.

"I'm sure you won't. Elin, however, will not understand." Geira shrugged. "I cannot promise you anything."

"Father will be angry when he learns you saw me. Will you be all right?"

"I'm sure he will find some way to punish me," Geira said with a sigh. A flash of pink tinted her cheeks. "Do not worry. I will do my best not to betray you."

Thora hugged her stepmother. "Thank you."

"Where are the wolves?"

"I sent them into the forest. They created too much of a ruckus."

Geira nodded then stepped up close to Ari. "If you don't protect her, her father will be the least of your troubles."

"You have my word she will be safe when she's with me. Always."

"I'll have to be satisfied with that for now." She faced Thora once more. "As soon as your business is finished, I expect you to find us and explain everything to your father. We are in one of the public longhouses. Promise me."

"I promise."

"Come along, children. We have much to do and it's almost time for you to go to sleep."

Geira strode back to the merchant and collected her wares, then guided her children away. Before she disappeared into the crowd, she turned and gave Thora one last look.

When her family had vanished from view, Thora allowed Ari to hold her close, needing to lean on his strength. Her legs trembled so much, she feared she might fall to the ground in a heap.

"Come, we must return to our camp now."

She nodded, still stunned by the confrontation with Geira. Her thoughts tumbled chaotically over each other, but one gained supremacy over the rest.

Her father would find her. Surely he would know Geira hid something of import. He would force his wife to tell him what secret she kept.

"Ari, he's going to find us."

He shook his head, his arm about her shoulder holding her close. "Even if he learns of your presence here in Tingwalla, by then it will already be too late. We will stand before the council and he cannot stop us."

Despite the assurance, Thora's worries maintained their persistent grasp. She remained silent, praying to Odin to keep her father unknowing. A few moments later, recollection poked and her dread multiplied, over and over.

"The sacrifice! We don't have anything to offer. We were supposed to give thanks and we didn't and now look what's happened!"

"Take ease, *ástin minn.* You are mine. As I am yours. I will never let anyone take you away."

How she wanted to believe, to trust his vow. His words flooded her with warmth, but her father had many men. Ari, even with his companions, would be vastly outnumbered. Her greatest fear seemed to be coming to pass.

***

Ari wished he knew of a way to soothe the trembling in Thora's body. No matter what words he offered, none would console her. Her panic remained tangible, seeping from her as if she bled. When they reached their camp, she let out a cry of joy to see the wolves had heeded her orders and returned to the shelter. He released her hand and she hurried to her pets, kneeling before them and hugging them both. Ari smiled at the giggles her animals drew with their licks and cuddles.

"How did you get close enough with those two standing guard?" Karsi's question drew Ari from the distraction of watching her.

"The female had been wounded by outlaws who attacked Thora. Kati killed one, and I dispatched the other."

"Earned their trust right off, eh?"

Ari shrugged. "I suppose so. And I helped Thora treat the injured wolf. They knew I meant no harm."

Karsi slapped him on the shoulder. "The gods appear to favor you these days."

"Let's hope their goodwill holds out through tomorrow."

The amusement faded from Karsi's grizzled face. "It will. There are enough of us to bear witness to his crimes, none will doubt you didn't poison Drengr or arrange for his murder."

Ari hesitated several moments, glancing around at the other men camped with them. They laughed and drank, ignoring Ari. He motioned to Leif, then drew both men a few paces from their shelter.

"Thora was seen by her stepmother tonight. She fears her father will learn she is here and find her before we go before the council. If I must... keep watch over her if I cannot."

He didn't voice his own worry that Thora's father would indeed find them and take her away. Ari refused to consider the possibility, even though the idea refused to be completely extinguished.

"You have my word," Karsi vowed.

"Mine, too," Leif agreed.

The three grasped hands to seal their oath and Ari turned back to Thora. With her pets beside her, she seemed much calmer and he took his place beside her on the fur pallet.

"Soon, this will all be over." He covered her hands, twisting in her lap.

She met his stare evenly. "Do you truly plan to wed me?"

Did she still doubt him? The twinge on hurt at her question was easily brushed aside when he read the uncertainty in her eyes.

"Of course. Perhaps as soon as the council has cleared me and named Hersir's sentence."

Her dark eyes glowed in the firelight and he pulled her close, brushing his lips across hers and ignoring the shouts and jibes from the others. While he had no plans for anything more than a few kisses, he cared more for Thora's ease than his own desires. All else had worked in his favor. She was his only concern tonight. He would not embarrass her before the others, much as his cock ached to be inside her.

He drew away and leaned back, settling her against him. A fluff of fur brushed across his face. He looked up as Kati took up a position beside him. It had been the end of the wolf's tail that had swiped his cheek. He chuckled. On Thora's other side, Kata rested, her head on her mistress' hip. Had Ari ever felt so at peace since, before his long banishment?

The temptation to dare the gods to try and take Thora from him now rose up, but he forced it aside. Now was not the time to draw Odin's ire. Especially not with her father nearby. He'd reassured her, but truthfully, the worry was never far from his thoughts.

Sleep eluded him for a long time, even as Thora still rested fitfully, half-waking every few minutes, mumbling about her father, her hand curled tightly into Ari's tunic. The others had finally settled, either too fatigued or too drunk to stay awake. The light from the fire grew smaller, until only crackling embers glowed in the pit.

"Thora!"

The shout jolted him from slumber and he blinked against the light of morning. Another call of her name and she bolted upright.

"It's my father!"

Ari looked heavenward, knowing full well he had let his confidence overshadow his gratitude. He made a silent apology and rose, grabbing his sword from where it lay beside him. Despite his trouble sleeping last night, the bright sun and the pumping of his heart made him instantly alert.

"Stay behind me."

By now, the others had also heard the shouts, getting louder as the man neared. Through the fog, a man on horseback finally emerged, sword raised. Two others also appeared, flanking him. Behind Ari, Thora gave a strangled cry and her hands curled into his sides.

"I won't let him take you."

The man reined his steed in and leapt from the saddle. He rushed toward their camp, but Ari's men immediately took up defensive positions. He scowled. Ari recognized the warrior in the expression.

"I am Kori Thorfinnson. Thora is my daughter." Kori pointed his sword behind Ari, making it clear he had seen her.

"I am Ari. Your daughter has been under my protection."

"Protection from what?"

Ari hesitated. How much should he share? He didn't want to speak of Hersir just yet. The other men accompanying Kori now neared, axes and swords at the ready. His men outnumbered them and he dismissed his initial concerns.

"Tell him how you saved me," Thora whispered in his ear.

He tilted his head toward her but never pulled his stare from her father. "Are you giving me orders, *ástin minn*?"

"Yes! Just do it!" she hissed.

Even in this dire situation, the woman had the capability of making him see humor.

"Very well." He fully faced Kori once more. "She was under attack and one of her wolves had been wounded. I... defeated the outlaws."

Now it was Kori's turn to stare curiously. He paced slowly, his fierce glare focused on Ari, clearly appraising him.

"Thora, come with me. Now." Her father pointed to her.

The shake of her head nudged against Ari's. "No."

Her refusal only served to infuriate her father more. He snarled and took several strides closer, stopping only when Karsi met him, well before he he had the chance to get closer than a few paces. The point of Karsi's sword aimed at his neck.

"Do not refuse me, Thora. You must come with me at once."

Ari tried to stop her, but Thora stepped out from behind him. His worst fear seemed to be coming to life, except she stopped when she stood only a few steps before him. She didn't go to her father! The realization eased the tight squeeze around his heart.

He drank in the sight of her, proud of the defiant tilt of her chin, her spine straight, arms folded. She looked formidable, and the thought of how he'd reacted when she'd faced him in such a manner briefly taunted him.

"I am staying with Ari."

The rest of his fear crumbled. Once again admiring her strength, he reined in the maelstrom of excitement threatening to dull his wits.

"You know I've made arrangements, alliances. You dishonor me by refusing."

The mention of her marriage to Hersir roused disgust, but Ari no longer worried Thora might suffer such a fate. He would fight to the death to prevent it.

Another shake of her head. "You dishonor me with these arrangements."

Ari's eyes widened. The hint of disrespect in her words drew some shocked murmurs among his men. And another snarling shout of fury from her father.

"How dare you? You've always been rebellious, but you go too far this time!"

"Thora, do not speak to your father that way!" One of the other men accompanying Kori shouted to her.

"Uncle Hradi, you don't know. Ari goes before the council today. After that, you will understand. All of you."

"No! I will not accept this!" Kori faced Ari again. "She is not your wife, you have no claim. I demand you return her to me."

"I will not go against Thora's choice."

The man's shoulders heaved with heavy breaths. Finally, with a glance to his allies, he lowered his sword a little. Ari remained in position, ready to shove Thora back behind him and face her enraged father if necessary. She still stood tall, head high. He noted the way her fingers clenched, hidden from her father's view due to the position she took. But Ari knew just how frightened Thora was and the urge to touch her in reassurance grew near impossible to fight. Somehow, he refrained, knowing to further anger Kori could prove disastrous for all of them.

"I will not leave you alone with him." Kori jerked his chin toward Ari.

"I am not alone." She waved one arm toward the assembled men. Did anyone else notice the tremor? "And I have Kata and Kati."

"You will be disgraced before all."

She shook her head, sending her long dark tresses into a soft sway. "You'll see. When Ari makes his claims, you'll know I do what is right and best for me. And for you too, Father."

Kori took another step, the sword lowering further. Anger still emanated from the man, like a fog rolling in from the ocean. But now he seemed a little calmer, less like the berserker he appeared to be when he first rode up to the camp.

"I will accompany you to the council."

The declaration knotted Ari's gut. He didn't relish the idea of dealing with an angry Kori while he prepared for his turn before the council. He didn't understand what game the gods played, but he gave thanks he and his men had prepared well last night. Gathering the packs containing the needed evidence, he took his place at the head of his men.

Ari understood Kori and his men needed careful watching, for the concern he might try and steal Thora back. He arranged for her father to walk between himself and Karsi, close enough to Thora to appease him, yet still give Ari the advantage in preventing any attempts to separate her from his side. The others would be encircled by the rest of Ari's men. Though there were grumbling complaints, all three men heeded his orders.

The trek through the market and back to the center of the city, to the longhouse where the council sat outside to hear cases, seemed to last days, though Ari knew it was only his nervous anticipation of what was to come. In a few short hours, his name would finally be cleared, his honor restored. The feel of Thora's hand in his as she walked beside him fed the confidence in his ultimate success.

"What have you done to her to make her refuse my orders?"

Kori's question cut into his thoughts. He met the other man's stare, grateful for the man who stood between them.

"I've done nothing to harm her." He raised his chin, daring Thora's father to refute his claim, perhaps draw him into a fight. Not that he planned to give in to any attempt Kori might make to incite him into combat now. If, after his appearance before the council was finished and justice claimed, Kori still chose to battle, Ari would accept the challenge.

"Thora, you can still come with me."

Kori's words held a plea, one to which Ari feared she might yield. Yet, when he turned to study her reaction to her father's declaration, he found her expression more stony than ever. He might laugh if the situation hadn't grown so dire. From the first time he'd seen it, her defiant nature had drawn him in, seduced him in a way he'd never expected. Made him love and respect her even more.

CHAPTER TWENTY-ONE

Thora avoided looking toward her father, much as she hated to admit a powerful sense of comfort had surged through her at the first sight of him. Refusing him hadn't been difficult, she'd rebelled against him often enough when she was younger, but somehow, this time seemed to create a chasm between them she feared they'd never bridge again. Still, despite the familiar comfort his arrival had stirred, apprehension overpowered the brief moment of happiness to see him again.

This morning, the crowds seemed bigger than ever, the merchants' shouts grating uncomfortably on her ears. She held tight to Ari's hand, forcing her attention anywhere but toward her father, who still tried to catch her attention.

The smoke from the cooking fires burned her eyes and her stomach rolled once more at the smells from the roasting pigs and goats. Kata pressed in closer and the feel of the wolf's fur beneath her fingers soothed her a little.

Sobs and pleas for mercy reached her and she turned, her gaze settling on the slave market. Several women and young men were held in a pen, hands bound while traders looked them over and made bargains for their sale. Thora shuddered, looking away as one trader savagely beat a young man. She wondered what the poor soul had done to earn such savage punishment.

She pressed a little closer to Ari, his nearness, as always, bringing the feeling of safety amid the chaos rioting both around and within her. The trek to the longhouse seemed to last hours, though she knew only a few minutes had passed. Each step closer to the council jarred through her, making her head pound. She gave a moment's thanks there had been no time to eat this morning, for surely she would lose anything she ate.

"Thora, are you unwell?"

Ari's voice broke through the internal tumult. She turned, the ground suddenly starting to spin. She reached for him, her fingers closing around his tunic, his hands tight on her arms.

"What have you done to her?" Her father's voice seemed a distant shout, the buzzing in her ears growing louder.

"Come, you must rest for a moment." Ari led her to a spot near the stables, pulling her close. She leaned into him, breathing deeply of his familiar masculine scent.

A hand on her shoulder drew her gaze up. She stared into her father's concerned face. She burrowed deeper into Ari's embrace.

"Are you ill?" Kori asked.

She shook her head. "Just... worried. I'm feeling better now."

She looked up at Ari, whose gaze possessed a similar concern.

"Are you sure?" he asked.

"Yes." She disentangled herself from his hold, feeling stronger once more. "You must finish this."

His smile chased the remainder of the chill still clinging to her. Once again, she fell into step beside him, Kata on her left and Kati beside Ari. The throngs of people thickened with each step closer to the longhouse. Ari pushed his way through those gathered in the courtyard until they stood amid the inner circle.

Five men sat upon a dais before the longhouse, their throne-like chairs large and imposing. The one in the center possessed a large set of antlers, making the man seated there look even more formidable. King Hemming, she supposed, assuming the other were local jarls or those close to the king.

Ari leaned close to her ear and confirmed her hunch. "King Hemming sits in the middle. Jarl Drengr is to his left."

Thora's gaze drifted from the fair-haired young king to the older man with long snowy white hair beside him. His fluffy beard was neatly groomed and the ornately embroidered cloak he wore had a collar of fine fur, the elegant garment revealing his wealth. He leaned over to the king and whispered something. Even from this distance, Thora recognized the sharpness in his eyes while he considered the three people standing before them, in an apparent dispute over land.

"Where is your brother?" Thora whispered.

When Ari didn't answer, she turned to find him glaring across the courtyard. She followed his stare, her stomach knotting to see Hersir standing amidst several men near the end of the dais. She'd only caught a glimpse of him that morning, but she still recognized him without any doubt. He also donned a finely woven cloak, and his leather boots gleamed. Though they stood far away from him and his companions, Thora read a malicious madness in his expression while he watched the proceedings.

"Hersir." Ari issued the name on a quiet growl.

Kori jumped in front of him. "Tell me how you know Hersir and Jarl Drengr."

The sudden movement left the wolves prancing about them in agitation. Thora flicked her fingers, urging them to sit beside her. Though they obeyed, Kati continued to paw at the ground, while Kata shifted from sitting to standing and back.

"He is my brother."

"You son of a whore! You are using my daughter against your own flesh and blood?"

Kori's shout drew the attention of the entire crowd, as well as the council. A strange silence settled over the assemblage. As if realizing the focus had fallen to them, Kori turned.

"Ari? Is that you?" Jarl Drengr stood, eyes wide and a hint of a smile lifting his beard.

Ari faced the man he'd been accused of trying to kill. His grip on her hand tightened almost painfully.

"Yes, it is I."

"I'd not thought to see you."

Ari took a step toward the dais. At the same time, Kori tugged on Thora's arm and her hand fell away.

"Ari!" she cried, trying without success to jerk free from her father's tight hold.

He turned, taking a step toward them, but Kori raised his sword. "Stay back."

Ari halted, his attention bouncing between Thora and the council. "Just a little while longer."

His assurance did little to calm her rising panic, but she nodded. He needed to finish what he'd come here for, without worrying for her. When this was all over, surely her father would be convinced and not insist on keeping them apart.

He turned and took several steps toward the dais. Hersir did the same until the two men stood only a few feet apart.

"What are you doing?" Hersir shouted.

"I have come to clear my name," Ari announced.

The strength in his vow sparked a surge of pride within Thora.

"Clear your name? None will believe you. You're lucky you weren't killed for your crimes." Hersir paced slowly, his smirk making him looking even more evil.

"They were not my crimes, and I am going to prove it."

Hersir laughed, a maniacal shout that sent a fearful shiver along Thora's spine. A moment of gratitude for her father's embrace was quickly chased by the reminder he intended to give her to this man. She tugged against the tight hands on her shoulders, but they held firm. She refused the urge to turn and plead with him to release her, folding her arms and taking several deep breaths in an attempt to steady her racing heart.

"You're nothing but a murderer!" Hersir sneered, his hand going to the hilt of his sword. "Everyone knows it."

"I demand an explanation for this!" King Hemming's booming voice rang out over the courtyard, sending the hushed murmurs into silence.

Drengr placed a hand on the king's arm and drew him into a conversation no one heard, not even Hersir who stomped his foot in a display of petulant anger. Thora shuddered. She finally dared a look at her father, but his bland expression revealed nothing of his thoughts. Did he know what his choice would cost her?

"I seek only to see you settled," Kori said.

She'd spoken aloud? Narrowing her eyes, she shook her head. "You seek an alliance for the clan, with me as the sacrifice!"

"He is wealthy and powerful and will be a jarl."

"He set Ari up to be executed as a criminal. Ari has the witnesses to prove it."

The skepticism in her father's eyes only grew stronger. Jaw clenched, glancing at the dais. The other jarls had joined the conversation between Drengr and Hemming. The case they had been hearing seemed to have disappeared. Had they issued a decision? A moment later, she sucked in a deep breath, her hand pressed against her lips to stifle a scream. Hersir stalked toward Ari, sword now drawn.

"Stop!" the king commanded.

Hersir's face mottled with rage but he obeyed and turned to face the council. "I merely mean to –"

"I don't care what you intended." This time Drengr's voice carried over the once again agitated crowd and their ever-growing murmurs. He faced Ari once more. "Tell me, boy, what you have come to say."

"I have proof that it was not I who commanded a murderer to kill you. It was Hersir."

Gasps and shouts filled the air. Thunder rumbled overhead, along with a flash of lightning, though the sun still shone bright. The crowd again fell silent. Clearly, the gods watched closely and none wished to draw their ire.

"You're a liar as well as a murderer!" Hersir's shout grew oddly high-pitched. He pointed his sword toward Ari, the blade wavering.

"Let me go!" she cried, pulling at her father's iron grip.

Ari turned and fixed her with a stern stare. "Stay."

The command in his voice, combined with his pointed stare, roused an immediate need to obey. She stopped fighting her father, closing her eyes against the threatening tears.

Ari returned his attention to the council, reaching into his pouch to withdraw several daggers and pieces of bark marked with runes.

"Along with this proof, I also brought witnesses." He turned and motioned toward his men.

"Karsi? Alarr? You too?" Drengr asked when the two men stepped forward.

"Who are these men?" Hemming asked.

"They were once part of my clan, but they left us. I never knew why."

"Because Hersir threatened us when we refused his request to commit murder in your name."

Karsi's announcement brought another round of muttering from those gathered in the courtyard. He took the evidence Ari held and brought it to the dais.

"Lies, all of it! He has convinced others to speak untruths against me!" Hersir continued to rail until Drengr once again ordered him to silence.

The jarl studied the items, showing them to Hemming and the others before facing Ari once more.

"What are these?" Hemming asked.

"They are claims from those unable or too afraid to come and speak before you," Ari explained to the king. "But I think you will find what these men have to say even more compelling."

After Karsi and Alarr related their tales of Hersir's intimidating pressure, the way he'd menaced them and their families if they didn't carry out the crimes he wanted, other men stepped forward and shared their tales. One after another, they described how they'd been either coerced into committing crimes, then driven from their homes when Hersir threatened their families, or threatened when they refused. In two cases, Hersir had even raped the men's wives. By the time the last man had given his account of how his children's lives had nearly been lost when Hersir had stolen them away, letting them loose in the forest on a particularly cold night, the crowd was completely silent.

The fury emanating from Drengr was almost palpable, the heat of his rage hovering over the assemblage. Thora again twisted in her father's grip. Skin ashen, he stared at the man he'd intended to be his son-in-law. His hold finally slackened and she pulled away.

"Do you see how despicable he is?" she whispered.

"I am sorry, Thora. He hid his crimes well." The bleak despair in his dark eyes shattered the icy anger she'd directed toward him.

"No longer." Her attention returned once more to Ari, who stood proudly before the council, flanked by his men. She would never get enough of the sight of him. She only hoped there would be time to look at him for years to come.

"Liars! Every one of you!" Hersir's shrill screams sent another apprehensive shiver along Thora's spine.

She inched closer to Ari, determined to stand beside him. When her father's hand again landed on her shoulder, she paused and turned. This time, he joined her instead of holding her back.

"Hold your tongue!" The echo of Drengr's roar echoed over the crowd for several moments. His eyes blazed with rage and he signaled to Hersir to stand before him.

Hersir continued to mutter threats toward the witnesses who exposed his crimes. His sword remained poised and ready, as if he anticipated an attack, or perhaps planned one of his own.

"It's quite clear you have committed many grievous crimes," King Hemming said. "I find it difficult to believe all of these men are lying."

"They are!" Hersir's shout held notes of madness, his face red with fury. "I've done nothing wrong! They envy me, my position, my wealth!"

Hersir turned, his enraged stare focusing on Thora for a few moments before landing on Kori then returning to Ari. Eyes narrowed, he looked positively evil.

"This is my bride, is she not?" he demanded.

"No longer. I am breaking the contract," Kori stated. "Had I known the truth before, I never would have agreed."

"You can't do that!" Hersir screamed. His face reddened further, spittle flying from his mouth. "She's mine!"

"I can and I have." Her father faced the dais, bowing to the council. "Jarl Drengr, I am sorry, but I cannot see my daughter wed to this... this –"

Drengr held up a hand. "I agree and I cannot blame you. I am sure King Hemming will not enforce the contract."

"I will not," the king agreed.

"Now that I know the truth," Drengr continued, "we must decide on Hersir's punishment."

Hersir's maniacal ranting continued, screaming about injustice. Thora wanted nothing more than to be beside Ari and headed toward him. Before she reached Ari's outstretched hand, Hersir ran over and grabbed her, pulling her tight against him as he backed away.

"She is to be *my* bride! I will wed her now."

Thora fought against the iron grip Hersir had around her waist, elbowing him in the gut. It had little effect, for his hold only tightened, forcing the breath from her lungs. Heart racing in panic, she clawed at the arm pinning her.

Swords drawn, both Kori and Ari lunged toward them, halting abruptly when the tip of Hersir's blade pointed at her neck. Thora tilted her head away from the danger, her breath caught in her throat. Surely the gods wouldn't betray her this way, not after all they'd put her through. A sob lodged in her throat but she refused to let it free.

"Bring the sacrifice and the *godi*! We do this now!"

A low growl drew Thora's attention. Her wolves! Trying to avoid the sword pointed ominously at her, she searched the area, but did not see her pets. But they were close. Hope sprang back to life and she could breathe again. Her gaze darted among the throngs of people in the courtyard. Yet, no one else seemed to have heard.

Hersir backed away, dragging her with him. When his arm slid from her waist, his hand tight on her shoulder, she turned and bit the closest finger. He howled in pain, but his grip loosened. Thora twisted free, ducking when Hersir's fist sailed toward her face. She ran toward Ari.

Hersir's ear-splitting scream halted her flight. She turned to see Kati clamping his jaws on Hersir's sword arm, forcing the man to drop the weapon. At the same time, Kata mauled his legs, sending the man to the ground. Barks and growls, accompanied by Hersir's inhuman howls drew the attention of everyone assembled.

"Thora!"

Ari held out his hand. She ran to him, falling easily into his embrace. Facing her pets once more, she covered her ears to drown out the ever-weakening shrieks from the mauled man. For several minutes, he attempted to fight the animals off, but his movements soon weakened, his cries fading to whimpers as the wolves tore at his flesh. Blood pooled on the ground, forming a thick, red mud. Finally, Kati dove with the final blow, his fangs gauging Hersir's throat and sending the last terrified sounds into a death gurgle. The wolves stopped their attack and stood over the still body, growling at anyone who neared.

"May his soul be prevented from entering Valhalla!"

The king's proclamation rang out over the silent crowd, his gaze, like everyone else's, fixed firmly on the two wolves in the courtyard. Stunned surprise lined his face, clearly caused by the unexpected turn of events. Thora snapped her fingers.

"Kata, Kati, come!"

The animals obeyed her command, trotting over to stand beside her and Ari. Blood still coated their snouts. She would need to take them to the river and... why were such inane thoughts running through her head?

"We had heard of a wolf woman arriving in Tingwalla," Drengr said. "She is your daughter, Thorfinnson?"

Thora looked over at her father. Disbelief and confusion lined his face. Behind him, Geira emerged from the crowd, coming to stand beside him. She gave Thora a wink and a smile before she turned to her husband.

"Acknowledge the king," Geira urged.

Kori focused his gaze on Thora. The love and assurance she read there soothed her. He smiled.

"Yes, Thora is my daughter." His pronouncement rang out clearly.

Drengr stroked his beard, clearly contemplating some idea or another. Thora leaned into Ari, savoring the feel of his lips against her forehead.

"I may have a solution that will please everyone." Drengr paused and motioned the other council members close. After several minutes, they separated and Drengr faced Ari, Thora and her father again.

"Clearly, I must proclaim a new heir," Drengr began. "I placed my faith in the wrong man, but now that I have learned the truth, I would like to now name Ari Hugisson as my new heir. As such, Thorfinnson, the contract between our clans can be amended. If you choose."

Thora met Ari's stare, a crazed laugh escaping her to see the surprise lining his face, which surely matched her own. A grin slowly spread across his face and he picked Thora up and swung her around. She laughed and hugged him tight, meeting his kiss with eagerness. Around them, cheers and shouts erupted, but she barely noticed, too intent on the feel of Ari's lips on hers, the burst of happiness lighting her from the inside.

When he drew away, carefully settling her back to her feet, she leaned into him, her grip around his neck tightening. She never wanted to let go.

"Thora," he whispered. "Your father."

Uncertainty dimmed the joy and she slowly turned. She met her father's stare, hoping his bland expression didn't mean he intended to refuse.

"Father?" Her voice cracked, fear that me might decide against the change in the contract.

Kori's gaze remained firmly on Ari. "Do you love her?"

"I do," Ari vowed.

Kori stepped close, now meeting Thora's gaze. Her heart hammered against her chest, fearful of his decision. Didn't matter. One way or another, she intended to stay with Ari, even if it meant she would be cast out of her clan, never to see her family again.

"And do you love him?" her father asked.

The lump in her throat nearly prevented her from speaking, She swallowed twice and lifted her chin, the feeling of Ari's comforting hand on her shoulder soothing the agitation setting her legs atremble. She lifted her chin.

"I do love him, Father. And no matter what you –"

Kori held up his hand, his dark stare warm and understanding. "Then I will agree to Drengr's terms."

Her breath eluded her, hear heart racing even faster. He'd given his blessing! Tears of joy blurred her vision and she turned back to Ari. She didn't care his embrace was so tight it forced the breath from her lungs. She clung to him, fearing if she let go, he might be taken from her forever. The pounding in her head nearly drowned the cheers and congratulations from the crowd.

"Again you cry," he murmured against her ear. "I'm beginning to think you don't want to be my wife."

She cupped his face in hers, drawing him close for another kiss, desperate to convey the love bursting within her heart. When she drew away, the twinkle in his blue-green eyes sparked another sting of happy tears.

"I do, Ari. I do!"

He grinned. "I know. And before Mani rises in the sky, we will be wed."

A hand on her arm drew her attention once more to her father.

"The *godi* has been summoned and a sacrifice will be prepared." His words, while spoken solemnly, still inspired another giddy rush of joy.

"Thank you, Father." She forced the words past her tight throat.

"Geira has sent for the children. The contract will be honored and a new alliance sealed."

Thora didn't hear anything else. Once again, Ari held her tight against him. She clung to him, never wanting to let go. His fingers under her chin tilted her head back so he could stare into her eyes.

"I am so very glad I saved you that day."

His words set off another rush of longing, one she didn't even try to contain. Shortly, she would become Ari's wife. Though their wedding would not be traditional, she didn't care. All that mattered now was that she would belong to Ari for all time.

"As am I. I love you, Ari."

"And I love you. I will spend the rest of my days loving you and the children you will bear me."

Another kiss and Thora found herself lost once more in the heat of his passion. She raised her eyes heavenward.

"Thank you," she whispered.

"Who are you speaking to?"

She almost laughed at Ari's confused expression. "I am thanking the gods for sending you to me. You saved me, in ways I never knew I needed saving."

His smile warmed all the corners of her heart. "And you saved me, as well. I will love you forever, Thora."

He sealed his declaration with a heat-filled kiss.

THE END

Thank you for taking the time to read Norseman's Deception. I hope you enjoyed it, and if so, please consider telling your friends or perhaps you wouldn't mind posting a short review. Word of mouth is an author's best friend and more appreciated than you know.

About the Author:

I'm a proud born-and-bred Jersey Girl with Brooklyn roots. And I still live where it all started - I married my very own alpha male many eons ago, and have an amazing college-age daughter and a 10 year old son who charms and frustrates me at every turn. Free time is always a luxury and I spend the bulk of what time I manage to scrounge up lost in the worlds of my own making. I love to read and write hot, sexy and emotional stories about people both glamorous and not-so-glamorous. Be warned - some of my characters are even downright un-heroic, which is part of what makes them so interestingly sexy, in my opinion!

On the rare occasions I'm not taking advantage of that valuable free time by writing, you can catch me poking around in my other favorite twisted historical worlds of Sleepy Hollow, Reign and the History Channel's Vikings. I'm also a huge fan of Harry Potter, Highlander,

Charmed, and DragonBall Z! Yeah, a strange fandom medley, but each one features some of the sexiest villains ever. Did I mention I love villains? And of course, let's not forget my beloved NY Rangers.

Find Gianna online:

"A Kinky Twist on History!"
"Magically Kinky!"
Website:
www.giannasimoneeroticromance.com
Blog: http://giannasimone.blogspot.com
Twitter: @Gianna_Simone
Facebook:
www.facebook.com/GiannaSimoneRomanceAuthor
Goodreads:
https://www.goodreads.com/author/show/4493720.Gianna_Simone
You can also find me on Pinterest, Google+, LinkedIn!
Don't hesitate to reach out and say hi!

The Norsemen Sagas

NORSEMAN'S REVENGE: Being kidnapped by a Viking raider on her wedding night might really be a blessing from the gods.

Geira Sorensdotter awaits her new husband, but she's filled with doubts about the man and the marriage. Those doubts are forgotten when the village is attacked, her husband is struck down and she is tied up and carried off amidst the raid.

Kori Thorfinnson has waited years to take revenge against the man who murdered his wife. But he soon finds the innocent young woman he's taken as his personal slave is not his enemy, despite her marriage to his foe. Her courage in defying him, her caring heart, and the fiery passion she shares stirs feelings Kori hasn't known since his wife died. Afraid to lose Geira, he binds her to him in many ways – not only with rope, but with his body, his collar and his brand.

Geira quickly learns just how despicable her husband was, and despite her difficult circumstances, grows to care deeply for Kori, her captor. Still, dreams of freedom linger. But once she finds herself with child, she must plan her escape, to save herself and her baby. However, Kori has plans of his own.

** Contains explicit love sce
Kinky Twist on History! bondag
ménage à trois scenes and more!

COMING SOON!

...ASE OF

...R'S LEGENDS

...SION: Upon her ... n Marlowe is ordered ... d Royce Langley, the Earl of Mon... Worried she is being offered up as little more than a sacrifice in a political game, Gillian is surprised to find herself intrigued by her arrogant and infuriating husband.

Tasked with ridding the border along Wales of rebels who seek to unseat the king, Royce finds subterfuge and secrets everywhere, even with his beautiful wife. Though he only agreed to the marriage because of the king's order, he finds himself both fascinated and incensed by Gillian at every turn. She tries his patience, defies his orders and places herself in danger. To keep her in line, he spanks her, binds her to his bed and uses dominating sexual games to torment her, in an effort to get her to reveal her secrets. But even that is not enough to subdue her stubborn determination to stand beside him and defend her home and people.

Discovering his wife enjoys the same dark

pleasures as Royce does only stirs more confusion. He has sworn never to fall for a woman's wiles, but his wife captivates him and stirs a desire deeper than any he has ever known. Trusting her is another matter, as he fears Gillian may bring about his downfall with her continued secrets, which he views as an attempt to undermine his authority.

As the rebel attacks increase and danger lurks everywhere, Gillian falls under suspicion as the traitor, despite her vows of loyalty. Royce must overcome his mistrust and find a way to maintain his possession of Gillian as they battle the enemies both within and without, if there is any hope for them to save each other.

Featuring A Kinky Twist on History! including male domination, bondage, spanking, anal sex and so much more!

WARRIOR'S VENGEANCE: Near the Scottish border during the reign of Edward I, Marissa Langley, daughter of a powerful English earl is captured by a band of marauding Scotsmen. Completely at their mercy, she is desperate to escape. When the leader of the group saves her from certain rape, she believes she will be freed.

But Ian MacCallum is no savior. He takes her for his own, seduces her then makes her a submissive. Her collar and chains are part of his vengeance on her father—the man Ian claims is responsible for the death of his beloved wife and son.

But her immediate death is not Ian's plan. He subjects her to daily suffering and punishments and goes so far as sharing her with another clansman. Yet, her spirit will not be broken. He finds himself drawn to that core of strength within her; finding it most exquisite as it cannot be violated.

When danger from within his clan threatens her, Ian protects her, discovering at the same time that he does not want to lose her, ever.

Marissa makes her own discovery: she comes to crave Ian's torturous touch. When she learns the source of his hatred, she is certain he is wrong. Her father would not commit atrocities. She waits for the moment when she can escape and prove her father's innocence. But that would mean leaving Ian when she is no longer sure she wants to be free.

Featuring A Kinky Twist on History, including bondage, collars, spanking, multiple partners and so much more!

WARRIOR'S WRATH: In 14th century England, a long-kept secret devastates Rowan Langley. Anger sends him on a quest for truth. He trusts no one, keeping others away, except fellow knight Gerard.

Aeron Dawkyns, fleeing Wales and a charge of murder, lives on the street, pickpocketing. She steals Rowan's coin. Later, Rowan catches her attempting to steal his horse. She has a choice – sexual slavery, or be handed over to be hanged. She chooses Rowan and Gerard.

Serving an angry Rowan has dark pleasures Aeron learns to crave. She feels safe, despite the knights' wicked games. When Rowan drags her back to Wales, she fears that safety will be destroyed.

Rowan learns Aeron's plight and vows to hunt down her enemies, promising to protect and keep her. Yet he worries he's no better than her enemy. Still, he craves his slave's touch, as much as he craves her heart.

Staying with Rowan becomes Aeron's heart's

desire – but could mean her death.

Featuring a Kinky Twist on History! including bondage, spanking, multiple partners and so much more!

THE BAYOU MAGISTE CHRONICLES

CLAIMED BY THE DEVIL: Helene Gaudet finds the perfect Dom in an internet chat room. It's as if he can read her mind – and he knows how to make her beg. When they agree to meet in the real world, Helene realizes why her Dom knows her so well – he is none other than Devlin Marchand, the same man who handed her over years ago to a dark sorcerer – to be killed.

She thought she was free from suffering – including a rageful ex-husband who cursed her, leaving her unable to bear children. She wants to forget the past – but her lust for Devlin is so intense after each tormenting, releasing encounter, she doesn't want to leave him.

Devlin wants to repair his past wrongs – but guilt over his past betrayal is multiplied when he learns the curse that has dogged Helene for years comes from the trove of magic created by his very own family. Devlin fears the tentative relationship they've built will be destroyed – and he cannot allow that.

Can they overcome the past to have a future together?

** Contains lots of explicit Magically Kinky! love scenes of the paranormal kind, including magical sex toys, potions, bondage, spanking and more!

CLAIMED BY THE MAGE: Lily Prentiss wishes she could ignore her inborn healing magic so she can live life on her terms, not follow the path her Magiste family chose for her. But when she stumbles across Aidan Marchand in the excruciating throes of evolving into a Mage, her touch is all that stops his pain and she can no longer deny her powers. When the sexy Dom seduces her into willing submission, she finds she doesn't want to resist and actually enjoys giving up control.

Aidan has more to worry about than just his rapidly maturing powers – his business partner is blackmailing him into funding a venture that involves kidnapping young girls both magical and mortal, and selling them as sex slaves. Even as Lily's touch eases Aidan's pain, he knows staying with her puts her in danger from his enemies. But the gift of her sexual submission helps him even more than her healing magic...so how can he let her go?

** Contains lots of explicit Magically Kinky! love scenes of the paranormal kind, including magical sex toys, potions, bondage, spanking and more!

CLAIMED BY THE ENCHANTER: Regine Marchand loves being in control – and the role of domme is the perfect way for her to exert that control. An accomplished equestrian, she has her goals of championship in sight and no one will get in her way. Her life and future are in her hands, she doesn't need to depend on anyone for success and happiness.

Cameron McIntyre is fascinated by the cool façade Regine displays, but he senses the depth of her passion lurking under the surface. Despite her protests to the contrary, he recognizes in her a desire to submit and be dominated. But when he is forced to suspend her from competition due to performance enhancement spells used on her horse, he worries he may drive her away, instead of back into his arms. Believing her innocent of the charges, he vows to help her uncover who set her up while convincing her that submission to him is what she truly wants and needs. Submitting to the tall Irishman brings a new level of pleasure Regine has never known, at the same time making her question everything she knew about herself.

Regine is unaware an enemy from her past has targeted her for revenge. Together she and Cameron must discover who wants to knock her out of competition for good, possibly killing her in the process.

** Contains lots of explicit Magically Kinky! love scenes of the paranormal kind, including magical sex toys, potions, bondage, spanking and more!

CLAIMED BY THE ZYNDEVINE: In 13th century France, attacked by those carrying out the Papal Inquisition, *Magiste* Enchantress Chantal Belliveau is thankful for rescue from certain torture and death. But she never expected it to be at the hands of Henri Marchand, one of a powerful pureblooded line of ancient *Magiste*, the Zyndevines. Henri holds the key to her survival, but the danger he poses to her heart and soul could turn out to be even more perilous.

Henri is part of *Il Resistasse*, a handful of powerful *Magiste* fighting the atrocities the Catholic Church inflicts on their race. Saving Chantal becomes more than a simple rescue - the innocent young woman with half-trained powers enchants him more than he has ever been before. That she enjoys the dark side of pleasure he inflicts her makes him question his determination to never give another his heart.

Chantal is horrified when Henri invokes an ancient spell, the *Possede Puissant*. The incantation leaves her little more than his possession. While she finds herself enjoying his dark and wicked sensual delights, she determines to free herself. Still, the security she finds with Henri encourages her to stay by his side, claiming spell or not.

Resentment toward her from Henri's family convinces Chantal she must ultimately break free of Henri's possession. But when the Inquisitioners attack, Henri convinces Chantal to embark on a journey to a new land, a journey that may well mean the survival of the entire *Magiste* race but the loss of her freedom forever.

** Contains lots of explicit Magically Kinky! love scenes of the paranormal kind, including magical sex toys, potions, bondage, spanking and more!

Made in the USA
Columbia, SC
05 November 2023

25535294R00157